Drea

The wind wailed and shrieked and died, only to return stronger than ever. It seemed to break through the walls and bombard me with icy needles. What a strange wind! Miss Isabel must be made of stern stuff to live alone up here.

It's not always like this, I told myself. *It's Brent's sound effects, and wouldn't you think he'd switch to eerie music? Something appropriate for the night like* The Sorcerer's Apprentice*?*

At the end of the hall, my image in the mirror confronted me. Dark hair swathed in a blue hood, raincoat flapping, eyes luminous. One hand raised to my mouth.

My hands were at my side!

The image stepped out of the mirror and glided toward me.

I froze.

There was no mirror hanging on the wall at the end of the hall. Nothing was there, no window, not even a painting. Just dark wood paneling and the blue thing that had materialized in front of my eyes.

The ghost.

It was moving.

The cold bombarded me again, impossible winds cutting through solid walls, making my hands shake violently.

Dear God! I had seen ghosts before, but this one was different. She was fully formed and looked as real as anyone in the dining room downstairs.

Where had it—or she—come from then?

Rational thought fled. I'd forgotten that I wanted to solve the mystery of Cynthia's murder and find out if Rachel's ghost really haunted the Spirit Lamp Inn. I forgot I was Jennet, solver of mysteries, who took pride in being courageous. I was holding my breath, and my mouth felt as if it were filled with sand.

Close your eyes. Look again. If it's still walking toward you, run.

When I did look again, nothing was there. A blue haze hung in the air. It looked like smoke, but it smelled, faintly, of lilacs.

I ran anyway.

What They Are Saying About

Dreams and Bones

A mysterious ghost known as the Lady in the Blue Raincoat, old bones found on the grounds of the Spirit Lamp Inn, the Lakeview Collie Rescue League's error that could result in a lawsuit—all of this and more in Dorothy Bodoin's newest Foxglove Corners mystery. Her seventeenth book in this series is entitled *Dreams and Bones* and is definitely a must read.

Bodoin's intricate skill in weaving a series of mysteries is brilliant, for once again I found myself in a race to the end to discover who the killer is and whether Jennet would escape with her life intact.

Bodoin's Foxglove mysteries have become a huge part of my life and I look forward to the next one. They are definitely worth reading, and spending time in Foxglove Corners is an adventure you won't want to miss out on. I heartily recommend this book.

Suzanne Hurley

Other Works From The Pen Of
Dorothy Bodoin

The Secret Room of Eidt House—March 2012
    A rabid dog that should have died months ago from the dread disease runs free in the woods of Foxglove Corners, and the library's long-kept secret unleashes a series of other strange events.

Follow a Shadow—September 2012
    A shadowy intruder haunts Jennet's woods by night, and a woman who can't accept the death of her collie asks Jennet to help her find Rainbow Bridge where she believes her dog waits for her.

The Snow Queen's Collie—March 2013
    During a Christmas Eve snowstorm, a white collie appears on the porch of the Ferguson farmhouse, and the painting Jennet's sister gives her for Christmas begins to exhibit strange qualities.

The Door in the Fog—November, 2013
    A wounded dog disappears in the fog. A blue door on the side of a barn vanishes. Strange wildflowers and a sound of weeping haunt a meadow. And a curse refuses to die. It's another typical summer in Foxglove Corners

Wings

DREAMS AND BONES

Dorothy Bodoin

A Wings ePress, Inc.

Cozy Mystery Novel

Wings ePress, Inc.

Edited by: Jeanne Smith
Copy Edited by: Joan Powell
Senior Editor: Jeanne Smith
Executive Editor: Marilyn Kapp
Cover Artist: Pat Evans

All rights reserved

Wings ePress Books
http://www.wings-press.com

Copyright © 2014 by Dorothy Bodoin
ISBN 978-1-61309-814-1

Published In the United States Of America

May 2014

Wings ePress Inc.
403 Wallace Court
Richmond, KY 40475

Dedication

To my lunch companions and high school classmates: Mary Lynn Buckley, Linda Eder, Kathie Purslow, Sue Kelly, and Shirley Schenkel.

One

"Sparrow?"

The voice had the clarity of a bell coaxed to life in the humid autumn air. Its source eluded me as we appeared to be alone on Sagramore Lake Road, I and three of my collies.

Candy froze in her tracks, ears at attention, eyes fixed on a gabled white cottage half-hidden behind a towering blue spruce.

"Sparrow!"

A figure in black stood in front of an open window, a young woman with streaming yellow hair and a rag in her hand. The next moment the face was gone and the front door burst open. She hurried down the walkway toward us on an intercept course.

Candy strained at her leash while Sky, the skittish blue merle, pressed her body close to mine and Misty, my rambunctious white collie puppy, started barking.

I smiled at the stranger, not sure if that was the best response.

"You have such beautiful collies," she said. "The tri is absolutely gorgeous. May I pet her?"

She was looking at Candy whose tail was wagging energetically.

I was tempted to say no. There was something about her that set an alarm bell ringing. Something about her excessive enthusiasm. Perhaps the glitter in her cat-bright green eyes. Who comes bounding out of her house to talk to a passerby's dog? What if she were a nut? Suppose she later claimed that Candy had bitten her?

1

Don't overreact, Jennet, I told myself.

She'd already extended her hand for Candy to sniff.

"I guess so," I said and added, "Be careful. Candy has sharp teeth."

The woman stroked Candy's soft black head. "She's so beautiful. What's her name?"

"Candy."

"Where did you get her?"

I paused. Candy had been a stray brought to me by an unknown boy during that unhappy time when Halley, my first collie, was lost. He had his eye on the reward. I'd kept her even though she wasn't Halley.

"I found her locally," I said with a possessive touch on Candy's neck. "Who is Sparrow?"

The girl ignored my inquiry. "I'm in the market for a tricolor female."

What a coincidence! No wonder she was interested in Candy.

"I belong to the Lakeville Collie Rescue League," I said. "You might check out the dogs we have available for adoption."

"Rescue? No." An edge crept into her voice. "I want a dog of my own, not someone else's castaway."

I couldn't let that pass. Of my collies, five were rescues, and they were all unique and wonderful, each in her own way.

"All kinds of dogs end up in Rescue through no fault of their own," I said. "We have a website…"

"I want a collie with a good pedigree," she said. "One I can show."

It was futile to try to change somebody's mind and unfair to the dogs who hoped to find a forever home. "There are several fine kennels in the area. Colliegrove has a beautiful blue merle at stud."

"Yes, well, I'll look."

Seeing she couldn't convince the stranger to pay attention to her, Misty began to pull on her leash. She could smell the lake water and

2

the scent of smoke in the air. So could I. Someone was burning leaves.

"Nice talking to you," I said, giving the leads a light tug.

I sensed that the girl stood rooted to the sidewalk, felt her gaze on me and my dogs as we walked on.

It was foolish to let a chance encounter unsettle me, so I wouldn't; and there down the street I spied another diversion, friends this time. Molly and Jennifer, the little blonde girls whose lemonade stand had become a summer fixture in Foxglove Corners, saw us and waved. The admiring stranger already forgotten, Candy urged us onward. She knew the girls had cookies for sale as well as lemonade. Dogs remember.

~ * ~

The last time I'd seen Molly and Jennifer, Molly was the taller of the two girls. They were the same height now. They looked more grown up with fingernail polish and a touch of pink lipstick.

Well, it had been two summers ago. At least the stand and the menu hadn't changed, and Jennifer's whimsical lion's head shirt hearkened back to little girlhood.

I told the dogs to sit and they obeyed. Candy chose a spot close to a paper plate of cookies.

"How's business?" I asked.

"Good," Jennifer said. "Everybody's going to the beach today. They stop here on the way."

"We couldn't set up last Saturday because it rained," Molly added.

There was a hint of rain in the sky this morning. A gathering of clouds, a thickness in the air, and a dampness stealing over my skin. I pushed back a strand of hair that had fallen forward over my eye.

"I'll have a lemonade," I said, "and three cookies for the dogs."

They were oatmeal. No raisins. It was the collies' lucky day.

Jennifer counted them out. "One for Sky, one for Candy, one for Snow White."

"Her name is Misty," I said. "She's new."

"Where's Gemmy?" Molly asked.

"At home with Halley and Raven."

These days I walked the dogs in shifts, three at a time, thanks to Candy, my wild child, who had incited a canine riot when she'd broken free of her leash to chase a deer. My husband, Crane, and I both agreed that walking six large dogs together was asking for trouble, unless he was with me. Certainly I'd never lead my entire brood onto a residential street.

"They must hate being left behind," Jennifer said.

"I'll take them out this afternoon."

Double trouble. Double time. But also double exercise, and I felt more in control with three.

Jennifer poured lemonade in a tall cup while I sifted through the coins in my pocket for change and dropped fifty-five cents into the girls' canning jar bank.

"We're going to have caramel apples next week," Molly said.

I took a long sip. The weather was warm for late September, and the lemonade was on the warm side, too. But no one would hear me complain about these temperatures. Fortunately it was Saturday. That meant no school and perhaps one of my last chances for a leisurely stroll by the lake. In other words, it was a good day.

"What's been going on in the neighborhood?" I asked.

"A new boy moved in next door to Jennifer," Molly said. "He's real cute."

"And there's a new dog in the corner house," Jennifer added.

"His name is Douglas," Molly said.

"The boy or the dog?" I asked.

That elicited a burst of hilarity, rather out of proportion to the statement, but it was good to laugh in the sun, to exult in the joy of freedom and the mere mention of a new boy on Sagramore Lake Road.

Molly was the first to regain her composure. "The boy, silly."

"There's something else," Jennifer said. "We have a mystery of our own."

"Yeah. We're going to be detectives like you when we grow up," Molly added.

"You girls know I'm an English teacher, don't you? Nouns and verbs and writing and literature."

Molly made a face. "But you solve mysteries, too, and that's more fun."

I smiled. "Sometimes. Tell me about your mystery."

The girls exchanged glances.

"We can't," Molly said. "Not yet. It's a secret."

"Well, I guess you can't then."

I was mildly curious but didn't press them for details. They'd tell me when they were ready, although the lemonade stand's days were numbered. I might not see the girls again until next summer.

Their mystery couldn't be an earthshaking one but a puzzle tailored to their age and interests. *Jennifer and Molly and the Mystical Jewel.* Or maybe it concerned a boy named Douglas.

The dogs had finished their cookies, licked up every fallen crumb, and Candy was eyeing the still-heaping plate as if it were the most precious treasure in her world.

I glanced back down the street. The young woman who had fussed over Candy had gone, presumably back into her house. She was no mystery, but the incident was a little strange, and her prejudice against rescue collies saddened me. Still, people want what they want.

It occurred to me that she hadn't mentioned her name.

"Do you know the girl who lives in the house with the tall spruce tree in the front yard?" I asked. "She has long blonde hair."

"Is she our age?" Jennifer asked.

"No, older. Probably twenty or so."

Molly shook her head. "She must be new, too. Don't you want a cookie for yourself, Jennet?"

I did, but I'd have to share it, as all three dogs were begging for second helpings. While I debated, thunder rumbled in the distance. Should we walk on to the lake or go home? I calculated distances, scanned the sky, and decided the storm was still far enough away for safety. We could easily make it home before the storm.

"Come back next week and bring the others," Molly shouted as she gathered paper cups.

"If we can," I said.

Who knew what would happen in Foxglove Corners from one week to another? I'd learned it was best not to plan ahead. If possible.

Two

The rest of the day was uneventful. Thunder continued to rumble, but the storm didn't reach Foxglove Corners, although light rain fell at intervals, turning the landscape soggy. I was able to take the other three dogs for their walk. Because Crane was out of town on sheriff's business, I didn't have to cook dinner. A long evening lay ahead of me, one filled with infinite possibilities.

But how dull the house was without him. How lonely.

I imagined him coming home from a long stint of patrolling the roads and by-roads, locking his gun in its special cabinet, and sitting by the fire after dinner with his newspaper while Candy slept at his feet.

A typical evening in our green Victorian farmhouse on Jonquil Lane.

I could almost see the sparkle in his frosty gray eyes. Any minute I would hear his voice, so powerful was the imprint of his personality.

Candy tilted her head. It was as if she heard his footsteps coming up the walkway. She was always the first to greet him.

I, of course, heard nothing. Crane was far away in another part of the state. As the wife of a deputy sheriff, I had grown used to his long absences. Which didn't mean I had to like them.

So quit fantasizing and enjoy this evening alone.

I would feed the dogs, make a sandwich for dinner, and revel in the knowledge that nothing needed to be done tonight. I could settle down in the rocker and read my new Gothic novel instead of the dry-as-dust Puritan sermon slated for tomorrow's American Literature lesson. I could always do schoolwork tomorrow.

A melodious ring tone floated into the deep silence that had settled over the house. I found my cell phone on the kitchen table and snapped it open.

"Hi, Jen. What are you doing?"

Leonora, my friend and fellow English teacher at Marston High School, sounded a trifle dispirited, which was unlike her. Usually invisible bubbles formed around her words.

I glanced at the loaf of bread on the counter. "Thinking about dinner. What's wrong?"

"My date stood me up."

Leonora was seeing Deputy Sheriff Jake Brown, a handsome rogue who liked beautiful blondes. He courted both Leonora and my sister, Julia, and appeared to be happy with either one.

"And on a Saturday night," she added.

"Sheriff's business?" I asked.

"Who knows? I hope so."

"Do you want to come over?"

"I thought I could talk you into going out for dinner."

I glanced again at the loaf of bread. What did I have to put inside a sandwich?

"That sounds like fun." Immediately I thought of my favorite restaurant with its comfort food menu, so fitting for a rainy fall day. "Clovers?" I said.

"Some place a little nicer. After all, it *is* Saturday." She paused. "How about the Spirit Lamp Inn?"

My second favorite restaurant, the atmospheric Inn was an appealing autumn destination with a history to rival any Gothic novel and a documented haunting as well.

"Perfect," I said. "Maybe we'll see a ghost."

"We can only hope. I'll drive. Say an hour?"

"I'll be ready."

I considered my long dark denim skirt and white shirt. An evening at the Inn called for a dress. Something black. I had the ideal one in mind.

~ * ~

"The Haver House," Leonora said softly as we passed the old white farmhouse on Deer Leap Trail en route to the Inn. "It looks so lonely."

"No one comes here anymore."

With the change of seasons, the vibrant colors had drained out of the wildflowers that had flourished throughout the summer. Stalks, ferns crumbled to powder, once tall perennials caved in on themselves, loneliness was inherent in the scene, almost palpable. Loneliness, sadness, grief, and loss.

The acreage was indistinguishable from other tracts of land along Deer Leap Trail. An abandoned white house, a barn sitting in the midst of fields, woods. A 'For Sale by Owner' sign in the front yard. A 'No Trespassing" sign nailed to a tree. Its story was finished.

Quickly I turned my thoughts to the Spirit Lamp Inn where life and light still existed.

~ * ~

The Inn had an extravaganza of brown gables and a picturesque wooded setting that lent an air of mystery to the place. Lights in the first floor dining room did their best to attract and welcome a select clientele, for in truth the Inn was quite literally off the beaten path.

Leonora and I had first known the Inn as a refuge from a summer storm. In time we learned a few of its secrets. I suspected a few more waited to be uncovered.

"What's that?" she asked as she pulled into the drive. "Oh, no!"

The lamp post cast a yellow pool around the 'For Sale' sign that had sprung up like a noxious white mushroom in the grass after rain. It hadn't been there the last time we'd dined at the Inn. Last summer.

"We can't lose this place," Leonora said. "We just found it."

"Everything changes." I tried to look on the bright side. "It's not closing down. It's just for sale."

"What if someone wants it for a private residence?"

That was what it had been at one time. This was, I had to admit, an out-of-the-way location for a restaurant but a good one for a country home. "Then I guess we lose it," I said. "But I hope we won't."

"There aren't many people here." Leonora found a parking place near the front door and we walked up to the porch. "This reminds me of our first visit. We were the only customers."

And like the first time, the hostess' station was deserted. A sign invited us to seat ourselves, and a menu board promised Michigan pasties with mashed potatoes and gravy and for dessert pumpkin or apple pie.

I peered into the dining room. There were eight people sitting at three tables. By mutual agreement, we chose a booth by the window with a view of the garden in vibrant autumn color.

Please, I thought, *don't let the Inn pass into history.*

According to an old story kept alive by the owner, whom I had never met, a ghost known as the Lady in the Blue Raincoat haunted the Inn. Supposedly she wandered the hall on the second floor searching for her traveling companion who had disappeared one stormy night in 1955, never to be seen again.

I didn't know of anybody who had seen the Lady, but the Inn's wait staff and hostesses came and left at a dizzying rate. Once I'd heard a terrified scream that was glibly explained away by an employee. I didn't believe the explanation. Knowing Foxglove Corners' reputation for unearthly happenings, I didn't doubt that the Lady had made an appearance.

"I wonder what the blue phantom will think when she comes back to find the Inn closed," Leonora said.

"Being a ghost, she probably knows already."

"Then she won't come back."

"She hasn't found her friend yet. I think she'll keep looking for her."

"Even if they demolish the Inn?" Leonora asked.

"This is too fine a house to tear down."

But I didn't know that for certain. In Oakpoint, where I taught at the local high school, I'd seen several sound houses razed to make room for larger, fancier ones. The new structures swallowed up every square inch of the lot. A developer might look at the Spirit Lamp Inn and see an eyesore.

"Well," Leonora said. "Here we are on a Saturday night without our men. You look terrific, Jen," she added.

"So do you."

I'd added a rhinestone pin to my black sheath. Leonora's dress had similar styling but it was ice green and accessorized with a king's ransom of crystal jewelry. This was undoubtedly the dress she'd intended to wear for her date with Jake.

"I don't think I'll ever have Jake the way you have Crane," she said.

This was an obvious invitation for me to disagree with her, but I couldn't. It wouldn't be kind to give her false hope.

"He seems to like to play the field," I said. "But you never know what the future will bring. For a long time, I wasn't sure of Crane's intentions."

"Change."

"What?"

"You said it. Everything changes."

"That's true. Maybe Jake will realize that he can't live without you. One day."

A waitress dressed in coffee brown and white filled our water glass and handed us large menus. "I'm Gillian," she said. "Can I get you something to drink?"

"Root beer later with my meal," I said.

"Same here," Leonora added.

Dutifully I scanned the offerings, although I'd already made my decision. "I'll have the pasty and mashed potatoes."

"Oh, I'm sorry." Gillian looked truly regretful. "We ran out of pasties. Everyone wanted them."

"Then…" What was like a pasty? Meat with mixed vegetables and crust? "Chicken pie. and garden salad."

"Same for me," Leonora said. "Although I *did* want a pasty," she added with a fleeting pout. "I guess I'll have to make my own."

"That's an idea. They say the way to a man's heart is through his stomach."

When Gillian returned, I said, "I was surprised to see the 'For Sale' sign out in front. Why is the owner selling?"

"Personal reasons," she said in a clipped tone. "We'll be here a while longer. Through Halloween, I think."

Ah, Halloween! That magical time for haunted houses. The mysterious owner wouldn't want to vacate the Inn before Halloween. That would be the night to come back to the Inn for dinner. Maybe Crane would be able to join us. Brent Fowler, Foxglove Corners' other elusive bachelor, would. And we'd invite Lucy Hazen, our celebrated horror story writer who seemed to have captured Brent's interest.

On my desk at home I had the beginning of a manuscript narrating my own supernatural experiences in Foxglove Corners. It had stalled for want of material. I had enough for several chapters but wanted an entire book.

I wasn't the first to write about the Lady in the Blue Raincoat. Rachel Carroll, her name was, and her companion was Cynthia Lauren. The Foxglove Corners Public Library had a modicum of information about the case and subsequent hauntings dating back several decades.

No one had seen the Lady in ages, and her search for her missing friend remained as wispy as fog on an autumn morning.

Maybe it was time for that to change.

Three

"We have a problem," Sue Appleton said. "It's serious, and I'll admit I have no idea how to solve it."

Sue, recently elected president of the Lakeville Collie Rescue League, sat at the oak table in my kitchen the next day pretending to eat her apple muffin. Obviously she didn't want it. No one was more aware of that than Candy, who had stationed herself as close to Sue as possible without being in her lap.

Sue had walked over from her horse farm on Squill Lane, arriving windblown and breathless. I'd known immediately that something was wrong.

"I made a mistake," she added. "But how could I be expected to know?"

"Tell me about it," I said, pouring tea in our cups.

She speared a piece of muffin on her fork and moved it to the side of her plate. "Yesterday out of the blue this girl, Deanna Reid, came to visit me. She claims we let her collie be adopted without her permission. She's going to sue us if we don't return the dog to her."

People had threatened the League with lawsuits in the past, ignoring the fact that the organization operated solely on the generosity of donors and, at times, the personal resources of the members. Collies in need of food and veterinary care severely taxed the modest sums in the treasury.

"How did that happen?" I asked.

"It's a complicated story, and I don't know whether to believe every part of it." She reached for her teacup and knocked a piece of muffin off the table. Candy caught it in mid-fall and licked her chops for more.

"When Ms. Reid was in the hospital, she asked a friend to keep her dog for two weeks and paid him for board. Apparently she paid him well. Come to find out, he surrendered the dog to Rescue. He told her he gave it away."

I saw why Sue had reservations. The story seemed far-fetched. Or, if credible, crucial details were missing.

"What kind of friend would do something like that?" I asked.

"A former boyfriend, she says."

A disgruntled, vengeful one.

"She seemed sincerely distressed," Sue said, "but it's all so outrageous there has to be more to it."

I took a sip of my tea, feeling I needed fortification. This situation was indeed dire. How would I feel if somebody had given one of my dogs away without my knowledge?

Sue took a paper from her purse. "I made a copy of the adoption. The alleged owner, Alex Blaine, claimed he had been laid off and couldn't afford to feed a dog. He didn't have her papers."

"Did he say he owned the collie?"

"I didn't ask him. I just assumed…"

"Oh, dear."

"Why would he surrender someone else's dog?"

"That's the question," I said. "I'd like to talk to this Deanna Reid. Is there anything else you can tell me?"

"The collie went to the Summerton family in Lakeville on July third. They've given her a wonderful home." Sue read from the paper: *Collie, tricolor female. Two years old. Sixty pounds. In good health. Obvious good breeding. Appears friendly. Name, Sparrow.*

Sparrow!

The young woman we'd met on Sagramore Lake Road had called Candy Sparrow and come dashing out of her house to make an inordinate fuss over her. Now this odd behavior made sense. To a point. Hadn't she said she was in the market for a tri female, a show prospect?

"This is a coincidence, but I think I know who Deanna Reid is," I said. "Does she have long blonde hair and green eyes?"

"She's a blonde, but she was wearing sunglasses."

"I'll bet it's the same girl." I told Sue what had happened on our walk. "She made me a little uneasy. I'm not sure why."

Sue folded the paper and slipped it back into her purse. "Could you talk to her, as a representative of the League? Maybe you can reason with her. How can we take Sparrow away from the Summertons? They've had her for over two months. Their three little girls love her."

"On the other hand, how can we keep her away from her rightful owner? If Deanna Reid *is* the rightful owner. If the story is true."

"Anyway you look at it, this is bad for the League," Sue said. "This should never have happened, and it's all my fault. If you can somehow turn this around, Jennet, I'll be forever indebted to you."

"All I can do is try."

Poor Sue. This wasn't the first misstep she'd taken since accepting the leadership of the Rescue League, and she took every failure to heart. In her place, though, I might have assumed the former boyfriend was telling the truth, too. Most of our rescues came to us without papers.

I wondered if anyone else had ever summarily disposed of another person's pet? Maybe Alex Blaine could be charged with theft. I had minimal knowledge of the law and couldn't imagine what a judge would say. If only Crane were here. Oh, well, he'd be home soon. This problem wasn't going to be resolved in a day.

"She left me her phone number," Sue said. "She expects to have her dog back by the end of the week."

That gave me about six days to find a solution. I'd have to try very, very hard.

~ * ~

Deanna Reid wasn't answering her phone. If she had an answering machine, it was turned off. No matter. I knew where she lived and could walk over to her house anytime. But not with the collies. I had a hunch that wasn't a good idea.

I began to wonder why I'd agreed to get involved in this conflict. On the surface, it seemed like an impossible dilemma. How could I convince Deanna Reid not to hold the Rescue League responsible for the loss of her collie? Who should keep Sparrow? Her former owner or the new family who had given Sparrow a home, believing it would be forever?

What could I do? No, what should I do?

Well, the members of the Rescue League stuck together. But I needed more facts, true facts, and the obvious first step was to meet with Ms. Reid as soon as I could contact her.

Setting the problem aside, I spent the rest of Sunday preparing for the coming week. Lesson plans, grocery shopping for Crane's homecoming on Tuesday, ironing, walks and playtime for the dogs. It was a busy agenda, as always, and the day flew by.

When I wasn't planning how to approach Deanna Reid, I spared a thought for the Spirit Lamp Inn. It seemed they were already winding down. Last night Leonora and I had ordered pumpkin pie only to find they were out of every dessert except vanilla ice cream. Which was good, but I could have that at home. Also, we had lingered in the booth talking until eight o'clock, and in that time only two other parties had come in.

If I were going to pursue the Inn's mystery, I had better hurry, lest some evening I'd arrive for dinner and find the place shuttered.

Four

Once upon a time when the clock struck ten, I stopped whatever I was doing to sit on the porch of a green Victorian farmhouse with tea and muffins gazing at Jonquil Lane and savoring country peace and quiet. Birds sang, the sun shone, and an occasional deer wandered into view. All was serenity and loveliness.

That was in another lifetime. Back to school, back to work changes everything.

Flash forward to September. Sweltering in a blue turtleneck dress, I stood in front of my restless fourth hour class taking attendance. My surroundings were far from relaxing, and there were no refreshments.

My section of American Literature Survey was loud and chaotic. It was a constant struggle to make the literature of Colonial America appealing and relevant. Merely to keep students in their seats was a chore.

And I was usually ravenous by this time. I tried not to think about my sandwich—turkey on rye—and the California peach in my desk drawer. That reviving mid-morning snack would have made a tremendous difference in my energy level.

The 1600s. A pilgrim describes the hardships and deaths during the first winter in the new world. Colonists shiver at the thought of hell and damnation. Last night I'd decided I couldn't face the Puritan sermon.

'Hang on,' I wanted to tell them. 'Better stories are coming. *The Legend of Sleepy Hollow*, the works of Edgar Allan Poe and Ambrose Bierce.'

I closed the attendance book, initialed the absence slip, and set it on the desk to be picked up by an office aide. Most of the faces in front of me were still unfamiliar, except the one belonging to my old nemesis, Denver Armstrong. He'd failed my last two American Literature classes and bounced back like a boomerang. Same time, same book, same diabolical smirk. The difference was this was his third attempt to pass the course, required for graduation. I assumed at some point Denver wanted a high school diploma.

"Hi, Teach," he'd said the first day of class. "Have a nice summer?"

I'd been appalled to find his name on my class list when school started. Couldn't the computer spread the trouble around?

Well, you failed him, I told myself.

Of course I'd had no choice.

Nonetheless, I was determined that we would start with a new slate. To be sure, Denver appeared more presentable, had been on time for class (so far), and hadn't yet instigated one of his famous confrontations. He also hadn't turned in a single assignment.

I opened the American Literature text that seemed heavier than usual on a Monday morning and found the day's selection.

About half of the class was with me. The others were elsewhere. From Day One this particular class had been my least favorite.

New groups were often reasonably subdued until they scouted the lay of the land. This happened in the first few days. Then one by one they began talking, adding their voices to the cacophony until the atmosphere grew and remained rowdy. Some groups were unruly from the beginning. Like this one.

Fourth hour had a preponderance of girls. One of them, Katrina Clark, had already distinguished herself—not in a good way. A girl with the delicate features and short hair of a pixie and a wardrobe of bright tee-shirts, she had a screechy voice and was constantly in motion—to the pencil sharpener, the waste paper basket, a desk closer to a friend. She had an impressive store of excuses to leave the room.

Today she was surreptitiously applying gloss to her lips. I frowned. She dropped the silver cylinder into her purse and ostentatiously picked up a pen.

"See, it's a pen," she announced.

I strode up and down the rows, checking to see that all or most of my students were copying the background notes I'd written on the board. Some were; some weren't. Typical.

Denver was drawing palm trees, not on the desk as he'd been last semester but on a sheet of copy paper.

"Mr. Armstrong," I said. "Did you finish the notes? They won't be on the board tomorrow."

"I got 'em last year," he said. "Don't you remember I took this course twice already? They're the same notes."

That was a blatant lie. Last year Denver had drawn dragons and named them 'Jennet.' Then he'd been suspended and didn't bother to return to school. I'd never seen his notebook which was to have been handed in for an extra credit grade. It probably didn't exist.

"These are different notes," I said.

"They look the same to me."

I sighed. "Put the art work away and start copying."

With a grumble, he slapped a sheet of lined note paper on top of the beach scene and squinted at the board.

"I can't read your writing," he said.

"It's printing."

I moved on. How long Denver would even pretend to participate in class was anyone's guess. At any rate it was time to read the day's selection. If I assigned it for homework, only a few students would read it.

Before introducing the narrative, I glanced up. Denver was working on his palm grove again. The only new leaf was the one on his paper.

~ * ~

"How goes the battle?"

Leonora set her tray on the long table we used to lay out the school newspaper in Journalism. She had a barbequed beef sandwich and French fries. Suddenly my turkey sandwich seemed inadequate.

"Need you ask?" I said. "I have Denver Armstrong again."

"Your resident artist. How can you be so lucky?"

"The computer has it in for me. I'm hoping he grew up a little over the summer."

But I was breaking a cardinal rule. We'd agreed not to discuss any aspect of school during our twenty-minute lunch period.

That left a host of fascinating topics: the Spirit Lamp Inn, Deputy Sheriff Jake Brown, ghosts, our collies, Leonora's new dress, her wish to visit the Grand Hotel on Mackinac Island for her birthday, and the Collie League's dilemma. Leonora was a new member of the League.

"It's too bad you can't divide a dog in two," she said.

"How morbid."

"I was thinking of Solomon in the Bible and the two mothers who wanted the same baby."

"He never intended to do that, I don't think."

"I can't decide who should have Sparrow," she said. "Not that it's up to me."

"My opinion is that she should go back to her original owner. Sue can find another collie for the Summerton family."

"The Summertons will be devastated," she said. "They adopted her in good faith."

"True enough, but someone is going to be hurt whatever happens."

20

It'll be the dog, I thought.

Shadow, separated from her mistress, given to the boyfriend, then to the Rescue League, then to a foster home, then to a forever family. Given away four times. Every dog deserves love, care, and a stable home. A dog should never be passed from one human to another like an unwanted lamp.

I'd been dreading getting involved in the bizarre impasse, but suddenly I found myself looking at the situation in a different way. By entering the fray, I would be helping a collie who desperately needed a champion. After all, wasn't that why I had joined the Collie Rescue League?

Yes, of course it was, but I never imagined it would be so hard.

Five

I shied away from the acidic tone of Deanna Reid's voice. "Unless you're prepared to return my dog, we don't have anything to talk about."

"The situation is complicated," I said. "Sparrow's new owners have bonded with her. They're not willing to give her back."

I didn't know that for certain, but it was a safe assumption. Sue Appleton hadn't told them about Deanna's claim yet. She was holding out for a happy-ever-after solution for everybody. That wasn't going to happen.

"That's *their* problem," Deanna said. "It has nothing to do with me."

But it did. I'd already decided that I didn't like Deanna Reid. She had lost my sympathy with her hard line. On the other hand, how would I feel if our positions were reversed and I had to fight for ownership of one of my collies? I still felt that Deanna should have her dog back.

But why had she told me she was in the market for another one?

"Before I can proceed, I need more details," I said. "Was there anything in writing? Did you give this man a time limit on Sparrow's stay?"

"I told the other woman everything you need to know," she said. "He had no right to give Sparrow to the Rescue League. He stole her from me."

"Didn't you place her in his care?" I asked.

"Temporarily, yes. He understood that. He was supposed to return her to me as soon as I got out of the hospital."

"Then why…"

She didn't let me continue. "Because he's crazy. That's why. That's what he does. Goes around stirring up trouble for innocent people and helpless animals."

She paused; the pause lengthened. I glanced at the cell phone screen, wondering if I'd lost the connection.

"In other words, Alex Blaine is a first class jerk," she said.

"He sure stirred up a kettle full of misery this time," I said. "I'd like to talk to him, too."

"What good will that do?"

"You say he's the one who surrendered the collie to the League."

The acid turned belligerent. "Do you think I'm lying?"

Five minutes into the conversation I could see why Sue had been so eager to have me handle the matter.

"As I said, I need to have all the facts. Can we meet somewhere?"

"I suppose so, but it can't be at my house."

Well. I didn't want her to come to my house either.

"How about coffee at Clovers?" I asked. "Do you know where it is?"

"Sure. On Crispian Road. That'll be okay if we can do it on Friday at five."

"I'll be there. And would you please bring your friend's contact information?"

"He's no friend of mine," she snapped. "I thought you understood that. See you then."

~ * ~

"Life is good," Brent Fowler said. "Life couldn't be better. Wait till you hear my news."

This was the old Brent, before an unfortunate acquisition had brought him a string of bad luck. The hearty fox hunting bachelor of Foxglove Corners who had hair the color of a certain kind of autumn maple leaf. The family friend who had an uncanny knack for knowing when I had a savory dinner in the oven or when I needed help. Invariably he showed up on our doorstep unannounced bearing a contribution to the meal or one for our home. Tonight's gifts were a bottle of wine and a box of maple candy from Canada, little soldiers that looked too much like toys for their own safety.

I set the candy on the mantel out of the dogs' reach, and Brent settled in the rocking chair with Sky on one side and Misty on the other. For a moment I thought he was going to hoist Misty into his lap, but apparently he thought the better of it. She weighed almost as much as Candy.

Crane's frosty eyes glittered with humor. "You have a new stuffed fox head on your wall?"

"Better than that. Much better."

I set another place at the table. "Are you going to tell us?"

"I'm officially out of the hot air balloon business and about to embark on a brand new enterprise."

More horses for his stable? A new stable in another location? Something had energized him. His enthusiasm was contagious.

"I'm going to be an innkeeper," he said. "Did you know the Spirit Lamp Inn was for sale?"

"I saw the sign when Leonora and I had dinner there last Saturday night."

"It's gone. You're looking at the new owner."

"How did this happen?" I asked as Crane said, "What made you decide to buy an inn?"

"Lucy and I were having dinner there Sunday night. We got to talking about the ghost and the girl who disappeared from the Inn in the fifties. Lucy said it would be fun to own a haunted house."

Lucy was right. It would be, and it would appeal to Brent's penchant for adventure, for the unique.

"It turns out that the current owner wants to unload the place immediately if not sooner," he said. "So I decided to buy it. I'll have some renovations done, repainting and redecorating—stuff like that. And I want to update the landscaping. It's boring."

"I thought you were going to concentrate on horses," I said.

"I can do both. I thought we'd have a grand opening on Halloween. Tell me what you think of this idea, Jennet. You can dress up as the Lady in the Blue Raincoat and mingle with the guests."

"You're out of your mind, Fowler," Crane said.

I added three wine goblets to the table and lit the candles in the heirloom candlesticks that had belonged to Crane's Civil War ancestress, Rebecca Ferguson. This was Crane's first night home. I was glad he was on hand for support before Brent swept me away on his wave of euphoria.

"I don't think I want to do that, Brent," I said. "Maybe Lucy will. Or Annica. They both have a flair for the dramatic."

"You have a blue raincoat with a hood," Brent reminded me. "I've seen you wear it."

"Talk about outdated and boring."

"Then I'll get someone to play the part of the gal who disappeared. What was her name again?"

"Cynthia Lauren."

"Are you going to make Jennet disappear?" Crane asked.

"I haven't thought it all through. I'll have to rehire a staff. They're all leaving with the owner."

"Even the cook?" I asked.

"She's retiring."

I'd never met her, but she'd responded to a note I'd sent her by returning the lost collie, Breezy, to her owner.

"She was a master cook," I said.

"I'll find another one."

This was exactly what Brent needed: a new project. And it could open doors for me. The mystery of Cynthia's disappearance had never been solved. With Brent owning the Inn, I'd have free rein to investigate the premises.

If any clues had survived the inevitable changes of decades.

I remembered a drawback. "The room the girls rented that night was lost in a prior renovation."

"How handy," Crane said. "Maybe that was deliberate."

That one observation ignited my curiosity. The room was gone, but evidence might have been overlooked in some other part of the Inn. An old house must have many nooks and crannies.

"When do you take possession of the Inn?" I asked.

"Anytime. The owner's already gone. I changed the locks."

"But one of the waitresses said they'd be there till Halloween. How could you arrange everything so fast?"

"I offered the owner cash."

Of course. How wonderful to have that kind of money. To redecorate every room and spiff up the garden with bright fall plants, transforming every inch of the place according to your own vision. I didn't agree with Brent that the landscaping was boring, but he wanted to give the Inn a new look inside and out.

I suspected the ghost wouldn't like that.

Six

I sipped coffee and alternately gazed at the piece of pecan pie on my plate and at Annica as she wandered through the rows of Clovers tending to the needs of her customers.

To celebrate the season, the decorative clovers that decorated the restaurant year round were interspersed with paper leaves in autumn colors of orange, yellow, red, and brown. Bouquets of dried flowers in painted pumpkin centerpieces adorned the tables. Best of all, comfort food filled the menu with one of my favorites, beef stew, at the top of the list.

It was five-thirty, and Deanna Reid hadn't showed up yet. She'd been so precise about the time that I was beginning to think she didn't intend to keep our appointment. If she didn't, what would the next step be? Wait for her or her lawyer to contact us?

Annica swung by my table, coffeepot in hand. Her eyes were bright with suppressed excitement and saucy pumpkin earrings gleamed amid tendrils of red-gold hair. "Is something wrong with your pie?" she asked.

"I'm waiting for someone," I said. "If she doesn't show up soon, I'll give her up as a lost cause."

"A new friend?"

"It's business. I'm here as a Collie Rescue representative."

"So—it's confidential?"

She filled my cup to the top. Thank heavens the coffee was hot again. After a string of warm sunny days, winter had slipped quietly into Foxglove Corners. Well, wintry weather. It was still technically fall. The red dress I'd chosen so that Deanna would know me was one I usually wore in December.

"For now," I said. "It's what you might call a conundrum. I'm hoping to negotiate a settlement."

"Who knew rescue work could be so complicated?" Annica said. "I thought it was just save a collie, find it a new home."

"Sometimes it is."

Annica scanned the room quickly and, apparently satisfied that all was well, slipped into a vacant chair. "Did Brent tell you he bought the Spirit Lamp Inn?"

"Yes. Last night."

"Isn't it exciting? Now we can investigate the disappearance and the ghost with the blessing of the owner."

"If I know Brent, he'll insist on being part of the team."

"Well, he should. He's the boss. We won't have to make up stories to venture beyond the dining room. We can go anywhere we like. Do you know what I think?" She didn't wait for an answer. "All that renovation he's going to do may turn up more than dust."

"I had the same thought, but the police must have searched the Inn thoroughly at the time."

"You'd think so. Maybe they missed something."

That was what I hoped. "Wouldn't it be amazing if we found out what happened to Cynthia all those years ago?"

"Excuse me."

I looked up to see a young blonde woman in jeans and a burgundy tunic sweater standing uncertainly at the table. Her long hair hung straight down past her shoulders, caught in a large barrette with a gaudy green stone. Deanna Reid. Finally.

As she stared at me, her eyes widened. "You," she said, making it sound like an accusation.

"I'm Jennet Ferguson," I said, "a member of the Lakeville Collie Rescue League. We talked on the phone. You must be Deanna Reid."

She gave me a hard stare that turned her green eyes into emeralds. "You walked past my house with your collies the other day. Is this some kind of trick?"

"Not at all. I often walk my dogs to the lake. I didn't know who you were then or about your problem. I'm a kind of troubleshooter for the Rescue League," I added.

"Do you think I'm trouble?"

Annica sprang to her feet and said brightly, "Can I get you a cup of coffee, Miss? A piece of pie? Dinner?"

"Just coffee," Deanna said. "Cream and sugar." She perched on the edge of the chair Annica had vacated. "Do you have my collie?"

"Well, no. Weren't we going to talk today?"

She drew a card from a denim clutch. "This is the address of the man who stole my dog. Can you tell me where she is now?"

Sue had warned me that she was going to ask this question, had told me what to say.

"I'm afraid I can't give you that information. Our adoption records are confidential."

"I can find out for myself, you know."

"Be my guest."

She gave me an exasperated sigh. "How long will this take?"

I turned the card around in my hand. It was a plain white index card cut in half with a name and phone number printed on it.

"I can't say, Ms. Reid. The new owners don't even know there's been a complication."

Annica took her time about pouring coffee and pointing Deanna to the basket containing cream and sugar.

"Then we're finished here." She stood. "You have the name of the thief. Call me again when you have real news."

Leaving her coffee untouched, she stalked off, setting the clover chimes on the door ringing.

Annica stared after her. "She didn't pay me."

"She didn't touch the coffee."

"So what? She ordered it. Oh, why pour it down the drain?" She sank into Deanna's chair. "What a witch!"

"Ms. Reid is upset, and rightly so. You gathered the nature of the problem, I take it."

"Sure. You people stole her dog. Aren't there enough strays running around in Foxglove Corners?"

"It wasn't like that."

"Forget her." Annica stirred sugar into the coffee and tasted it. "Delicious! So when can we go back to the Spirit Lamp Inn? Brent says we can come by anytime, but he's closing the doors for two or three weeks."

"How about tomorrow? It's Saturday."

"It's a date. We can explore the entire building first, then make a map and zero in on likely areas."

I smiled. "Nooks and crannies. Cellars and attics."

"That old ghost won't have a chance," Annica said.

~ * ~

On the way home, I stopped at Sue Appleton's horse ranch on Squill Lane to give her my report. I found her in the barn working on a beautiful chestnut horse.

"All I accomplished was this." I handed her the index card. "Maybe we have a reprieve. She didn't mention a deadline."

Sue gave the card a cursory glance. "This isn't the address he gave us. What should we do now?"

"Call him, I guess. Arrange a meeting. Hear his side of the story."

"Will you go with me?" she asked.

"If I can."

We walked on a hay-strewn floor outside, shivering in the chilled air. The sunlight was rapidly fading, reminding me I'd better not linger here. The dogs were waiting for me, and Crane would be home soon.

He had listened to my recounting of the League's newest dilemma with only one comment. "Don't get too involved, Jennet. There may be more going on here than meets the eye."

How would he react if I interviewed the man who had set this sad affair into motion? The man referred to as crazy and a jerk?

I knew the answer to that.

However, if Sue and I approached him together, as a team, that should be safe.

Sue slipped the card into her jacket pocket. "I'll give him a call," she said.

Seven

Trucks from Earth's Garden Landscaping and a radio blaring rock music stripped the Spirit Lamp Inn of its mysterious aura. Behind the Inn, a man shouted an order, and another sang his own song off-key. Set against the stillness of the neighboring woods, the noise was an abomination.

I longed to silence the radio or at least muzzle it.

"This is a work in progress," Annica said as we made our way past a load of topsoil to the front porch. She carried a picnic basket filled with sandwiches and lemonade from Clovers.

I viewed the brown-gabled house so accustomed to country tranquility. It looked apprehensive. "The ghost will be running for cover and taking our mystery with her."

We passed Brent's blue convertible, its top down in spite of the brisk September air. Our host was inside. We could ignore the black lettered sign that announced the Inn's closing for renovation. Brent was having all of the rooms repainted and the hardwood floors refinished. But he'd changed his mind about adding a wing and buying new furniture for the second story.

"The antiques are in great shape," he'd said. "I bought the Inn as is, lock, stock, and barrel, and got a good deal if I do say so myself."

I wondered again why the previous owner had been so quick to unload the property. If Brent got a good deal, she must have sold at a loss. 'Personal reasons' didn't quite satisfy me.

Annica set the basket on the top stair. "It's heavier than it looks. Must be the pound cake."

"Wait!" I said. "Let's see what they're doing to the garden."

She followed me around the side of the house to the back where dozens of chrysanthemum plants lay in makeshift rows waiting attention. Misty mauve, bright yellow, rust red, autumn colors like the paper leaves that decorated Clovers. Among the new additions were an elegant three-tier birdbath and a pair of white iron benches. Fortunately the workmen hadn't dug out the hydrangea bushes in their zeal.

"Next year Brent is going to have an old fashioned rose garden," Annica said, "and he's talking about a maze."

He must be thinking about next Halloween. I imagined a corn maze designed to entice and befuddle guests, an attraction to add to the mystique of his personal haunted house. In many ways Brent was a boy at heart.

Two workmen were digging holes while a third dragged a long hose across the grass. The man with the hose frowned at us. "Inn's closed, ladies. Didn't you see the sign?"

Annica tossed her head. Her silver bell earrings tinkled their defiance. "We're guests of the new owner. He's expecting us."

The man shrugged and dragged the hose a little closer to the excavation.

"Let's see what Brent is doing," I said.

We found him in the dining room shuffling papers and drinking coffee from a tall paper cup. He wore jeans and a forest green sweater that complemented his dark red hair.

"We've come to explore," I said.

"And we brought lunch," Annica added.

"Morning, girls. Sit down." Taking his coffee with him, he moved to a larger table with a view of the garden and the ongoing activity.

I settled myself in a chair and glanced around. The dining room had a different ambience. Without tablecloths, china, and floral centerpieces, without smiling waitresses in their gingham uniforms, the vast cavernous space seemed as inviting as a mausoleum. Our voices bounced back to us as echoes. I slipped my jacket off and felt a sudden urge to put it on again.

"Are we the only ones in the Inn?" I asked.

"The painters will be here this afternoon." He set the empty cup on the table with a force that almost crumpled it. "It seems I inherited a lady when I bought the Inn."

Annica's eyes sparkled. "The ghost?"

"That too, but I'm talking about a real lady, Miss Isabel Bryte. She's a permanent guest of the Inn. I had the devil's own time convincing her to move out of her suite while it's being repainted."

"How long has she lived here?" Annica asked.

"Ten years, she says. Turns out she wants to live in the country but can't keep up a house of her own. What could I do?"

I couldn't imagine Brent turning any lady out of her home. "What *did* you do?"

"I put her up in the Lakeville Lodge, free of charge, and let her choose the new color. It's lavender."

"She can't object to that," I said.

"Lavender." Annica stifled a giggle. "As in *Lavender and Old Lace*. She sounds like an old lady."

"That's *Arsenic and Old Lace*," I said.

"Miss Isabel is a retired French teacher. Yes, you could describe her as elderly. She's interesting. A real character."

Annica sighed happily. I could read her thought: no competition there.

"In all that time, she may have seen something out of the ordinary," I said. "Can we meet her?"

"As soon as she comes back. In the meantime, I think I figured out where the missing room must have been. I came across an old floor plan in some papers the last owner left me."

He meant the room from which Cynthia had vanished. I recalled the details, the few I'd been able to gather.

Cynthia Lauren and her friend, Rachel Carroll, had checked into the Inn on their way home from a vacation in the northern part of the state. While Rachel went down to the dining room for dinner, Cynthia, who complained of a headache, remained behind to rest. After dinner, Rachel returned to the room to find her companion missing. Some of her possessions were still strewn around, but Cynthia was never seen again.

The disappearance of Cynthia, along with Rachel's return to the Inn as a spirit clad in a blue raincoat, were part of the ghost-history of Foxglove Corners.

"It was Room Two Thirteen," Brent said. "Do you want to see where it used to be now or should we eat lunch first?"

"Let's see the room," Annica said quickly.

"We'll do that then." He led the way to the staircase to the second floor.

"Are you going to install an elevator?" I asked, as I eyed the shadowy expanse of stairs. The staircase twisted in dramatic fashion, blocking off the view beyond the bend. The area received little light and the steps were uncarpeted. I reached for the railing.

"I considered it, but my goal is to retain as much of the old-time original flavor as possible." He grasped the railing and shook it. It didn't move. "I'll make repairs to ensure safety as needed."

"An older person might have trouble with the stairs."

"Miss Isabel seems pretty spry, but you have a point. I want to attract other guests."

We reached the second story where slivers of light found their way through small dusty windows. There were echoes up here too: our voices, our footsteps. Something else.

"The last step will be to hire a cleaning crew," Brent said.

"Do you plan to accomplish all this by Halloween?" I asked.

"Barring any setback." He turned left and came to a sudden stop. "This suite belongs to Miss Isabel. We'll leave her door closed, but here…" He opened another door leading to a room furnished in cool greens and blues. It looked like space carved out of a garden.

"Part of this suite used to be Room Two Thirteen." Brent indicated four boundaries with his hands. "Walls were knocked down to form two rooms in an earlier renovation."

To conceal a crime? After all these years, who could know? The renovation had effectively erased Room Two Thirteen from the canvas.

"It's lovely." I noted with appreciation the rug, pink cabbage roses splashed on a rich black background. The focal point of the suite was a charming spinet.

With no one but the ghost to play it.

A spinet was a strange item to have in a suite in the Inn. Perhaps it had been added solely for atmosphere.

Long years ago, there'd been a bed in this space. Or a double bed, or perhaps two twin beds. I let my imagination wander.

Beyond the windows, the storm raged on. Inside, Cynthia pressed her hand to her throbbing forehead and lay back against the pillows. She closed her eyes. A short nap might make her feel better. Then she'd be able to eat.

This scene had transpired decades ago. And then? What happened afterward?

"These other rooms are nice, but less impressive." Brent opened a third door. "You can see why I want to leave them the way they are. Just change the colors and refinish the floors."

I peered into a room well suited to Foxglove Corners with its penchant for fox hunting. It was decorated in earth tones. Horse prints and hunting scenes adorned the wall. Forest green curtains matched the comforter. Placed alongside a window, a Tiffany lamp on a mahogany desk invited a guest to scribble messages on post cards, or make an entry in a travel journal.

Once again I wondered how the previous owner could walk away from such an enchanting place.

Brent showed us the other rooms on the second story, then suggested that we have lunch. Afterward, if we wished, we could explore to our hearts' content.

"What's above?" Annica asked with a glance at the ceiling.

"The attic, with more furniture and the usual discards. The last owner didn't seem interested in what she was giving away. I haven't had time to check everything out yet."

"There's where we can look for a clue," I said.

Brent shook his head. "Not without me. It might be dangerous."

I'd expected him to say something like that. "Well, I don't think Cynthia would go up to the attic in a strange inn."

"She went somewhere," Annica said.

"That she did."

And she didn't come back.

Eight

On Monday I was back in school, but during the occasional lull, my thoughts drifted to the Spirit Lamp Inn. Our investigation had been incomplete and fruitless. After a picnic lunch in the empty dining room, we'd hardly begun to stake out the Inn's nooks and crannies when the painters arrived with their own radio and more noise.

Ladders were dragged up the stairs, paint fumes invaded the halls, and male voices shattered the silence. In general, chaos reigned.

Brent showed us the stairs that led to the attic, after which he returned to the dining room to interview applicants for the position of cook. We left the Inn reluctantly.

"When the workers are finished and before the Inn reopens, we'll go back," I said.

"Let's hope they don't paint over a clue."

"A clue on the walls?"

"You know what I mean."

I did, sort of. So ended our first exploration of the Spirit Lamp Inn.

A few restless murmurs—this was my good World Literature class—indicated that the pages of the *Odyssey* assigned for silent reading had been finished, leaving ten minutes until bell time. And what could we do in ten minutes?

Not much. Wind down. Principal Grimsley believed that every single minute of the period, which wasn't quite an hour, should be devoted to learning. I was more realistic. Let them learn to communicate with one another without shouting.

I closed one text book and opened another. My next class was American Literature Survey. Denver Armstrong's class. Today's selection was an account of a witch trial, a teacher's giant leap from ancient Greece to colonial America.

Could any true narrative compete with the latest horror movie?

Of course not. The selections in the textbook weren't intended to entertain but to preserve a certain dark moment in history. Nevertheless the title alone might spark their curiosity.

The bell rang. The sophomores raced to the door, and the juniors and a few stray seniors streamed in. It was time to switch gears. This morning before my first class I'd drawn a rough depiction of the witch tests in stick figures on the blackboard. I counted on them to elicit a comment or two from the more observant students.

"Whoa!" Denver exclaimed as he paused to view my artwork. "Comics."

Not what I'd hoped for.

I ignored him and pulled the seating chart out of the grade book. The bell rang again, and the latecomers found their desks, most of them seated before the bell's echo faded.

Everyone was accounted for. What a rare occurrence. To begin the class I had a brief unannounced quiz on yesterday's material. I set six copies on the first desk of each row and stood back to watch the fireworks.

"No fair!" Katrina screamed. "You didn't tell us."

"Can we use our books?" Dale asked.

"No books or notes," I said. "It's a surprise quiz. Everybody quiet now. You have ten minutes."

"I don't have to do it," Denver announced in a loud voice. He turned the quiz over and began to draw on the blank side.

"Excuse me," I said. "You all have to do it—if you want a grade. If you plan to pass this class, you have to do the assignments. This quiz, for example."

"I did it twice already. Last semester and the semester before that."

He didn't have to remind me that this was his third attempt to pass American Literature. Denver wasn't stupid, but he lost class time through suspensions and unexcused absences, and he only did assignments when he felt like it.

"This is a different quiz," I said. "Turn the paper over. Remember, use pens for work to be graded. No pencils."

I sounded like a drill sergeant. Denver was obviously planning to ignore me.

Well, it would be his grade. A zero. The other students were scribbling answers or staring blankly at the questions. I walked to the front of the room and glanced at the clock.

After class, I'd talk to Denver about his attitude. If he refused to wait, I'd write yet another discipline referral.

After collecting the quizzes, I launched into a lecture about the witch trials of the time. When the bell rang, to my surprised, Denver stopped at my desk. Ostensibly he handed me a completed drawing of a witch with a pointed hat undergoing the water test.

"If you plan to pass the class, you'll have to do the work," I said.

"You should give me other assignments. It's your job to keep me interested."

It was a struggle to rein in my indignation. "It's not my job to design a special course for a student who fails the original one."

"I bet the principal will side with me," he said.

Oh, no. Would Grimsley agree to Denver's demand? Would I find myself creating a whole new course for this mouthy delinquent?

I struggled to keep my expression neutral as Denver sauntered out the door.

There's nothing like a heated confrontation with a student to pave the way for a relaxing lunch.

~ * ~

I unwrapped my sandwich and regarded it with indifference. Chicken and lettuce on whole wheat bread. Healthy but boring.

Leonora passed me a square of devil's food cake. "I brought one for you from the cafeteria," she said.

"Thanks. That's more appealing than an apple."

"I know what you can do about Denver," she said. "Have him outline each selection. We used to do that in history when I was in high school. It may not meet with new-fangled teaching methods, but I learned a lot that way."

"I could. If I'm forced to give him special work."

"Then substitute another novel for the one you read as a class. Say *Uncle Tom's Cabin.*"

Turn the tables on my arrogant nemesis. I smiled at the thought of Denver plowing through that dated classic. "He'll soon be begging to do regular class work."

I swallowed the last bite of my uninspired sandwich and turned to the cake.

Once my American Literature class dispersed, I looked forward to an enjoyable and relaxing afternoon: Journalism, another World Literature section with a return to ancient Greece, and my conference hour, which amounted to free time unless I found a summons to Grimsley's office in my mail box.

Would Denver take his grievance to the principal? They had a thorny relationship. Denver must have a personal file several inches thick, filled with discipline referrals from all his teachers.

Don't worry about it now, I told myself. *Enjoy the last bite of cake.*

All too soon the bell rang, signaling the end of our lunch minutes. Leonora sprang up. She had to take her tray to the teacher's lounge and hurry back to beat her students to class. I stuffed my trash in the brown paper bag. Invariably I felt more energetic after lunch, more equipped to meet whatever challenges the rest of the day had in store for me.

But I hoped the challenges wouldn't include a trip to the principal's office.

~ * ~

The problems that waited for me at home were quite different from those at Marston High School but every bit as challenging. I'd hardly had time for an afterschool cup of tea when my cell phone rang. It was Sue, sounding her usual agitated self. She came right to the point.

"That man, Alex Blaine, refuses to meet with us," she said.

I needed a second to catch up. Alex Blaine. Deanne Reid's former boyfriend.

"He says he doesn't have anything to say to us. He turned Sparrow over to the Rescue League, and that's the end of the matter. What we did with her is our business."

"But he has to talk to us," I said. "We need all the information available before making a final decision."

"I still haven't let the Summertons know there's a problem."

"You have to, Sue. They may have to give her up."

"I'm hoping it won't come to that. Hoping Ms. Reid will be reasonable and leave Sparrow where she's happy.

"Don't forget the lawsuit she threatened," I said. "We can't just spring it on them."

Sue sighed. "I wish I'd never accepted this job, Jennet. You'd have been so much better at it."

There we differed. I thanked my lucky stars I'd had the good sense to refuse the Rescue League's nomination. Still I was involved anyway. Sue needed help. She was clearly floundering.

I had to say something. "Blaine isn't going to tell us he gave away a dog placed in his care. Where would that leave him?"

"Liable."

I took the phone into the living room and sank into the rocking chair. If there was a way out of this conundrum, I couldn't see it.

"Either this man or Deanna may be lying, and the new owners are caught in the middle," I said.

"So what can we do?" Sue asked.

"At the moment I have no idea."

"Will you think about it and get back to me? Soon? I expect to hear from Deanna Reid again."

"I can think," I said. "But no promises."

Nine

"I have something for Jennet," Brent said. "If you don't mind my giving a gift to your wife, Sheriff."

A present for me? And he was talking to Crane? Practically asking his permission? I didn't see anything.

"And if I did?" Crane's frosty eyes sparkled. He attempted a severe tone that didn't fool either of us.

"I'd give it to her anyway."

He drew an object wrapped in white tissue paper from his pocket. It jingled faintly. Thinking it was a new toy for her, Misty fixed her gaze on his hand.

"It's a bracelet," Brent said as he removed the paper wrapping. "One of the gardeners found it when he was planting the chrysanthemum bed."

He laid it on the coffee table where it shimmered in the lamplight. It was a silver chain heavy with charms. Brent tapped a tiny bell with his finger, and it jingled obligingly. All the dogs came to attention and gathered around him.

"It has all sorts of charms on it," he said. "A crown, a windmill, a fan, a leprechaun…"

I picked it up. A tiny cuckoo clock, a gondola, the bell with the word 'Capri' engraved on it… "Your worker found this buried in the garden?"

"Deep down in the ground. He was chopping away at a root. No telling how long it's been there."

"This is a valuable piece of jewelry," I said.

"Yeah, it's sterling silver. I had it cleaned and appraised."

"It must be old," I said. "No one wears charm bracelets anymore."

"Then you don't want it?" He looked disappointed.

"I didn't say that, but think about the woman who lost it. She'll want it back."

"It could have been in the ground for years," Crane pointed out. "Could be it dates all the way back to the time of that mystery you and Annica are so keen on solving."

"That's a thought," I said. "It could be a clue."

I fastened the clasp around my wrist. "These charms represent different countries. Germany, Italy and Holland, to name a few. Whoever lost it must have been a world traveler. Look, here's a little ship. It could represent the one she sailed on."

Rachel Carroll and Cynthia Lauren had visited the Upper Peninsula of Michigan. Perhaps they had taken other trips together, traveling all over the world, only to come to grief in a rustic Michigan inn on a stormy night. But I was letting my imagination run free as usual. Anyone could have lost this bracelet at any time, although the clasp seemed secure enough. How devastated she must have been when she realized it was gone.

And yet with all those charms, it couldn't just slip off the wearer's wrist without her knowing it.

"I think you should hold on to it for a little while, Brent," I said. "Maybe when you reopen the Inn, one of the customers will recognize it. Or you could start building a display of artifacts from the Inn's past."

Brent nodded. "Good idea, Jennet. I wonder if the former owner remembers whose bracelet went missing."

"You can ask her."

"She may have left town. Why don't you keep it for the time being? It'll be safer here, and you can wear it on Halloween night when you dress up as the Lady in the Blue Raincoat."

"She's not going to do that," Crane said.

"I'm still thinking about it."

That last was to spare Brent's feelings. I had no intention of putting together a ghost costume and pretending to be the Inn's resident spirit. He didn't have to know that yet.

I shook my arm and listened to the music the little charms made as they touched one another.

The bracelet was lovely and unique. Of course it would be; it was a record of the owner's personal memories of faraway lands. They weren't my memories, but somehow the bracelet looked right on my wrist. Certainly it was more at home now than it had been buried in the earth.

That night, when I tried to open the clasp, just for a moment, it seemed that the bracelet didn't want to leave my wrist. Weird.

~ * ~

The next day at school I found a note from Principal Grimsley in my mailbox. *See me today during your conference period.* It was the summons I'd hoped wouldn't come.

I had misjudged Denver Armstrong. He'd taken his case to Grimsley after all. All day I fretted about the appointment and marshaled my arguments for requiring Denver to do the regular classwork.

He'd been tardy today and once again drew witches instead of answering the essay question I'd written on the board.

As soon as the sixth hour bell rang, I took my grade book and hurried to the principal's office. I hoped this wouldn't take all hour as I wanted to start reading my essays.

Just get it over with.

Grimsley pasted his signature smile on and set aside the *Free Press* sports section he'd been reading. "Have a seat Mrs. Ferguson. It appears you have a problem."

This wasn't starting well.

"Denver Armstrong came to me with a complaint. He doesn't think he should be doing your assignments since he did them in previous courses."

"I know," I said. "Denver has been in my American Literature class twice before. Since he did very little work the first two times, they should be new to him."

Grimsley made a steeple of his hands. "It's to everyone's advantage to help this young man graduate."

"He certainly isn't a candidate for Independent Study," I said.

"No, that's for our best students, the cream of the crop."

"What do you suggest then?"

Transfer him to another teacher's class?

He shrugged. "Keep encouraging him. Give him special help but no special work. Perhaps he can do a project for extra credit. Not to take the place of your assignments, of course."

"Did you tell him that?" I asked.

"I told him I'd consult with you."

"I see."

Well, at least Grimsley had sided with me, and I could happily inform Denver Armstrong of our decision. Would it alter his attitude? Probably not. He'd keep drawing witches and peaked hats and broomsticks—I wondered if he was in art class—and sooner or later there'd be another incident. I'd have to bounce him back to the assistant principal who would suspend him.

It was sad, but I didn't see any other outcome. Maybe Denver would have done better with another teacher, but the all-wise computer kept giving him to me.

"Is that all?" I asked.

He rose. "I think so. I want to check on him in a few weeks. Good luck, Mrs. Ferguson."

He should have added, 'You'll need it.'

Ten

With the problem of Denver Armstrong more or less solved, I hoped to cross another one off my list. To that end, I took Halley, Sky, and Raven for a walk on Squill Lane after school, destination Sue Appleton's horse farm.

That other matter, the ultimate fate of the collie Sparrow, was a cloud hanging over the Rescue League's head. It might burst at any moment.

This moment, however, was lovely and carefree.

The leaves on Squill Lane were flame-red and gold, blazing against a deep blue sky, and the light wind created a mesmerizing rustling sound all around us. It was easy to set life's cares aside and simply enjoying being part of nature for this sliver of time.

Sue was in her barn as usual, working with her horses. Raven bounded up to greet her, while Halley and Sky, my quiet ones, walked sedately with me past curious equine eyes and friendly whinnies. The inside of the stable was dim and cool. It smelled of hay and horse and freshly picked apples. Good autumn smells.

"Hi, Jennet," Sue said. "What brings you out this way?"

I hated to dash the hope in her voice. "I wondered if you had any news. Good news, that is."

"I haven't heard a word from Deanna Reid," Sue said. "And after she was so insistent on giving me a week to return Sparrow to her, too. Well, that week has passed."

"How about Alex Blaine?" I asked. "Did he have a change of heart?"

"I wouldn't know. He hasn't called either, and I didn't call him again. He made it clear. He doesn't have anything more to say about Sparrow."

"That isn't good," I said.

"Not at all. We're in Limbo. I keep expecting to be notified of a lawsuit any day now."

"It may not come to that."

But that could be wishful thinking. Still, the one-week deadline had passed. When last I'd spoken to Deanna, she hadn't mentioned any timeline.

From the far end of the barn, I heard Raven barking and an enraged hiss. Sue kept at least four cats, all black. I was surprised it had taken Raven so long to find one.

"Raven, come," I said and was surprised again when she trotted up to me, wagging her tail.

"I went ahead and told Mrs. Summerton what's going on," Sue said. "Now we have one more indignant person to contend with. She refuses to give Sparrow up."

"I didn't suppose she'd hand her over willingly."

"I think I'd better call an emergency meeting of the League. The members deserve to know what we might be up against."

"That's a good idea. Maybe someone can suggest a way out of this tangle."

"In the meantime, all we can do is wait for something to happen," Sue said. "That's always the hard part. Waiting."

"I wish there were some way we could find out what really happened between Deanna and her former boyfriend. Until we do, how can we make a fair decision?"

And having arrived at a judgment, how would we ever implement it?

"I just hope Deanna doesn't find out who has Sparrow," Sue said.

"How could she?"

"Nothing would surprise me. Suppose someone had taken one of your dogs? This pretty blue merle for instance." She let her hand fall on Sky's head and stroked it gently. "What would you do?"

"Move heaven and earth to find her."

"That's what I thought," she said.

I had a sudden memory of Deanna spying Candy from her window and rushing out to make a fuss over her. At first she may have thought Candy was Sparrow. From a distance, it was a natural mistake. But her intensity made me uneasy.

Then there was her story about wanting to buy a tricolor collie.

I suspected that neither Deanna nor Alex had told us the whole story.

~ * ~

The next day I wore the charm bracelet to school.

I hadn't intended to wear it—ever. But my gray dress looked too plain with only a sapphire wreath pin, and the bracelet lay on the dresser, shining in the light of the lamp, tempting me to pick it up, put it on.

The many charms would be a conversation piece. Girls always noticed what you wore. What would I tell them about my latest accessory when they asked, as I knew they would, if I had traveled to all the places represented by the charms?

England, Germany, Italy, Holland…

As it happened, I had. Except for Japan and Australia. I didn't have to add that I hadn't collected the charms myself.

I fastened the clasp around my wrist and went downstairs to join Crane for breakfast. He had made the coffee and fed the dogs, and I had set the table the night before.

"Are pancakes okay?" I asked.

He nodded. "Fine. And bacon."

As I gathered the ingredients, the charms clinked together, drawing the attention of the dogs—and Crane.

"I don't know that I like another man giving you presents," he said.

"Brent always brings presents," I pointed out.

"For both of us or for the house. This one is different."

"Brent didn't buy the bracelet for me," I said. "His landscaper found it."

"He could have given it to Lucy or Annica."

That was true. Annica liked jewelry that jingled. She had an impressive collection for all seasons.

I stirred the batter, considering. Possibly Brent didn't want to encourage Annica's crush. Lucy? I didn't know. He was more than a little fond of Lucy whose metal of choice was gold.

Then I had it. "I'm the senior detective in the group. Suppose the bracelet belonged to Cynthia or Rachel?"

"You'll never know for sure."

"I guess it doesn't matter." I stepped over Candy and spilled the batter onto the grill, forming sizzling golden-brown circles. "I won't wear it often. Just on occasion."

Like today.

~ * ~

"Can I see your charms, Mrs. Ferguson?"

Linda Kierston, one of my Journalism students, eyed my bracelet eagerly.

I'd heard variations of this inquiry all day. It was as if my students had never seen a charm bracelet before. Well, maybe they hadn't. I couldn't remember the last time I'd seen one myself.

"Is that a real bell? Does it ring?"

"Yes to both. It's from the Isle of Capri, which is off the coast of Italy."

Capri was a place I'd explored one rainy weekend, falling under its spell and buying jewelry of my own. I remembered the vivid blues, a grotto, and the touch of rain that couldn't dampen my enthusiasm.

"If I had one, I'd collect ice skates and ballet slippers and cats," Linda said. "All the things I love. Do they make those kinds of charms?"

"I'm sure they do."

I had a fleeting thought of the charms I might collect for a bracelet of my own: a collie, a tiny Victorian house, a wedding ring...

"Why don't you look on the Internet?" I said.

Journalism was the one class I could relax with. The students worked with textbooks and copies of the *Detroit Free Press,* learning the trade. Overall they were congenial and cooperative, and the assignments were fun.

Today, for instance, they were clipping interesting news stories that would probably be followed up in future editions. The sole drawback to a clipping assignment was that it made a mess. It's the rare student who thinks about clean up.

I stooped to retrieve a page that had fallen on the floor. Someone had clipped a story but overlooked another that immediately caught my attention: *Human Remains Unearthed in Foxglove Corners.*

Oh, yes. My attention was most certainly caught.

Eleven

Bones Uncovered during Inn Renovation
I read the article quickly, disappointed that it offered so few details. Workmen installing a fountain on the grounds of the Spirit Lamp Inn had discovered the bones buried deep in the ground beneath a line of hydrangea bushes.

I remembered those hydrangeas in bloom, those gorgeous showy flowers. Who could have guessed they were hiding a grim secret?

"Did you find something good in the paper, Mrs. Ferguson?" Linda asked.

"Something interesting. Is there anyone who hasn't found a story yet? This one will definitely have a follow-up."

Several students raised their hands. I gave the page to the one nearest to me. The *Banner* would have a more substantial article.

Dozens of questions spun around in my mind. Was anything else found with the bones? Like remnants of clothing? A watch or a ring? Had the bones belonged to an adult or a child? To a male or a female? Was there any sign of trauma? A blow to the head or a bullet hole?

And, of course, if the bones belonged to a female, had I found the owner of the charm bracelet?

Naturally my speculation settled on a person known to have gone missing from the Spirit Lamp Inn, Cynthia Lauren, the friend for whom the Lady in the Blue Raincoat conducted her never-ending search.

Wait, I told myself. *You don't know enough about the discovery yet.*

Only Brent could answer my questions, assuming he knew more than the *Free Press* reporter. But how much could he know at this point? It depended on whether he had been at the Inn when the bones were uncovered.

What would happen to them? I imagined the police would take charge of the remains and try to identify the hapless soul who had lain all these years in an unmarked grave. If there were any hope of identifying remains that old.

I had to find out. One way or the other, I needed to talk to Brent.

~ * ~

That was easier said than done. My messages ended up in his voicemail. I could stop at the Inn, but at this time of day, he'd probably have gone home or to his barn. I hoped he'd show up at our house for dinner. Certainly he'd be eager to talk about the discovery.

After school I stopped at Blackbourne's Grocers for milk and eggs and bought the late edition of the *Banner*. Unable to wait, I read the story in the parking lot. It contained a few embellishments but no additional facts.

Their article alluded to Brent Fowler's recent purchase of the Spirit Lamp Inn and mentioned the name of the previous longtime owner, Marin Courtland. This was the first time I'd come across her name.

Did she have any knowledge of a body buried on the grounds of the Inn? The police would want to talk to her. Was there any connection, I wondered, between her hasty departure and the grave? I didn't see how there could be, unless she feared what Brent's planned renovation of the house and replanting the garden might reveal.

What had been a curiosity had developed overnight into a full blown murder mystery. Murder because who buries a body in a garden if not to hide evidence of a homicide?

I folded the paper and drove on to Clovers, intending to buy three take-home dinners in case Brent joined us tonight and possibly talk to Annica. This proved to be a good decision. The Specials included stuffed cabbages, a favorite at our house. Annica was on a break, drinking coffee in a booth toward the back. In a forest green sweater and copper leaf earrings, she looked like an autumn spirit. The *Banner* was open to the page that featured the bones story.

"Cool bracelet," she said. "Crane is the most generous husband on earth. I'd like to have one just like him some day."

That was true, but I didn't want to mislead Annica. "Actually Brent gave me the bracelet—on loan," I said. "One of his men found it buried in the garden. I couldn't resist wearing it today."

Her eyes took on a sparkle I knew well. "It belongs with the bones," she said.

"Maybe."

"You'll have to give it back to him then. Or turn it over to the police."

I hadn't thought of that. I did now and was unprepared for the sense of possessiveness that surged through me.

It's mine. I don't have to give it to anybody.

Good grief. Was I going to obsess about this admittedly beautiful piece of jewelry?

"While you still have it, may I see the charms?" she asked.

"Be my guest." I laid my arm on the table, and Annica examined each charm more closely than I had.

"This little castle opens up. Look!" She pried the base with a frosty pink fingernail, and two miniature figures appeared inside. "It's the Tower of London, and here are the Princes in the Tower. We're reading *Richard III* in one of my classes," she added.

"I didn't realize it opened," I said. "The spinning wheel turns and the bell rings…"

"It's too bad you can't keep it." She drained her cup. "Can I get you a cup of coffee? A piece of pie? We have chocolate meringue."

"Coffee in a minute. I came in for take-out."

"I almost forgot to tell you my news," she said. "Brent hired me for the hostess job. I'm going to work at the Inn on weekends." She patted an errant red-gold curl behind her earring. "He said I'm so pretty people will come for dinner just to see me."

I suppressed a smile. What a line! And Annica believed him. I thought Brent was more innovative. Well, she *was* pretty and bright and warm. She'd be an asset to any establishment.

"So I have to buy a new wardrobe," she said.

"Won't it be too much—going to school, working at Clovers and the Inn?"

"I can manage. It'll be fun seeing Brent every weekend. And when I have breaks, you can help me solve the mystery."

I help *her*?

"Which one?" I asked.

"Is there really a ghost?"

"Well, of course there is," I said. "People have seen her."

"Then we're going to find out what she wants." Annica stared off into space. "What if she wanted Cynthia's body to be discovered? That's already happened. What's left for us to do?"

"I'm surprised at you, Annica," I said. "We can try to find out what happened to Cynthia. Who buried her, why she was killed. The discovery of the bones gives us a head start."

We were both assuming that the bones would prove to be the remains of the mysterious Cynthia Lauren. Well, speculation was free. We weren't officially on the case. Otherwise, we would have to consider other possibilities.

~ * ~

The next day I learned more about the discovery at the Spirit Lamp Inn. The bones belonged to a woman in her late twenties or early thirties. Badly deteriorated brown material might have been a dress or a skirt. When she'd been placed in her grave, she wasn't wearing jewelry. The cause of death hadn't been determined.

These facts were sufficient to bolster my belief that the woman was Cynthia Lauren. And the bracelet? It had fallen off her wrist before the murder.

I tested the clasp. It was strong and wouldn't likely have come loose. Suppose she'd taken the bracelet off for some reason, or someone had removed it from the body? Or maybe her wrist was thinner than mine and it had slipped off at some point to be ultimately lost in the Inn's garden. It might or might not have any tie to the murder.

And what if the murdered woman were someone else?

Annica was right. I should turn the bracelet over to the police. Better still, I would return it to Brent who had given it to me.

Then I could keep it a little longer.

Twelve

Brent didn't have any additional facts, even though he'd been at the Inn when his men uncovered the bones. The discovery in the Inn's garden affected him profoundly.

"It makes me wonder what else is buried in that land I bought," he said. "Are there any other bodies waiting to be dug up? Was the Inn built on an old graveyard?"

"One set of bones is quite enough," I pointed out. "And one bracelet."

He had joined us for a spaghetti dinner the evening following the discovery. Afterward, we sat in the living room over coffee speculating on the possible identity of the murdered woman. Brent agreed with me that she might be the long-lost Cynthia Lauren. But none of us could come up with a motive for murder or a method.

"Remember," I reminded them, "According to every account I've read, Cynthia disappeared in the time it took Rachel to walk down to the dining room and eat dinner. That's about an hour."

"Which doesn't necessarily mean she was murdered in that time frame," Crane said. "She might have been lured away and killed later."

His observation led to more speculation. How one managed to get murdered during a stop in a rural inn was a true mystery.

"I asked the police to keep the story out of the papers, at least till we know a little more," Brent said. "You can see how they listen to me."

I couldn't understand his desire for secrecy. "This is free publicity for the Inn and the Halloween bash you're planning," I said. "You have a ready-made mystery and a ghost."

"I thought of that, but…" He trailed off, taking possession of the tug-of-war stocking toy Misty pushed at him. "Maybe somebody out there didn't want the body to be found. The bones, I mean."

"A murderer still lurking around. I never thought of that."

"Besides, ever since the story broke, gawkers have been tramping all over the grounds, taking pictures and leaving a mess. It's annoying."

"What's there to see?" I asked.

"Crime scene tape and a stalled landscaping project. I don't let them inside the Inn."

"Do they bother the workmen?"

"The landscaping company rescheduled, and the painters are almost finished on the second story. Miss Isabel wants to move back to her suite."

"While you're still closed?" Crane asked. "That could be dangerous."

"And lonely," I added.

Even I, in the grip of mystery-solving fever, wouldn't brave the shadows of the Spirit Lamp Inn without a companion, let alone spend the night in a room on its second floor. I couldn't wait to meet the indomitable Miss Isabel Bryte.

"It's impossible for her to come back at this time," Brent said. "There's no cook. She'd have to have her meals at a nearby restaurant. There's no laundry service. No one around if she were to get sick."

"Does she have transportation?" I asked.

"An ancient Plymouth Fury, but she doesn't go out much. I'm encouraging her to stay put for a while."

"Is it all right if Annica and I visit the Inn again before it opens for business?" I asked.

"Sure. How about tomorrow after school, or whenever Annica is free? Ask her to put together another picnic lunch. There shouldn't be as much commotion as we had the last time."

"Maybe you can take us up to the attic," I said.

"We'll see, but I'd like to deal with what's on the other floors first."

"What I'd like are some answers."

Attics and basements were the obvious places to search for a clue. They were the dark, silent places where unwanted items and other curiosities were stored and subsequently forgotten while in the main part of a house, life continued and the years rolled on.

"Oh, before I forget..." I reached for the bracelet on the mantel, setting the Capri bell in motion. Misty dropped the stocking and lunged for it.

"You'd better have this back, Brent," I said.

He didn't take it.

"Keep it for now, Jennet. Even if it turns out to be a clue, no one has asked about it."

"Nobody knows about it," Crane reminded us.

"Except Luke, the guy who found it," Brent said. "And whoever was near him at the time and whoever he told. You, me, Crane..."

"Annica and Leonora. At least the newspapers didn't get wind of it."

"Besides what would the cops do with it?" Brent seized his opportunity to grab the toy from under Misty's nose. "Lock it away in an evidence room where it'd never see the light of day? It might as well have stayed buried in the ground."

I tapped the spinning wheel lightly, and the wheel turned. Well, I'd offered to return the bracelet, and my offer had been rejected. It was mine now. I set it back on the mantel. Later I'd take it upstairs, and maybe in a few days I'd wear it again.

"If anyone wants a free clue, you'll know where to find it," I said.

~ * ~

How could I be so naïve as to think my problem with Denver Armstrong was solved just because Principal Grimsley had spoken?

Apparently he hadn't spoken to Denver. No, I remembered. He'd left that for me to do.

"So where's my special assignment?" he asked as I passed out a Colonial Writers worksheet.

He was drawing again, a witch with straggly hair, a peaked hat—and a bracelet. I set a worksheet on top of his artwork.

"This is it."

"No way, lady. Grimsley said I could have other stuff to do."

"No, he didn't."

"I'm not going to do this dumb worksheet again."

I didn't feel like arguing with him so early in the day, or ever. In fact my head was starting to ache, a dull pinpoint of pain behind my right eye.

Denver had rested his pencil on the witch's face, over her eye.

"That's your choice," I said. "I can't make you do the assignment. I can only grade what's turned in."

I walked on, resisting the urge to look back and see what he was doing. Denver Armstrong wasn't the only student in my fourth period class. Sometimes it just seemed that way.

At lunchtime, I took two headache pills, hoping to feel better for the rest of the day. I told Leonora about Denver's drawing and the sharp pencil point aimed at the witch's eye.

"He's the cause of this headache," I said.

"Don't be ridiculous. It's probably the change in weather."

"I felt fine this morning. Last semester he drew a dragon and named it Jennet. This year I'm a witch."

"You don't know that the witch is supposed to represent you. You're reading about the Salem Witch Trials."

"I'm not serious," I said quickly. "It was just a thought. Denver Armstrong is the most potent stress maker in all my classes, and stress can bring on a headache."

"Forget about him. Have half my brownie."

She cut it with a plastic knife, giving me the larger piece. It was frosted, with a walnut in the center. An antidote for anything, even a rebel student.

I thanked her and set the rest of my sandwich aside uneaten.

I'd read that chocolate was bad for headache sufferers. It had the opposite effect on me, and by the time my Journalism class arrived, the pain behind my eye had abated. A little.

Thirteen

Every day in Journalism class, I scoured the *Free Press* for updates on the bones story. I never saw a follow-up article, nor did the *Banner* have any further information. I listened to the evening news and checked the Internet. That only meant nothing was happening.

I could see the mystery being shelved while the police dealt with current happenings. That was understandable. How many people wanted to know more about the woman buried and forgotten for so many decades?

The story mattered to me, though, and to Brent, and presumably to the killer who might still be alive and desperate to keep his crime a secret. Even at this late date he or she could still be prosecuted for the murder.

A secret murderer! The idea turned my blood to ice. Apparently it hadn't yet occurred to Crane to warn me away from the mystery at the Spirit Lamp Inn. With luck it never would.

Realistically, the killer might be long dead, in which case there was no need for undue concern. But suppose he wasn't?

We weren't able to return to the Inn until Saturday as Annica was either working a late shift at Clovers or studying for an exam. But Saturday was free for both of us. As soon as I took the dogs for their walks, I set out to meet Annica at the Inn. She had packed a picnic lunch again, and I'd filled a cooler with beverages. On an impulse I slipped my mystery notebook into my purse along with my cell phone. I planned to take pictures.

I was surprised that the Lady in the Blue Raincoat hadn't made an appearance now that Cynthia's remains had been unearthed. After her decades-long search for her friend, you'd think she'd be on hand or close by.

Maybe she was. Unfortunately I doubted that my cell phone camera was capable of photographing a spirit.

As I turned into the Inn's parking lot, I saw that Brent's painters had moved outside. They were turning the exterior of the Inn from dull brown to a glossy creamy white that, curiously, did little to minimize the effect of the spooky façade. It must be the gables. Gingerbread-trimmed gables and ghosts went together in my view, and the change in color made the Inn look as if it were illuminated from within. It was an inspired choice.

Brent came out to the porch to meet us. He stepped into the sunlight and took the picnic basket in one hand and the cooler in the other. "Let's take these right to the dining room," he said. "I'm starving."

"Can we see the grave?" Annica asked.

"If you'd like. There's nothing in it, though."

"Are they sure?"

"Reasonably. What do you think they overlooked?"

"Another piece of jewelry, maybe? A bloodstained dagger? Another body?"

"Let's assume the police did their job." I held the door open, and Annica fairly skipped across the threshold, preceding Brent to the dining room.

I stopped at the abandoned hostess station, remembering the first time I'd visited the Inn with Leonora, both of us drenched from a sudden storm, dripping on the floor and surrounded by silence.

No one had been there to greet us. The dining room was empty. We wondered what kind of place we'd come to. Then a single server appeared. The Spirit Lamp Inn was, then and now, a bastion of mystery.

Brent had opened the basket. He was asking Annica what kind of sandwiches she'd brought.

I heard her answer. "Turkey on whole wheat and corned beef on rye."

The unsettling mood that had taken hold of me lifted. In a few weeks, Annica would be standing at this station wearing one of her new dresses and earrings that clinked or clanged or jingled. Brent would welcome guests in his booming voice. The Inn would come to life again.

But I suspected nothing would change.

"Hey, Jennet!" Annica called. "What's keeping you? Brent has something to show us."

I joined the others. Annica was setting the contents of the basket on a table with a view of the grave. They included a whole pie.

"What is it?" I asked.

Brent whisked a tiny object out of his pocket, a silver heart embossed with graceful scrolls. "Another charm. I'm betting it came from the bracelet."

"I wonder," I said. "The other charms were souvenirs from different countries. I figured the owner bought a charm in each place she visited."

"A valentine heart is universal," Annica pointed out.

"Where did you find it?" I asked.

"One of the painters came across it in a closet. It was hiding in plain sight."

"That's incredible," Annica said. "In all the years you'd think someone would have seen it."

I held the charm to the sunlight, hoping one of the scrolls would prove to be an initial *C*. They were just scrolls.

"We don't know for certain it came from the bracelet," I said. "It could have been lost anytime. Someone might have hung a bracelet over a hook, and one of the charms fell off. It could even have been part of a necklace, although it seems a little too small."

When I got home, I'd examine my bracelet to see if there were any extraneous spaces between the charms.

My bracelet.

"I guess you're right," Annica said. "Things are always getting lost in my closet. How often do you look in corners?"

"Usually just when you're painting them."

Annica opened the cooler and surveyed the offerings: ginger ale, root beer, iced tea, bottled water, sparkling water. She chose a root beer for herself and said, "Let's hurry up and eat. I want to see if we can find anything else."

~ * ~

"Hello! Is anybody in there?"

The voice, low and melodious, echoed in the silent entrance. Startled, I almost dropped my sandwich. I'd been thinking about ghosts, wondering if we'd see one today, and here came a spirit as if on cue.

Annica must have had a similar thought. "What was that?" she asked, a barely discernible quiver in her voice.

The unknown arrival spoke again. "Mr. Fowler? Are you in the dining room?"

Not a ghost.

"Uh oh," Brent said. "It's Miss Isabel."

She drifted through the door, a diminutive, silver-haired vision in flowery pink, bringing a potent scent of carnation with her. She wore white gloves, carried a small white handbag, and, incredibly, wore a blue straw hat set at a tilted angle on her head.

She might have drifted in from another season, another decade. Brent rallied quickly. "How are you this morning, Miss Isabel? I didn't expect you."

"I came for my white ruffled cardigan." Her eyes swept over Annica and me. "Am I interrupting an intimate lunch?"

"These are my friends, Jennet and Annica," he said. "They're interested in the history of the Inn. Ladies, meet Miss Isabel Bryte."

"We're psychic investigators," Annica said.

Miss Isabel bestowed a bright smile on us. She pulled off her gloves. I couldn't help staring at them. I'd never owned a pair of white cotton gloves, nor a dainty summer hat, come to think of it.

"You've come to the right place," she said. "We take pride in our household ghost."

"Please join us for lunch," Brent said. "There's plenty."

She glanced at the table. "I *would* like a drink. Spring water will be perfect."

He pulled up a chair for her, opened a bottle of Michigan Pure, and offered her a paper cup.

"I had another reason for stopping in today," she said. "I want to move back to the Inn. The lodge is so noisy with people coming and going constantly. I can't get any rest and can't even concentrate to read."

"You'll be back as soon as the Inn reopens. That's a promise."

"That won't be until Halloween. It's too long to wait."

"It may be sooner," Brent said. "We've gone over and over this, Miss Isabel. It isn't safe for you to stay in the Inn alone. I don't know why you'd want to."

"Because it's my home. I love the woods and the solitude. There's no other place I want to be."

He took a deep breath. It wasn't often that Brent lost an argument, and he didn't intend to lose this one. "I'm responsible for the well-being of the people under my roof now," he said. "I won't take a chance with your life. What if a thief broke in? What if he had a gun? You could be dead for hours before anyone discovered your body."

"Oh, don't be so dramatic, Mr. Fowler. I'll be perfectly okay."

"Have a piece of pie, Miss Isabel," Annica said. "It's raspberry." That diverted her. Brent cast Annica a grateful look.

"I believe I will, if you're sure I'm not intruding," she said.

As Annica divided the pie into neat slices, I said, "Have you ever seen the Lady in the Blue Raincoat, Miss Isabel?"

"Never, I'm sorry to say. But I don't have to see her to know she exists. She lives here." Miss Isabel cut a small piece of pie with a plastic fork and tasted it. "Delicious! So I won't really be alone, Mr. Fowler. You don't have to worry about me."

Fourteen

We lingered over our pie, not only because Annica had cut enormous pieces, but because Miss Isabel started talking about her ghostly experiences at the Spirit Lamp Inn and didn't seem inclined to stop. She might not have actually seen the Lady in the Blue Raincoat, but over the years she'd heard inexplicable sounds.

"Such as?" I asked.

"Footsteps in the hall, swishings like the sound material makes when someone passes by, faraway music, rain..."

"Rain?" Annica asked. "What's spooky about that?"

"Yes, rain beating on the windows when there isn't a cloud in the sky. Ghost rain."

"Well, that *is* scary," Annica said.

As for footsteps, swishing sounds, and music, there was nothing unusual about that in an Inn.

Then Miss Isabel added, "I'd hurry to the door, but there was never anyone in the hall, and the music would stop."

Well then, that, too, was scary.

"Sometimes when it's absolutely quiet I can hear people talking," she added, "but I can't make out what they're saying. It's like the walls have absorbed conversations from those who stayed at the Inn in the past. You can see why I never feel alone here."

"Miss Isabel," Brent said in a tone that brooked no argument, "that's insane. Walls can't record conversations."

"Now, Brent, you want a supernatural atmosphere for your Halloween bash," I reminded him. "What would be better than unearthly sound effects?"

Brent laid his hand on Miss Isabel's arm. He was frowning. Clearly her belief in a phantom guest and spirit noises disturbed him.

"A ghost doesn't make an adequate guardian," he said. "The Lady wouldn't be able to stop our hypothetical thief."

Miss Isabel gave him a coy smile. "She could materialize and scare him to death."

"You can't count on that."

"I wish that collie dog were still here. She would protect me. We were best friends."

She was talking about Breezy, the dog the cook had rescued and ultimately returned to her real owner. She'd had the run of the grounds and the Inn itself. Naturally Breezy would have become attached to an animal-loving guest.

"I have no intentions of changing my mind, Miss Isabel," Brent said. "I'll welcome you back with open arms when I reopen the Inn. Until then it's off limits."

"Does anyone want that last piece of pie?" she asked.

No one did. "And may I have a bottle of iced tea, please?"

Annica gave her one. While she devoured the pie with gusto, I jotted down notes in my mystery book. Footsteps, swishings, music, rain, talking. It was a beginning.

~ * ~

When the pie was gone and Brent had eaten the last sandwich, Miss Isabel left us to go up to her suite and retrieve her cardigan.

"Do you think I convinced her?" Bremt asked.

"No," I said. "She'll be back with another argument. She's sweet but obstinate."

"I don't want anything to happen to her."

"She looks so fragile." Annica gathered unused paper products and stashed them back in the picnic basket. "You just want to protect her."

"I think she's stronger than she looks," I said. "She'd have to be to contemplate staying in an isolated Inn alone. Well, fellow psychic investigator, shall we begin our tour?"

Annica closed the basket. "I want to see the attic first."

"You'll get dirty," Brent said. "You'll get cobwebs in your hair. Are you ready for that?"

"Not really." Annica patted the red-gold curls that peeked out from behind her coral earrings. "But I'm willing to make the sacrifice for science."

We waited until Miss Isabel came down, the white cardigan draped over her shoulders. Brent walked her to the door. When he rejoined us, he said. "I wouldn't put it past her to stay up in her room till we all leave. I watched her drive away and locked the front door."

"How do we get to the attic?" Annica asked.

"Follow me," he said.

There was a railing to hold on to, but the stairs were dark. When Brent switched on the overhead light, nothing happened.

"I'll have to change that bulb," he said.

One of us should have thought to bring a flashlight. What detective goes sleuthing without a flashlight...or a candle?

Brent reached the top step and pushed on a panel set in the ceiling. It creaked open to a blast of cold air and faint slivers of light stealing through the vents. All we could see was an intimidating vista of trunks, stacks of boxes, floor lamps, chairs, and all kinds of small tables.

Discards, in other words, from the floors below. In all likelihood, they were antiques. They had been stored on either side of a makeshift row, crammed together so that it would be inconvenient if not impossible to browse among them.

And it was still up here. As still as a mausoleum.

Brent led the way, about six feet into the attic and came to a stop, gazing at the jumble of items. "I guess I bought all of this stuff along with the Inn. The owner didn't want to move it, wasn't even curious about what she was giving away."

"I wonder why," I said. "I can't imagine she'd leave everything behind. Some of it may be valuable."

"Who knows? I thought she was on the nutty side."

Suddenly Annica said, "I didn't see a squirrel cage on the chimney. Could there be bats in the attic?"

"It wouldn't surprise me," Brent said.

She paused. "Well, I *am* afraid of bats."

"I don't hear anything suspicious." I stepped around her. "Don't be a baby, Annica. You're the one who wanted to see the attic."

I moved a few steps farther, brushing a suspicious substance away from my face.

"Watch your step, Jennet," Brent said, reaching for my hand. "The floor is unfinished."

"Can't we bring some of these boxes down and look through them in comfort, where there's some light?" Annica asked.

"Then what do we do with whatever's inside? I'm trying to get the rooms ready for occupancy. I don't want junk lying around."

"Who says it's junk? Maybe you'll find something that fits right into one of the rooms."

I took a deep breath and listened. Was that muted music? Not in the attic, but somewhere beneath us?

No, I decided. It was the power of suggestion, but that power was potent. I could almost smell the fear and feel an alien heaviness descend on me. Almost…

Get away!

Was that my trusty inner voice or another spectral one? No one else appeared to hear anything.

Brent's hand tightened on mine as I slid into a wide space between the boards. Shaken, I regained my footing.

Behind me, Annica sneezed. "Ugh. I'm allergic to something up here."

"Dust," Brent said. "Cleaning an attic is at the bottom of my list. Okay, Annica, you've seen it. Ready to go?"

"But there are so many places to look up here," she said.

"You don't know what you're looking for," he pointed out. "We can come back sometime. How about searching through the closets? Maybe we'll find more jewelry."

He opened the door, and Annica skittered out, half protesting.

"That's funny," he said. "I thought I left that door open. Coming, Jennet?"

"Coming," I said and added, "I think you have a haunted attic, Brent."

Fifteen

On the way home, we passed the Haver House on Deer Leap Road. I glanced out the window as the surrounding acres flew by. Leaves had fallen, covering the dead wildflowers in a russet and gold blanket. The 'For Sale by Owner' sign had tipped over into a mound of leaves. It was barely visible in the shadow cast by the house, and the barn loomed over all. It seemed taller than it had been before.

In my view the place was still haunted.

"The house looks so lonely," I said.

"And sad," Annica added. "Whoever buys it should paint it a light color, like the Spirit Lamp Inn, then paint the barn to match."

And in the summer, the wildflowers would be back. The explosion of color would make a difference in the scene. Superficially.

After a while Annica said, "We have to go back to the attic, Jennet. Brent didn't give us a chance to explore it properly."

I hid a smile. "You told Brent you wanted to *see* it. He took you at your word."

"The next time I'll wear jeans and an old sweater and tie a scarf around my head. I'll be ready for anything."

Her anything, I suspected, was a live creature.

"If there were bats in the attic, they'd have made some kind of noise," I pointed out.

"What kind?"

"Oh, a flapping. A hissing... Fortunately I've never met up with a bat."

She shuddered. "Still, if you wanted to conceal evidence of a crime, what better place is there than an old overcrowded attic?"

I thought about that. "If I killed somebody, I'd destroy the evidence."

And bury the body. But in the woods, not the flower garden.

"I've been thinking about a suitcase," I said. "People don't travel without one. What happened to Cynthia's clothes and toilet articles?"

"The killer stashed them in the attic."

"No, I don't think so." I remembered the books I'd read about the disappearance. "According to Rachel, Cynthia's nightgown was on the bed and various other possessions in the room. There was no mention of a suitcase. Wherever she went, she left in a hurry. It makes sense that Rachel took Cynthia's property with her when she left the Inn."

"Except for her bracelet and the heart charm Brent found."

"We don't know for sure they belonged to Cynthia. Especially the heart charm."

"Isn't it strange, though, that Brent is finding jewelry all over the place?"

"Maybe not so strange when you consider all the people who stayed in the Inn over the years."

Annica set her coral drop earring spinning. "If I lost one of my bracelets or an earring, I'd do everything in my power to find it."

"Unless you were already dead," I said.

~ * ~

I dropped Annica off at Clovers where she planned to buy a take-out dinner and drove on to Jonquil Lane. As soon as I went through the door, wading through a pack of excited collies, my cell phone rang.

It was Sue Appleton.

"I just got off the phone with Joyann," she said. "She's upset."

"Who's Joyann?" I asked.

"Joyann Summerton. Sparrow's new owner."

"Oh." With my thoughts still on the attic at the Spirit Lamp Inn, I'd almost forgotten that the Rescue League had a major issue to deal with.

"What happened now?"

"A chance encounter with Deanna Reid at the park in Lakeville. Joyann was there with her kids and Sparrow. Deanna saw them and made a horrible scene."

"So now Deanna knows who has Sparrow. That isn't good."

"But she doesn't know her name or where she lives."

"She could find out," I said.

"Anyway, Deanna screamed at Joyann and accused her of stealing Sparrow. Called her a thief. A crowd gathered. The kids started to cry. A cop happened to be at the park, or it could have escalated. It was bad enough. What was worse…"

There was more?

"Sparrow was overjoyed to see Deanna. She lay down, crossed her paws, and refused to walk on. That upset Joyann more than Deanna's outburst."

Good girl, I thought. *You know your mistress.*

I'd definitely taken sides in the ongoing dispute. A dog belongs with the person who first captures her heart. I believed that. Of course, as a member of the Rescue League, I should be impartial. We still didn't know the whole story.

But Sparrow knows it.

"She must have gotten up," I said. "Unless they're all still in the park."

"She did, but Joyann had to yank on the leash and drag her. Sparrow choked. Then Deanna accused Joyann of abusing her dog. She threatened Joyann."

"With a lawsuit again?"

"With physical injury and death. What are we going to do, Jennet?"

I reached into space for an idea. There were none there. But we had to do something to end this debacle before Joyann or Deanna or Sparrow got hurt.

"You were going to call a meeting of the Rescue League to discuss the problem, Sue," I said. "Do it. We can't just let this situation drag on."

"I will. I'll try to get everybody together on Friday at my place."

"I'll be there. Let's hope someone can suggest a solution that will satisfy everybody."

I snapped the phone shut and thought about what I'd just said. I feared we'd reached a point of no return. Anything could happen. Both women felt justified in claiming the collie. The man at the heart of the problem refused to talk to us. Deanna had showed she was capable of volatile behavior. Joyann Summerton and her family appeared tenacious.

If ever a conflict called for mediation, this was it.

~ * ~

I kept thinking about suitcases. Overnight bags. Hat boxes because the disappearance had happened in the nineteen fifties.

And I thought about a nightgown folded on the bed. That was what Rachel Carroll found when she returned to the room after dinner.

Cynthia had never put that nightgown on, never gone to bed.

I tried to re-create the scene, using the scant facts mentioned in the printed accounts I'd read.

After searching the room and reporting Cynthia missing, Rachel would have stayed on at the Inn, hoping to find a trace of Cynthia, but eventually she would have gathered their possessions and continued her journey home.

If Cynthia's luggage had been missing, the disappearance would have turned in a different direction, indicating she'd left of her own volition. But why? I could only think of one scenario: by chance Cynthia met an old boyfriend and decided to drive home with him.

No, not likely. Even without knowing Cynthia, I rejected the idea. If she changed her plans, she would have let Rachel know. Certainly she would have taken her nightgown.

It didn't happen that way.

However the disappearance played out, the suitcase couldn't be in the attic. Could it?

I recalled the music I thought I'd heard while standing in the attic and the strange heaviness I'd felt falling over me.

Was it imagination? Symptoms of physical discomfort in the cold, airless space? Something more sinister?

I needed more information. Specifically, I needed to reread those books I'd found in the Foxglove Corners Public Library. Maybe I'd missed an important clue.

Sixteen

The next day after school I made a stop at the Foxglove Corners Public Library. The old white Victorian, once the family home of librarian Miss Elizabeth Eidt, sat drowsing on an undulating sea of leaves. Miss Eidt's black cat, Blackberry, kept her tireless vigil on the porch, lying in one of the vintage wicker chairs that gave the place its cozy old-time look.

Blackberry was an unfriendly animal with the innate superiority complex and glittering green eyes of her kind. I walked past her with a hasty "Hi, cat," and stepped into the cool, silent vestibule.

Miss Eidt was expecting me. I'd called from school asking her to set aside the library's collection of books on local hauntings for me.

She sat at her desk surrounded by Halloween decorations, reading and twisting the double strand of pearls that brightened her pale lavender suit. At this hour the library was practically deserted, but soon people would begin to drift in and stay until closing time.

"Hello, Miss Eidt," I said. "You're looking well."

She'd been under the weather the last time I'd seen her.

"Jennet! I'm feeling much better, thank you." She closed her book and gave me the warm smile reserved for her special friends. "I have a surprise for you. It's a book you haven't seen yet. I didn't even know we had it."

She took a large thin volume from the stack on her desk and opened it to a page she'd marked. "It's called *Memorable Tales from Foxglove*

Corners," she said. "Debby found it shelved with the fiction. Look on page one hundred and seven."

I opened the book and stared down at an incredible illustration, a reproduction of a *Banner* front page, dated August twentieth, nineteen sixty-five. Under the heading, 'Missing Tourist Case Remains a Mystery' was the picture of a girl with wavy hair parted in the middle.

"Cynthia," I said.

"It's that story you were researching about the girl who vanished from the Spirit Lamp Inn. Ten years later, they still hadn't found her."

The girl in the photograph was smiling slightly as if leery of the camera's power to capture a person's essence. I studied her features in the light.

What can you tell from a picture? I could surmise that Cynthia was serious, quiet, unflappable. She must have been adventurous, but there was no trace of a restless spirit in her eyes.

In my mind I saw the girl who traveled around the world and bought a silver charm for her bracelet in every country she visited.

"This is how I imagined she'd look," I said. "Young. Quite Pretty. Blonde. It helps to have a face to match with the name."

Miss Eidt sighed. "So now they've found her, after all these years. She's nothing but dry bones in an unmarked grave."

"You've heard about the discovery at the Inn, I take it."

"From Mr. Fowler. Those remains have to belong to Cynthia. Who else went missing in Foxglove Corners?"

"A lot of people," I said.

"Yes, but who else vanished from the Spirit Lamp Inn? Just think. All these people writing about that story down through the years, and we finally have the answer."

"That's what I think, but there's no proof yet," I said. "At least none that we know. Crane is always cautioning me not to jump to conclusions."

"Well this conclusion is pretty clear, as far as I'm concerned. Crane is a lawman. He has to be careful. We don't."

"Everything points to the murder victim being Cynthia," I said.

"I read the chapter. There's quite a bit of information about the case in it. Maybe you'll find something you didn't know."

"I know very little, Miss Eidt," I said. "Mostly I was concentrating on Rachel Carroll, the friend she left behind."

"The ghost who haunts the Inn, you mean? The one they call the Lady in the Blue Raincoat."

"The same."

"Now I suppose you're going to try to find out who murdered the poor girl and also solve the mystery of the ghost."

"I guess I am, in my spare time. Suddenly the Inn's lure has become irresistible. Did you know that Brent Fowler is the new owner?"

"He told me when he was in here the other day. Mr. Fowler is such a kind man. He stops in regularly to see that everything is okay."

I smiled at the thought of the boisterous Brent in a library. "Not to take out a book?"

"Sometimes. He reads non-fiction. Books about horses mostly. He's given me money to buy new ones. Uh oh, I shouldn't have said anything. Don't tell him."

The door opened and two girls came in. They ended their chatter and walked past us to a prominent display of Halloween-themed paperbacks for teenagers, many of them with garish covers. I supposed Lucy Hazen's work was well represented.

This year for Halloween I'd be reading a real life horror story.

I signed out the book. If there was new information in it, I'd only take a few of the other ones. I scanned the titles and chose two that I remembered being especially informative.

"Can you stay for tea and cake?" Miss Eidt asked. "Debby's around somewhere. She can watch the library."

The offer was tempting, and I was hungry; but I was already going to be late getting home.

"Not today," I said. "The dogs are waiting. I'll take a rain check, though."

"Anytime," she said. "Let me know what you find out about the bones and the ghost and the killer and... Oh, my, Jennet, I can't keep up with you. You lead such an exciting life."

"I do," I said.

In more ways than one.

~ * ~

I didn't expect to hear from Deanna Reid again. I assumed she'd deal directly with Sue Appleton. But I had a message from her on my answering machine when I came home. She needed to talk to me as soon as possible. It was urgent.

Odd. How did she get that number?

I delayed returning the call until I'd fed the dogs and made a beef stew for dinner. I hadn't had an opportunity to read my chapter yet, and Crane would be home before long.

Well, I'd read it after dinner, postponing the pleasure of dipping into a new source. But I didn't want to put off unpleasantness.

While the stew bubbled on the stove, I dialed Deanna's number. She answered on the third ring, as if she'd been waiting by the telephone.

"Mrs. Ferguson," she said, "I've found my dog, Sparrow, and she's in trouble. I have to get her away from those people. Please, won't you help me?"

This change in attitude shocked me. I could almost like this young woman and certainly empathize with her, although I couldn't let her know my true feelings. And I couldn't tell her I already knew about the meeting in the park.

It would be interesting to hear another version of that volatile encounter.

"How did you find her?" I asked.

"By chance. We were in the same place at the same time. Sort of like when you walked past my house with your tri. Mrs. Ferguson, Sparrow is thin. Her coat is matted. She's being abused. Don't you people investigate homes before you place dogs in them?"

"Someone does. That's not my job at this time." Realizing how inadequate that sounded, I added, "How do you know she's being abused after one short meeting?"

"The way that woman yanked on her leash. Sparrow almost choked. Who knows what goes on behind closed doors? She probably has to eat junk food, and she hasn't been groomed since I had her."

"I see."

I hesitated, unsure how much of this to believe. I'd have to see Sparrow. Maybe Sue would let me pay a visit to the Summertons. Let me? She'd be overjoyed at any help I offered.

"I'll look into it, Ms. Reid," I said. "We have a clause in our contract. If the home proves unsatisfactory, the dog comes back to us."

"That's all I ask," she said. "Can you do it soon?"

"Not until sometime next week," I said. "But I *will* do it. Or see that it's done."

She thanked me, and I went back to check on my stew. Now I had another call to make, to Sue. Assuming she okayed my visit to Joyann Summerton, I intended to wait until the League Meeting on Friday. In the meantime I could only hope Deanna had exaggerated Sparrow's plight.

If she hadn't... That would be terrible, but it would solve one problem. Joyann Summerton would no longer be eligible to adopt a collie from our League and the threat of a lawsuit would evaporate. Deanna's former friend—I'd forgotten his name—would no longer be involved.

Seventeen

After dinner I read the chapter on Cynthia's disappearance in *Memorable Tales* while Crane built a fire with the dubious help of Candy and Misty. That done, he settled back on the sofa with a cup of coffee and the *Banner*.

The crackle of the fireplace flames blended with the rustle of the pages and created a soothing, safe background for a harrowing story of loss and mystery. As Miss Eidt had suggested, the account contained information new to me.

Ten years after Cynthia's disappearance, Rachel Carroll was still making annual pilgrimages to the Oaken Bucket Inn—as it was then called—staying in the room she had shared so briefly with Cynthia and encouraging the police to keep working on the case.

That was difficult for them to do as there wasn't a single clue. There were no suspects and no conceivable motive for the incident. They didn't refer to it as a crime.

During this time, two theories arose: that Rachel herself had had a hand in Cynthia's disappearance and that Cynthia had left the Inn without notifying anybody for some unfathomable reason. Both soon were debunked.

On a few of these visits, Rachel had another companion, Cynthia's younger sister, Catherine. That was a detail to follow up. Catherine might still be alive. If she were, possibly she could tell me more about the case. I made a note to find out where she was living.

A quotation from Catherine echoed one of my thoughts. "Cynthia traveled all over the world. How could this happen to her in a little town in our own state?"

Also I learned that both Rachel and Cynthia lived in Oakpoint. They were teachers at Amelia Earhart Middle School, an institution that had long since closed its doors. I was slowly becoming aware of an invisible bond between Cynthia and me. I was a teacher in an Oakpoint school.

No mention was made of a silver charm bracelet, but what world traveler wouldn't want to collect a souvenir from each port of call she visited? Cynthia would almost certainly have showed her sister the charm bracelet.

If it had belonged to her. I still thought it had.

There was no picture of Rachel in the news story. It would have been helpful to know what the Lady in the Blue Raincoat looked like when she walked the earth. I knew now that she had been alive ten years after Cynthia's disappearance. I made another note to find out when Rachel had died.

When Crane folded the *Banner* and deigned to notice Misty and her tug-of-war toy, I summarized the new information for him and showed him Cynthia's picture.

"She looks too young to be a world traveler," he said.

"She was twenty-six."

"Maybe she took a tour, one of those around-the-world trips."

I didn't have any problem with that aspect of the story.

"Rachel and Cynthia were teachers. They must have spent summers traveling in far-off places. Lots of teachers do that." I recalled Catherine's remark. "The Oaken Bucket Inn nestled in the woods of Foxglove Corners seems relatively safe, compared to Africa and Shanghai."

Crane smiled. "More likely it was England and France."

"If we find out that the remains in the grave *are* Cynthia's, someone is going to have to update the story," I said.

And I was the person to do it. I'd begun writing a book about my supernatural experiences in Foxglove Corners but had run out of material. Here was my chance to add to it. The next time Annica and I visited the Spirit Lamp Inn, I'd take pictures of the gravesite.

Of course I couldn't write a new version until we were sure that Cynthia had been found at last. And what a coup if I could solve the mystery and name her killer. However unlikely that seemed at the moment.

"It looks like that bracelet Brent gave you might have belonged to Cynthia," Crane said. "You should turn it over to Mac, honey."

Lieutenant Mac Dalby was Crane's friend and my nemesis who thought, not without justification, that I meddled in police matters. I could anticipate his reaction. "He'd wonder why it took me so long to get around to it," I said.

"Probably. So do I."

"I will," I said. "Sometime. I only wore it once, but I've grown attached to it."

I kept the bracelet on the dresser and often, while getting ready for school, I picked it up—and put it down again. I didn't know why. There was always a good excuse, always a necklace or brooch that would go better with the day's dress or sweater and a bracelet would be overkill.

Crane was right. I should be a conscientious citizen and give it to Mac. I'd tell him I'd forgotten about it. He'd never believe me, but so what?

Wear it once more then decide, I told myself. *Wear it tomorrow.*

~ * ~

The next morning, I fastened the charm bracelet around my wrist and added a silver leaf pin to my black dress. The charms jingled every time I moved my arm, attracting the collies' attention and later, that of more than one curious student.

All morning I fielded questions about the bracelet and eventually found myself telling classes about my own travels to Germany and France without actually saying I collected the charms myself. The tiny beer stein with the top that opened was the most popular charm.

By the time the bell announced the beginning of fourth hour, I was craving sauerbraten and strudel.

My American Literature class roared into the room with the unbridled energy of a hurricane. Denver Armstrong was the last to enter, without a book or notebook. Just himself with a pencil tucked into the pocket of his red shirt and a smirk on his face.

Without a single sign, I knew something bad was going to happen in fourth hour today. I glanced out the window at the stretch of wooded property that belonged to the school district. Wild winds had stripped the trees. They rose, gaunt and gloomy, against a slate gray sky. A perfect backdrop for trouble.

Today I was returning the Colonial Era essays I'd graded last night. They reflected a week's worth of research, and on the whole they were good. Sometimes the smartest students can be the worst behaved.

As I handed out the last paper, Denver called out, "Where's mine?"

He hadn't turned in an essay. He hadn't done a single assignment since I'd informed him of the principal's decree.

"You didn't give me one," I said.

He swore. "I put it on your desk. You lost it."

This was an old ploy and really I should devise a better system for collecting assignments. Hand in a paper, get a receipt. Something like that.

"That didn't happen," I said.

"He did," Katrina piped up. "I saw him. It was on top of mine."

"If you lost my report, you have to give me an 'A' for it," Denver said.

"I didn't lose it, and you're not getting a free 'A'."

"That isn't fair," Katrina shouted.

"No fair," somebody yelled.

I caught the look Katrina exchanged with Denver. Sly, ingratiating, triumphant. They must have planned this.

"That's the last work I do for you, lady." Denver marched out of the room without a backward look.

Now the question remained. Would Denver leave the building for an early lunch or take his new complaint to the principal? And would Grimsley believe me?

He'd sided with me the last time. Surely as a former teacher—he had taught science—Grimsley would be familiar with the 'You lost my paper' line.

"That isn't fair, Mrs. Ferguson," Katrina repeated.

A few minutes had elapsed. I knew it was crucial to stop any rebellious grumbling in its track.

I walked to the podium and opened the heavy literature book. "We're starting a new section today," I said. *"The American Imagination.* I can promise you there'll be some exciting stories to read."

"Yeah, right," someone said.

I ignored the voice and gave the shamrock charm on my bracelet a light tap.

Bring me luck, I thought.

Eighteen

The end of the day arrived with no summons to the principal's office. Furthermore, I'd passed him in the hall, and we'd exchanged smiles, mine fleeting and his permanently pasted on.

Obviously Denver Armstrong hadn't taken his grievance to Grimsley. He'd been bluffing. With his abysmal track record, who would believe him?

I was too experienced an educator to let a malcontented bully push me over the edge into paranoia. The way to avoid a repeat performance was simply not to allow students to drop assignments on my desk. Collect them personally and perhaps give out a receipt of sorts, a slip of paper with a check or 'turned in' on it. A pity it should come to that, but such was the school environment we lived in.

So forget about Denver until the next incident, I told myself. I didn't doubt there'd be one.

With that settled, I took a detour to Clovers after dropping Leonora off at home. It was a night for take-out dinners, something hot and comforting, and Clovers had never let me down.

The wind was powerful as I walked around the building to the entrance. It blew swirls of leaves in my face and would have taken the decorative green clovers that banded the restaurant as well if they hadn't been painted on.

I entered on a wave of cold air. Annica was working, dressed in orange for Halloween with scarecrow earrings and a matching pin. She smiled at me, nodding toward a table with a view of the woods across Crispian Road. It was empty and set with leaf-patterned dishes. Clovers' owner, Mary Jeanne, liked to celebrate the seasons.

As soon as Annica finished serving her customer, she joined me.

"What can I get for you?" she asked.

"Take-out dinners. What's good today?"

"Everything, as usual, but I think you'd like the meatloaf and mashed potatoes."

"That sounds good. Do you have a minute to talk?"

She glanced around at the tables and booths and at Marcy, her fellow waitress, leisurely preparing a take-out order. "A few minutes unless we suddenly get busy."

"Then I'll have a quick cup of coffee. I have something to tell you."

She brought two cups of steaming coffee to the table. While I drank away the chill, I told her about the new information I'd found in *Memorable Tales*.

"Have you traced Cynthia's sister yet?" she asked.

"I haven't had time. I just learned about her existence yesterday."

Annica stirred sugar into her coffee slowly. "We'll have to talk to her. She's a direct link to the mystery."

"I wonder if the police know about her?"

She gave a sly smile. "Tell them. Prove you're not a meddler. That Lieutenant Dalby you're always talking about will be impressed."

I would. When I returned the charm bracelet. Maybe they'd already contacted her, which would save me time and effort. Who knew when that would be, though? Subconsciously I moved the bracelet higher on my wrist.

"I've been wondering about something," Annica said. "Wouldn't you think Cynthia would be the ghost who haunts the Inn and not Rachel?"

"Good point. I suppose one was more disturbed than the other at the time of her death."

"What if there are two ghosts?"

"But there's only one story. People have seen the Lady in the Blue Raincoat. Nobody saw Cynthia."

"That we know of. I picture Rachel dying peacefully in her sleep."

"And Cynthia had a violent death. Well I suppose there's no rule book for ghosts."

"We have to go back to the attic," Annica said. "Brent said we could come anytime, but we'd better make it soon if we want privacy for our search. He's about ready to reopen the Inn."

"So soon? Miss Isabel will be happy."

I'd forgotten about her. If she knew what Annica and I were doing, she might want to accompany us. It'd be best to keep our quest a secret.

"How would this Saturday be?" Annica asked. "I don't have to work in the morning."

"Good. If it's okay with Brent."

"It will be. I hope we find something useful. Like a blood-stained dagger, or an ax with dried brains on it."

"Ugh," I said. "Even if we don't, it'll be fun going through those old boxes."

"And Brent will be with us, so we'll be perfectly safe." She glanced at my dress. "Black... You can't wear anything like that. It'll pick up every bit of dust and cobweb for miles around. Be sure to dress in old clothes and leave the bracelet at home."

As if I had to be told how to conduct an attic search. I couldn't resist teasing her. "And you make it a point to dress in a bat repellant outfit," I said.

~ * ~

Friday came and went with no note from the principal and no sign of Denver Armstrong in my American Literature class. I figured I was safe. Why should I be nervous about being accused of losing a student's paper? It wasn't true, and the student in question had handed in very few assignments.

At times I thought my teaching job cost more in aggravation and stress than it was worth. I'd considered leaving Marston for a school closer to home several times but in the end elected to stay put. This was my career, after all, the one I'd studied and worked hard to qualify for. Besides, I was attached to Marston High School, the staff, and most of my students.

So every fall I put up fresh bulletin boards, copied names in a grade book, and mapped out new paths for familiar courses.

For a Friday when even the best students tend to be fractious in anticipation of the weekend, the day had gone well. After school, following a brief stop at home to check on the dogs, I drove the short distance to Sue Appleton's horse farm on Squill Lane for the emergency meeting of the Rescue League.

We gathered in Sue's family room, perhaps the smallest group ever to assemble since its formation. Liz Melbourne was there with Emma Brock and Louann, along with others who were enthusiastic but for one reason or another not particularly active in League affairs.

The organization was definitely shrinking. Our former president had been murdered, one of our members had proved to be dishonest, and no one new had joined our team. I was afraid that one day it would be only Sue and me. Well, Sue and me and Leonora. Leonora hadn't rescued her first collie yet.

Sue came right to the point. "There's a major problem with one of our adoptions." She explained how the collie, Sparrow, had been surrendered by a man who had no legal right to do so and added Deanna's latest accusation. "I take full responsibility. I'm hoping someone has a helpful suggestion."

Her plea met with silence.

"Does anyone?" she asked.

"You couldn't know," Louann said. "What happened between Ms. Reid and her boyfriend was really bizarre."

Liz agreed. "Anyone of us could have made that mistake. But in the future, we should have a rule. Whoever brings a collie to Rescue should bring proof of ownership, too."

"Deanna Reid had a receipt from a kennel," Sue said. "But I saw it only after the fact. After she threatened to sue us."

No one else spoke. The clock in the living room chimed seven times. I thought of my six hungry collies and was grateful I lived so close to Sue.

Finally Louann broke the silence. "That rule is well and good for the future, but what are we going to do now?"

Sue nodded toward me. "The next stop is to pay a visit to Joyann Summerton. We need to find out if the accusations have any merit. Jennet has volunteered to do that. Thank you, Jennet."

"Are any of our other collies going to cause problems down the road?" Emma asked.

"We only have three, and they were found running free. Probably dumped. No one has claimed them."

"So the answer is no?"

"No. Yes, I mean. From now on, we should be okay, and I'll add that new rule to our questionnaire."

"Let's assume that the Summerton home is as perfect as we thought," Emma said. "What then?"

Sue shrugged. "We'll play it by ear, I guess."

It was no real answer. I gazed on Sue's collie and horse art and the arrangements of dried flowers in the family room, contemplated the refreshments that hadn't been touched and probably wouldn't. It was too close to most people's dinnertimes.

They say that every problem has a solution. It seemed that this one didn't.

~ * ~

Crane locked his gun in its cabinet and waded through the milling collies to grab me for a second kiss.

"Mmm. I could get used to this."

"I could, too."

He followed me into the kitchen and lifted the top of the Dutch oven. "And I could get used to pot roast."

Instead of going upstairs to change out of his uniform, he said, "I have some answers for you about the occupant of Brent's gave."

"Finally."

"It hasn't been so long. Here's what they know. The bones belonged to a female in her twenties. DNA testing shows she may have been the young woman who went missing in nineteen fifty-five."

"May have been?"

"The bones are so old they can't be sure."

"Mac must know about Cynthia's sister, then," I said. So much for impressing him. "How did they find out?"

"Superior detective work," he said. "Brent is going to have a burial for the girl at Roseridge Cemetery."

"All this had been happening behind the scenes and I didn't know about it."

"That's why you have me. Remember the phrase, *may have been*."

"It's counter-productive to be too careful," I said. "From now on, the bones in the grave were once Cynthia. Since she didn't put herself in that grave, we have a murder mystery to deal with."

Nineteen

Saturday was overcast and cool with a persistent wind that found more leaves to bring down. It would have been a depressing day if it weren't the weekend and if I didn't have something exciting to do.

I donned a denim skirt and a yellow turtleneck, both two years old, and met Annica at the Spirit Lamp Inn. She had packed another picnic basket for lunch and dressed appropriately for attic exploration in jeans and a red sweater. Except she'd added delicate silver bell earrings to this practical ensemble.

"It's my bat repellant gear," she said with a teasing smile.

"They'll hear you coming from a mile away."

"What's this?" Brent demanded as he strolled over to meet us. "There are no bats in my attic."

"How can you be sure?" I asked.

"I conducted a bat search this morning. No bats but lots of spiders." He took the basket from Annica, and we walked up to the porch and through the door that he'd left ajar. "What's on today's menu?"

"Fried chicken and roast beef sandwiches," Annica said. "And for dessert, apple tarts and lemon squares."

Real man pleasers. I suspected Annica's intent was to impress Brent with her domestic skills. Otherwise, she'd have thrown together a lunch of subs and chips.

"I guess you girls heard about the burial service for Cynthia," Brent said.

I nodded. "Crane told me, and I told Annica. It's a thoughtful gesture, Brent."

"Cynthia's sister, Catherine, doesn't have much money," he said. "Besides the bones were discovered on my property. We agreed that she should be buried nearby. Anyway, you're invited. It'll be next week on Saturday morning. I'll open the inn for dinner in the late afternoon."

"Will it be a gala opening night?" Annica asked.

"No, we'll celebrate on Halloween. I hired a good cook and a wait staff, and I have the prettiest hostess in Michigan."

Annica glowed as he patted her arm.

I said, "We'd better find our clue today then. I expect you'll soon be overrun with tourists."

Brent gave each of us a lantern flashlight and took one for himself, then led the way up the stairs to the attic. He had installed a new light bulb in the overhead fixture which made the ascent safer but at the same time created shadows that danced ahead of us.

One by one we stepped into the attic. Brent set his lantern down on a tall stack of boxes. "Whoever stored these boxes up here named their contents. This top one is labeled 'Broken Things'."

"We can bypass it then," I said.

"Or throw it away, sight unseen."

"No," Annica said. "Broken things can be fixed."

I found a box of my own that had once contained cereal. "This one is filled with books."

"If they're in good shape, I'll donate them—somewhere," he said. "Maybe Miss Eidt would like to have them for the library. Over here are Christmas ornaments and lights."

Next to them stood a life-sized Santa Claus doll that was too unique to be consigned to an attic.

Annica moved an ornate table lamp out of her way. "More books. Records. A Fisher stereo. Wow! I've never seen one of these."

"Over here's an old Singer sewing machine," I said. "Brent, you should have a yard sale."

"Or furnish a retro room," Annica added.

"They're all furnished," he said. "All ready for tenants. But that's a good idea. We'll have one in the spring. You and Jennet can help."

We continued to plow through boxes and promising antique trunks, most of which proved to be empty. Outside it started to rain, and the meager light that had slipped through the vents all but vanished. Thank goodness for our lanterns.

We worked steadily in the imperfect lighting with the rain as a backdrop and the shadows hovering over us. After an hour we had hardly made a dent in the boxes, and our clue or evidence or whatever we were looking for remained elusive.

A strange miasma seemed to settle over the attic. Slowly I became aware of a sense that we were trespassing in a forbidden place. With all the dust floating around, I wished I'd brought a bottle of water with me to soothe my dry throat.

"I have the weirdest feeling that we're not alone up here," Annica said.

Brent hummed the theme from the *Twilight Zone*. "Here's an old broken umbrella. Can the Lady in the Blue Raincoat be far behind?"

Impatiently I pushed back a strand of hair that was beginning to aggravate me. I felt crumpled and as gritty as if I hadn't showered in a week. And it was so quiet, a cold, deep silence broken periodically by the faint tinkling of Annica's bell earrings and the drumming of rain against the house.

It sounded more like hail than rain.

At that moment, when I was about to suggest that we break for lunch, I noticed a worn blue suitcase leaning against the outer wall. It hadn't been there before. At least I didn't think it had.

No, I'd swear that space had been empty save for a tarnished floor lamp without a shade and two matching end tables.

I rubbed my eyes and looked again.

Of course it had been there all along. It was just that the dark attic was deceptive with its looming shapes and shadows.

"Brent! Annica! Over here! I found something."

They joined me as rapidly as they could over the uneven floor.

"A suitcase!" Annica said. "The missing suitcase."

"Let's see." Brent dragged it out into the narrow space that served as a row. "It's too heavy to be empty." He tried the clasp. "We're in luck. It isn't locked."

"Open it!" Annica said.

"Have a little patience, Annica." He lifted the lid, and we stared down at an array of clothing: lingerie, dresses, sweaters, scarves, a pair of shoes, a cosmetic case.

"These belonged to Cynthia," I said.

At that moment I thought I heard a ghost-voice saying 'Yes'. Or was it Annica?

"Hold on. You don't know that." Brent sounded like Crane.

"Get real, Brent," Annica said. "Who else would leave a full suitcase behind except someone who didn't need her clothes anymore because she was dead?"

"Would you mind rephrasing that?" I asked. "You can't hide a suitcase when you're dead."

"We'd better notify the police," Brent said.

Annica couldn't mask her outrage. "Why? This is *our* clue."

He frowned at her.

"I don't think they're investigating the case," I said. "If the police couldn't solve Cynthia's disappearance in nineteen fifty-five, what makes you think today's police can solve her murder? Their involvement ended with their tentative identification."

"Can't we at least see what's in here?" Annica asked.

Without waiting for an answer, she lifted a pink pajama top. "This looks like it's never been worn. She must have bought it for the trip. And what on earth is this?" She held up a strange white undergarment.

"It looks like a girdle," I said.

"Horrible." She shuddered. "Imagine squeezing into one of these. I couldn't do it. And sheer stockings."

"They didn't have pantyhose in the nineteen fifties."

"I'm glad I didn't live then. These sweaters feel like real wool."

"They were coming back from a trip up north," I said. "To Mackinac Island."

Brent had had enough. "You girls are impossible. Annica, put that—that thing back. I'm going downstairs to call the police. Do you want to stay up here and keep looking?"

"No way," Annica said. "We found the suitcase. That's enough for one day."

"But not the murder weapon," I reminded her.

She picked up her lantern flashlight. "We can come back again, can't we, Brent?"

But he'd already gone through the door. If he heard her, he chose not to answer.

I thought I knew what his answer would be. But we had to return and continue our search. If a suitcase had been hidden in the dark recesses of the Inn's attic, what else might we find?

Twenty

Back downstairs, we washed the dust from our hands and faces and met in the dining room for lunch. The rain continued with flashes of lightning and violent thunder crashes. We might as well take our time eating. I didn't like to drive in a storm if at all possible.

I opened a can of ginger ale and took a long satisfying gulp. I couldn't remember a time when I was so thirsty.

Brent reached for a piece of fried chicken. "Lieutenant Dalby said he'll stop by when he can. Apparently there's an epidemic of crime in Foxglove Corners."

"What did I tell you? There's no urgency to solve an old case."

"We can do it," Annica said. "But we have to go through the suitcase and search the attic more thoroughly."

"Catherine is the only one who can tell whether the suitcase belonged to Cynthia," I said.

"And she should have it," Brent added. "I'll give it to her next week at the service if Dalby doesn't confiscate it."

"He won't."

I might be wrong, but I didn't think the police placed a high priority on the case of a young woman murdered so long ago who in their estimation might still be unidentified. As for a crime epidemic in Foxglove Corners, I didn't believe that. If it were true, Crane would have mentioned it to me.

"I find it hard to believe that the previous owner of the Inn didn't know the suitcase was in the attic," I said.

"Not every attic is neat and organized," Brent reminded me. "Some people just keep shoving boxes in an attic and over time forget what's stored there. How often does anyone go up to an attic anyway?"

"To check out a leaking roof?" Annica said.

"One time would be when the owner sells the house," I said.

"She told me I could do whatever I wanted with the stuff in the attic," Brent said. "She said it was all broken furniture and miscellaneous junk."

"I still think there's something strange about her haste. You make an offer, she accepts it, and she's gone."

"I didn't think of it at the time, but you're right," Brent said. "I wrote to her after I found the charm bracelet. She hasn't answered yet."

Annica waved the basket of chicken in front of our noses. "Have some chicken or a sandwich, Jennet. And Brent, here's another piece. I'm not taking this food back, and the new refrigerator hasn't come yet."

While Brent raved over the chicken, which *was* good, I sat back and thought about the suitcase and what might have happened on that stormy night when Cynthia disappeared.

I'd assumed Rachel had taken it with her, but the discovery had changed my developing scenario. Whoever killed Cynthia must have decided to hide all the evidence except for the few possessions left in the room. Why not hide everything? Maybe he'd run out of time.

The killer had to be familiar with the Inn. He or she would have had to know where the attic was located and would have moved through the halls in secret.

Why not simply take it out of the Inn? A suitcase was hardly an unusual object for a traveler to carry.

Because of the nature of the contents—sheer hose, that ghastly girdle, genuine wool sweaters—I had no doubt the suitcase belonged to a female; that meant to Cynthia.

Still it would be helpful if Catherine could give it a positive identification.

~ * ~

Saturday's storm ushered in a string of drab rainy days. Monday was especially gloomy with showers that came and went throughout the morning.

Partly in search of cheer, I wore my favorite red dress and, once again, the charm bracelet. I no longer felt as if it were mine on loan only. If the police weren't interested in an entire suitcase, a major clue in my view, why would they want my bracelet? Therefore, they didn't even have to know about it.

Once at school, I was too busy to think about the bracelet, the suitcase, or anything related to the mystery of the Spirit Lamp Inn.

Just as the fourth period bell rang to begin class, a lightning flash split open the low gray sky.

Talk about foreboding.

"Are they going to send us home?" asked Katrina, perching on the edge of her seat.

If only...

"I doubt it," I said and took advantage of their boisterous settling in time to close the windows. In an instant the rain had gone from drizzling to torrential.

"There's a tornado watch until three o'clock," Katrina added.

I hadn't heard that. It was late in the season for tornadoes to develop, almost the end of October, which didn't mean they couldn't. Weather this year had been strange and fickle.

"The superintendent will let us know if there's any danger," I said.

Denver sneered. "Yeah, right."

But Grimsley wouldn't release the students. They'd rush to the nearest fast food restaurant or to the mall instead of going straight home, no matter what he said. In school, with severe weather procedures in place, they'd be safe.

I hated being so far from my home in threatening weather. Besides, it would be a miracle if I could hold my students' attention for the day's story, *The Outcasts of Poker Flat.* But I'd try. It was a giant step above Puritan sermons, but the mere mention of school cancellation had thrown them into a frenzy.

I reached for my grade book—fumbled under the day's announcements, a flyer on a Creative Writing Workshop for teachers, and a page of background notes I'd written yesterday on the story.

It wasn't there.

Don't panic. It has to be. I used it just last hour.

I opened the middle desk drawer. Not there. The charms on my bracelet clicked frantically. The drawers on both sides. Not there. The closet, just in case I'd put it there in a non-thinking moment. No luck.

"Did you lose something, Mrs. Ferguson?"

"A tissue," I murmured and took one out of the box.

Don't let them know.

Fortunately by now I had the names of my students, even the good, quiet ones, memorized, and I could see the seating chart clearly in my mind.

Katrina, Dan, Sandy, Alison, Denver...

I grabbed an attendance slip, scribbled three names, then cast one last glance at my desk, hoping the grade book had magically appeared while I wasn't looking.

It hadn't, and I had no recourse but to start class. The page for the story was written on the board. I took my notes and set them on the podium, forced myself to speak calmly.

"It's a good day to read a story about conflict," I said. "In this story, it's man against nature. For Bret Harte's characters, it's a killer blizzard."

Thunder rumbled across the sky. Special effects. More foreboding. I could do without them.

~ * ~

"Sit down and eat your sandwich," Leonora said. "Time's flying by."

As soon as the bell rang to begin lunch, I had continued the search for my missing grade book. In truth, I was covering the same territory with the same results. Desk top, drawers, the closet, the waste paper basket... An old trick was to push something belonging to the teacher off her desk and into the basket. There was nothing heavier than loose paper inside.

Finally I was forced to admit that the grade book had disappeared.

No. It had been stolen. And this must have happened in my third or fourth hour class. Most likely in the American Literature class as my World Literature students were generally well behaved. And the black star of fourth period American Literature was Denver Armstrong who had sat quietly through class engrossed in his drawing.

Not that I could accuse him. Even though he had been locked in an ongoing conflict with me since his first day in my class. Even though he believed he had a reason to hold a grudge against me.

"Jen, you're going to be hungry later if you don't eat something," Leonora said.

With a sigh I collapsed into my chair. "If my grade book doesn't turn up, I'm going to have to report this."

To Principal Grimsley, who would no doubt blame me for being careless with the most precious item in a teacher's possession. Here was the only record of a student's absence and tardiness record and more important of his grades. Some teachers kept this information in computer files. I didn't because it had never occurred to me that my grade book wouldn't be safe. I always kept it near me during the school day and took it home at night.

Until today.

To be fair to myself, it had been within six feet of me at all times...

Except when I'd turned my back on fourth hour class to close the windows.

That's when it happened.

"Why don't you wait until tomorrow to report it?" Leonora said. "Maybe it'll turn up by then."

"I have a feeling I'll never see it again."

"Do you have any papers you haven't handed back yet?" she asked.

"Just one batch."

"You can record those grades and ask your classes to turn in their old papers again," she said.

"I'd rather they didn't know. It might lead to more trouble down the road. To challenges..." I trailed off. That trouble might be just beginning.

"You have your class lists, and the attendance office will have an absence record you can duplicate. If it were me, I'd ask for another grade book right away. As for Grimsley, I think this is a matter for the assistant principal. It's discipline. Grimsley may never have to know."

"With my luck he will," I said. "This is my fault for not keeping the grade book under lock and key."

"Nobody does that."

"You do if you have untrustworthy students in class. I will from now on."

Time was indeed flying by. I had five minutes of my lunch period left. I took a bite of my sandwich. Annica's roast beef and cheese should have been good. It tasted like sand.

If this had happened at the beginning of the course, it would have been easier to re-create. But report cards were due in two weeks, and on that day Parent-Teacher conferences were scheduled. Somehow I had to have an authentic duplicate grade book before then.

Twenty-one

Re-creating a grade book was surprisingly easy, if time-consuming and tedious. That evening I took the class lists from my file, together with the material I'd received from Eleanor in the attendance office, and entered them in a pristine new book. All that was missing were grades, but I planned to assign twice as many papers as I normally would.

I had one stroke of luck. The principal was out of town for three days. I could hope he'd never learn what had happened. In fact, besides the assistant principal, no one except Leonora and Eleanor had to know. Crisis averted. Sort of.

The next day after school, Katrina appeared at my door. She seemed nervous, unlike her usual boisterous self. I had my coat on and was gathering my books for a hasty departure.

"Can I see my grades, Mrs. Ferguson?" she asked without preamble.

"Not at the moment, Katrina," I said. "I'm in a hurry. And it's 'May I?'"

Her voice took on a grating, whiney tone. "It'll just take you a minute."

I couldn't let her see the new book. There was a chance she wouldn't notice the change, but I couldn't take it.

"I'll give them to you tomorrow in class," I said.

"The grade book is right there." She'd spied it under my purse. "Can't you just open it and look?"

"Ready, Jen?" Leonora stood in the doorway, wrapping her scarf around her neck. When she saw Katrina, she paused, hand on the doorknob.

"Tomorrow, Katrina. I'm sorry, but I really have to go."

She had no choice but to precede me out the door. I locked it, and she stalked off down the hall without a word.

"That," I said, "is suspicious. Katrina has never shown the slightest interest in her grades."

"Do you think she's the one who stole your grade book?" Leonora asked.

"Everyone in that class is a suspect."

Not even to Leonora would I admit that I was ninety-nine percent certain the culprit was Denver Armstrong. And Katrina was his girlfriend. I didn't have any proof, only a persistent inner feeling that he was guilty.

It was enough.

~ * ~

Relying heavily on memory, I decided that Katrina had a B minus average on previous assignments. On an index card, I wrote a string of B's and C's and handed it to her in class the following day. My new grade book stayed locked in the closet.

She took the card without a thank you or any acknowledgement whatsoever.

Well, what did I expect? I'd foiled her plan.

That day during my conference period, I looked up from the essay I was reading. Footsteps, whispers, a slight commotion in the hall had broken my concentration.

What now?

Two girls stood in the doorway, Kit and Marjorie from my fourth hour class. They were two of the good ones.

"Are you busy, Mrs. Ferguson?" Kit asked.

"Not very. Come in, girls. What's the problem?"

I knew there was one. Rarely did high school students drop in on a teacher just to chat.

Kit and Marjorie looked at each other. "We've got something to tell you," Marjorie said.

"Sit down, and we'll talk."

They remained standing.

"We know who stole the grade book," Kit said.

Uh oh. I hadn't fooled anyone. If these two knew the grade book was missing, so did the rest of the class.

"Who was it?" I asked.

"You can't ever let anyone know we told you," Kit said. "Not ever."

What was the point of knowing then? My visions of throwing the book at Denver Armstrong vanished in a puff of smoke. But I agreed to their condition. What else could I do?

"It was Denver and Katrina," Marjorie said. "Kit heard them bragging about it at lunch. They threw it in the dumpster behind Sun-up Donuts."

Oh, no! I imagined a quagmire of half-eaten doughnuts, coffee and hot chocolate spilled out of containers, tea bags, crumpled paper napkins... What else did they sell at the place?

"Well..." I didn't know what else to say.

"They were worried about their grades," Kit said.

Denver's non-existent grades. Now, he would think, the proof had drowned in a sea of garbage. He would claim that he had a B average. No would believe in A's.

"We got it back for you," Marjorie said. "We're thinking about our grades, too, and everybody else's."

"From the dumpster?" I was incredulous.

"We went down to Sun-up Donuts right after school and fished it out of the gunk," Kit said. "It's kind of beat up. Do you still want it?"

It took me a second to find my voice. I was thinking of their search through unthinkable debris. Who would do this for anything less than an envelope of money or a diamond ring?

"I certainly do," I said. Then "Where is it?"

"In my locker," Marjorie said. "We wrapped it in paper. It's pretty messed up."

"Remember," Kit said. "You can't tell anybody what we did."

I heard the fear in her voice. As much as I would like to see those two miscreants pay for their thievery, Denver would be able to find out who had betrayed him. I was suddenly overcome with gratitude that Marjorie and Kit would risk his payback.

"No one will know," I said. "That's a promise, and I can't tell you girls how much I appreciate this."

Kit slipped quietly out of the room and returned a few minutes later with a damp object wrapped in paper. I have seldom been so happy to see an inanimate object.

~ * ~

"You should nail them to the wall," Crane said that night. "They're criminals in the making."

"I can't. I promised. Who knows what would happen to them if Denver found out what they did?"

I had painstakingly copied the contents of the ruined grade book into the new one and discarded it in my own trash basket. I'd taken the additional precaution of opening a computer document to keep track of the grades of all my students.

"I don't know this Armstrong kid, but he sounds like a bully," Crane said. "Let him get away with this, and what will he do the next time?"

"I'm afraid to think," I said. "The semester is fairly new. He has a lot of time to make trouble, but I'll keep a close eye on those two. Believe me, I won't let this new grade book out of my sight. Katrina is just his pawn," I added.

"She's no less guilty."

"That's right," I said.

It would be so easy to lose faith in young people, but I remembered the chance Kit and Marjorie had taken to follow their consciences. Every class was a mixture of courteous, agreeable teens and defiant, dishonest ones.

As for Katrina, she craved Denver's attention. Only heaven knew why.

"From now on, I'll watch Denver Armstrong like a hawk," I said. "And Katrina too."

"It can't be easy teaching English in those circumstances."

"It isn't," I said. "It makes a little old murder mystery seem like a piece of cake."

Twenty-two

Saturday morning was tailor-made for a long delayed burial service. Gray clouds hung so low it seemed as if, with a little encouragement, they would brush the tops of our heads. A chilly wind swirled around the little party that had gathered at the gravesite, and every now and then a raindrop fell.

'A tear from heaven,' Annica said in an uncharacter-istic burst of sentimentality.

In a simple black dress with a crystal brooch pinned to the bodice, Catherine stood next to Brent, seemed at times to lean on him. A tall slender woman with neatly coiffed silvery blonde hair, she resembled the photograph of her sister, Cynthia, in the *Memories* book—a Cynthia grown older. Catherine was a widow with no family.

Brent had paid for the burial plot. He had chosen a pleasant, tranquil section of the hilly cemetery with three oak trees near enough to the grave to shade it in three seasons. He'd also ordered a headstone for Cynthia and was hosting a catered luncheon at the Spirit Lamp Inn after the service.

The rest of the mourners were women, and we all wore black. There were Leonora and Annica, who both felt a connection to Cynthia, and Miss Isabel Bryte, who had moved back to the Inn and wanted to be included in all activities.

"I might have stayed at the Inn when Rachel and Cynthia did," she'd said. "I might have passed them in the halls that night or seen Rachel in the dining room. Of course I didn't know that it would be important someday."

"Do you remember seeing two young women anywhere?" I asked. "One of them looked like Catherine."

"Not offhand," she said. "It was years and years ago, but let me think."

It would be unlikely that Miss Isabel had witnessed anything suspicious, even less likely that her stay had corresponded with Cynthia's. But I knew better than to discount any information, however trivial.

The priest said the final prayers over the grave, and it was done. I dabbed raindrops away from my face.

"Rest in peace, Cynthia," I said.

I felt that she would rest in this beautiful place. But it wouldn't really be done until her killer was brought to justice. If that killer still walked the earth.

Catherine turned away from the grave reluctantly, then looked back, wiping her eyes. "This brings it all back, the long years of waiting to know what happened to my sister. I always thought someday I'd find her. She'd knock on my door…"

Brent took her arm and escorted her slowly to the cars. We followed. I heard him say softly, "You did find her."

"We still don't know everything," Catherine added, echoing my earlier thought. "The person who did this got away with murder. He stole Cynthia's life and all her dreams. She wanted to see every country on the planet. She and Rachel were saving their money to go on a world cruise. After Cynthia disappeared, Rachel never took a vacation again."

Miss Isabel patted her arm. "Don't grieve. It happened a long time ago. It's the duty of those of us who are fortunately still on this earth to enjoy life to the fullest. Don't you agree, Mr. Fowler?"

"Hell, yes," Brent said. "That's my philosophy."

Catherine gave a scarcely audible gasp, and Miss Isabel said, "Don't forget, Mr. Fowler, we're in a holy place."

"Not for long."

Brent helped the ladies into his car, and led the procession out to the road.

"He's incorrigible," Leonora said as she settled into the back seat of the Taurus.

"But so wonderful." That was Annica, of course. "Just think. He's made all this possible."

"He can afford it," Leonora reminded her.

"But he didn't have to do anything once the police took the bones away. He got in touch with Catherine, bought the plot, arranged for the luncheon. Just like he was a member of the family."

"All right," Leonora said. "I agree. Brent is a wonder. The eighth wonder of the world."

I smiled, my first light-hearted moment of the morning. Leonora hadn't exactly agreed with Annica, but Annica didn't notice.

~ * ~

At the Spirit Lamp Inn, after the funeral luncheon, the priest and Leonora left, making the group even smaller. Annica refilled all the coffee cups, and Brent showed Catherine the suitcase we'd found in the attic.

"Oh, yes," she murmured, lifting the sweaters. "These were Cynthia's colors. Deep turquoise, purple, forest green. I gave her these pajamas for her birthday." She opened the makeup case. "Cynthia always wore dark pink lipstick. It looked so good on her. Did you notice how neatly everything is packed? What does that tell us?"

"That she only planned to stay at the Inn overnight," I said. "She'd have taken her nightgown out of the case—that's the gown Rachel saw on the bed—and probably a toothbrush and other things they found in the room…"

"She used Pond's Cleansing Cream," Catherine said. "I don't see it here."

"Maybe she used it up. I wonder what happened to that nightgown."

"Rachel must have taken it. Cynthia never went to bed that night." Catherine gazed out the window, appearing to create the scene as I had done. "Something happened. She left the room. Or she let someone in."

"The killer!" Annica said.

One by one Catherine set the contents of the suitcase on the table. "Her jewelry," she said, opening a small pink case that looked hand-crocheted. "Pearls, a ruby ring. That was her birthstone, the ruby. I don't recall seeing this pinecone pin, but it looks like something she might have found up north."

That reminded me. I took the charm bracelet out of my purse and added it to the collection on the table. "Have you ever seen this bracelet before?" I asked.

"That's Cynthia's!" Catherine exclaimed. "Whenever she visited a new country, she added a charm to it. Was it in the suitcase?"

"My landscaper found it buried in the ground," Brent said. "I gave it to Jennet for safekeeping. We didn't know who it belonged to."

"It's so pretty. Really unique. How did it get in the ground?" she asked.

Brent shrugged. "We don't know. It must have slipped off her wrist."

"Wait a minute, Brent," I said. "This bracelet turned up in the Inn's backyard. I can't see Cynthia wandering around outside on a stormy night."

"It fell off her body when the killer was burying her," Annica said.

"In the rain?" I asked.

Catherine sighed. "There's so much we don't know. How can we ever hope to solve Cynthia's murder at this late date?"

"We collect clues," I said. "Speaking of clues, show Catherine the silver heart, Brent."

"Right! The heart charm. I forgot about it."

Unfortunately he'd also forgotten where he'd stashed it.

"It's so small," he said, searching his pockets and his wallet. "Thin as a wafer. What did I do with it?"

"Was there a heart charm on the bracelet?" I asked Catherine.

"I don't think so. I can't be sure."

"Well, look for it, Brent. It can't just walk away."

"I'd like you to keep the bracelet, Jennet," Catherine said.

"If you're sure, thank you. I'll think of Cynthia when I wear it."

I'd always felt that it was meant for me; now it was official.

"Do you know the story about the Inn's ghost, the Lady in the Blue Raincoat?" Annica asked. "She's supposed to be Rachel."

"I've read about her," Catherine said.

"But you've never seen her?"

"No, and I can't picture Rachel coming back to haunt any place. She was very down-to-earth, very practical. She taught science and didn't believe in anything she couldn't see for herself."

"She *did* keep coming back to the Inn though," I said.

Catherine nodded. "It became an obsession. I drove up with her of few times, but even then, when the mystery was relatively new, it all seemed hopeless. Then Rachel died, and I gave up hope of ever learning anything about Cynthia until Mr. Fowler bought the Inn and decided to have the garden dug up."

"So you don't believe in the Lady in the Blue Raincoat," Annica said.

"I think it's just a story. How it started, I can't imagine."

"Every Inn worth its salt needs a ghost," Annica added. "The Lady is a particularly nice one. I'd prefer someone violent. A little scary. A spirit with a dripping dagger in her hand."

"That wouldn't fit the girls' story," I said.

Annica refilled our coffee cups. "Don't be a stranger, Catherine. Come back anytime."

"Yes," Brent added. "Anytime. You're always welcome."

"Maybe I'll do that," she said. "I think that something of Cynthia will always remain at the Inn."

Twenty-three

The rain continued through the rest of the week, guaranteeing a soggy Halloween. While disappointing for the trick-or-treaters, it was a boon for Brent's party at the Spirit Lamp Inn. He considered it free atmosphere and would have ordered thunder and lightning if he could.

Annica and Lucy helped him decorate the Inn with faux cobwebs and various Halloween novelties like scarecrows and giant pumpkins. On the night before Halloween, he made one last attempt to offer me the most unique costume in town.

"What is this?" I asked as he handed me an orange and black package.

"Your costume," Brent said.

Crane, no doubt in on the surprise, just smiled as I pulled a powder blue garment out into the light. It was a raincoat.

"I found it in that vintage shop in Lakeville, Old is New Again," he said. "It looked like it would fit you."

"It's like new," I said.

"Try it on."

"I was going to wear my witch costume," I said.

"You still can. Wear the raincoat over it. Look. It has a hood."

"A witch in a raincoat," I said. "That's as jarring as a mixed metaphor."

He looked puzzled. Intrigued, I slipped the raincoat on and found it wondrously comfortable. It felt right. Misty and Halley, equally intrigued, sniffed the material, tails wagging. Did the former owner's scent still remain on the coat? I supposed it depended on how vintage it was.

"I'm tempted," I said. "I could think of it as a tribute to Rachel. A sign of my belief in her. What do you think, Crane?"

"I never tell you what to do," he said with a wink.

I gave him a quick smile. "Since when? I guess it couldn't hurt. Okay, Brent, I'll do it."

I was thinking. I didn't have to dress as a witch. With the raincoat, I could wear one of my own dresses. Just as Rachel had. I'd choose one that wouldn't draw attention to itself by design or color so that everyone would focus on the raincoat. My gray knit with the turtleneck would do.

"But I won't drift through the rooms in a cloud of blue dust," I said.

"I don't expect you to. Anyway, I don't know where to lay my hands on blue dust."

I slipped the hood over my head and my hands into the deep pockets. The raincoat had no constricting belt unlike the one hanging in my closet. It was as comfortable as a robe. I'd wear blue eye shadow and maybe, in the spirit of All Hallows Eve, paint my fingernails sky blue.

"You can wear your charm bracelet," Brent said.

"The Lady in the Blue Raincoat doesn't have a charm bracelet," I reminded him. "It belonged to Cynthia."

"Consider it poetic license then and wear it in good health."

"By the way, did you ever find the heart charm?" I asked.

"No, and I can't remember where I put it. Oh, well, it doesn't go with a foreign country like the others."

Tiny objects had a way of vanishing. Still, I wondered. Was the charm misplaced or had it been stolen? This led to an obvious question: by whom? A theft seemed unlikely. Who even knew about the little silver heart except Annica, Catherine, me, and the man who'd found it in the first place?

Brent dipped into a dish of chocolate candy corn placed on the mantel out of the dogs' reach. "We're going to have these at the party," he said. "I love them."

Crane was still smiling.

~ * ~

On the night of the party, I stopped in front of the hall mirror to admire my transformation. In the hope of creating a ghostly illusion, I had applied make up with a light touch. Only blue eye shadow and lipstick with more gloss than color. The blue nail polish was a close match for the shade of the raincoat. Camille had lent me a pair of white cotton gloves from her own vintage collection.

Although I'd initially rejected the idea of dressing like a ghost, now that the deed was done, I looked on it as fun—that is if everyone attending knew the story of the Lady in the Blue Raincoat. Otherwise, I'd just look strange. I saw myself having to explain over and over again what I was supposed to be.

The collies gathered around me in anticipation of an evening walk.

"Later," I told them, giving each one a pat and instructions to be good.

Crane had promised he'd feed and walk them tonight, and there was a casserole in the refrigerator for him. Confident that I'd left my loved ones well provided for, I added a navy blue umbrella to my ensemble and left to celebrate the night with my friends. I only wished Crane could be with me, or at least make an appearance.

Driving proved to be tricky with light rain falling and mist that veiled the country roads in wisps of white. I passed the old Haver farmhouse on Deer Leap Trail where a light burned in a second floor window.

How curious. As far as I knew, the place was still for sale. No one should be inside.

Well, it was only one light. Perhaps the realtor had left it on to deter Halloween pranksters and vandals.

Forget the Haver House, I ordered myself. Its mystery had been solved, its fate remained uncertain. As for a light, it was a night when strange happenings were to be expected.

Brent knew how to throw a good party. He'd sent invitations, then changed his mind and declared his Halloween bash was an open house. Consequently the lot was crowded. I saw Annica's car in a prime parking place. I knew that she and Lucy had arrived early to help with last minute details. Finding a place of my own, I settled the hood over my head, took my umbrella and purse, and stepped out into the drizzle and fading light. Perfect Halloween weather.

It was the night for spirits to roam the earth, for frights and treats, and for a brief sojourn in the world of the unreal. Let the fun begin.

~ * ~

"Can I take your coat, Miss?"

I didn't know the woman in black and white who stood poised to divest me of my costume. But Brent had hired wait staff to help behind the scenes. She was obviously one of the temporary staff.

"Thank you," I said, brushing rain water off my sleeves. "I think I'll keep it on."

"It's warm in here."

"I'll be fine," I assured her. "But you can take the umbrella."

I surveyed the dining room. Annica and Lucy had been busy and creative, turning the room into a vast harvest field filled with haystacks and baskets of fruit. In the candlelight, the scarecrows looked bizarre, almost real, and the pumpkins were enormous, large orange ones mixed with the less frequently seen white. There wasn't a bat or a spider in sight.

To complete the illusion, an eerie wind sound blew through the room. Brent had arranged for sound effects after all.

"Hey, Jennet." Annica in red and white with a tiara of velvety valentine hearts on her red-gold curls, waved a wand. "I'm the Queen of Hearts. Check it out." She pressed a button on the wand, and a spray of tiny hearts shot out.

"You look fantastic," she added. "Where did you find a blue raincoat at this time of year?"

"Brent found it in a vintage shop," I said.

"A vintage shop? Oh, no!"

"What's wrong?"

"Don't you see? If it's old, really old, there's a good chance it belonged to Rachel. You could be wearing her raincoat!"

"I'd say that chance is one in a zillion," I said. "Blue has always been a popular color."

"But what if it *did* belong to Rachel? You're tempting Fate. Or something."

I couldn't help laughing. "Stop trying to scare me. It won't work. I'm wearing Cynthia's bracelet too." I shook my hand, and the Capri bell on the charm bracelet rang faintly.

"Maybe it'll be okay," she said.

"Brent wouldn't do anything to harm me."

"Not knowingly."

Abruptly she changed the subject. "Catherine is here with some woman friend, and guess what? They both have hunky dates. I have to run," she added. "See you later."

She drifted off, leaving a cloud of glittering red hearts in her wake, along with an annoying sense of apprehension.

Brent couldn't possibly have found Rachel's blue raincoat from the nineteen fifties in a vintage shop in Lakeville. And even if he had... A good many of the dresses and coats and accessories in that shop had once belong to people who had since passed on.

I had momentarily forgotten that Annica loved to tell gruesome tales, the more ghastly the better. This was vintage Annica.

But she had seemed sincere. Sincerely distressed.

It's part of the act, I told myself, and set out to find Catherine.

Twenty-four

Five members of the older generation sat together at my favorite table, the one with the best view of the garden: Catherine, all in black, her lady friend, and their escorts, together with Miss Isabel who must have thrown on every necklace she owned in an attempt to channel a gypsy. Every one of them had silvery gray hair.

This evening the window was draped in faux cobwebs and reflected the dining room with its blur of bright colors and fantastic shapes.

Happy to have a chance to talk to Catherine again, I wove around tables and standing groups, marveling at the innovative costumes Brent's guests had donned.

Catherine stared at me for a moment, wide-eyed; then her features relaxed in a welcoming expression. "You gave me quite a turn in that raincoat, Jennet," she said. "Did I mention that you resemble Rachel? A little?"

"You didn't," I said. "In what way?"

"She was about your height and wore her hair like you do, in a shoulder-length pageboy with bangs. Her hair was auburn, though. Seeing you in that blue raincoat... My goodness, my heart is still pounding."

I pushed the hood back and smoothed my hair. "I'm supposed to be Rachel's ghost. It was Brent Fowler's idea."

"Interesting," Catherine said, "but I simply cannot imagine Rachel as a ghost. I, for one, don't believe the dead come back."

One of the gentlemen commandeered a chair from an empty table.

"Sit down and meet my friends," Catherine said. "This is Marsha Anne. That's Ted with the chair and this is Bruce. Jennet is interested in the discovery of the grave," she added.

The men were both attractive in a rugged way and dressed in dark suits with Halloween themed ties. Owls and orange stripes. Except for Ted's slightly florid complexion and his cane leaning precariously on the wall behind him, it was going to be difficult to tell them apart.

Bruce said, "We used to drive out here for Sunday dinner when the place was the Oaken Bucket Inn. Their specialty was roast chicken. They had a secret ingredient."

"I remember," Ted added. "The light paint makes the place look new."

I couldn't help notice Marsha Anne staring at me. "You *do* resemble Rachel, Jennet. You would even if you took the raincoat off."

"It's part of my costume," I said. "I was going to be a witch. Now I'm glad I didn't."

I'd seen three witches on the way to the table, one of them glamorous, two hideous. No one likes to encounter anyone else wearing her outfit, even on Halloween. Witches were no exception.

I didn't see any other ghosts, only a tall skeleton, rather scary and oddly appropriate, considering the recent discovery of the bones.

"You look lovely, Jennet," Marsha Anne said. "I remember when we all wore white cotton gloves. You wouldn't feel dressed up without them."

Quietly I took the gloves off and slipped them in my pocket. They wouldn't fit in my evening purse, and I didn't want to lose them. As I did so, the charms on my bracelet jingled, and I explained how Brent had found the bracelet and given it to me and how Catherine had told me to keep it.

"I remember that bracelet," Marsha Anne said. "Cynthia always wore it, even though it kept getting heavier as she added more charms. It was her favorite. She said she'd brought a little piece of each country she visited home with her."

I was going to ask Marsha Anne if she had known Rachel or just seen a picture of her when I felt a pair of heavy hands on my shoulders. They could only belong to one man.

Brent's voice boomed out, "Happy Halloween, all. Glad you could make it. Nice costume, Jennet. I thought I saw a ghost come in out of the rain."

"Very funny," I said.

"The buffet will be ready in a half hour. In the meantime, enjoy the cider. It's my special brew."

"Is Lucy here?" I asked.

"She's around somewhere. Probably checking candles. She's worried about fire."

That gave me pause. I was afraid of fire. Any sensible person would be. The candle centerpieces at our table were pillars, reasonably safe, but I noticed the dining room was filled with tapers in single holders and elaborate candelabra, all of them different, all with an old-time look. Where had Brent found them?

Suddenly I remembered my question for Marsha. "Did you know Rachel, Marsha Anne?"

"Very well," Marsha said. "We roomed together for two years."

"The three girls rented a small house in Oakpoint," Catherine said. "They all taught at the same school."

"But it was always Cynthia and Rachel," I said, then realized how inane that sounded.

"Cynthia and Rachel were the travelers," Marsha Anne said. "I was a homebody. Still am."

I couldn't believe my luck in meeting people who had known Cynthia. I half-listened while the men continued the discussion of the Inn in the old days and formulated the questions I wanted to ask Marsha Anne.

When the conversation died down, I said, "Do you have any theories about what happened to Cynthia, Marsha Anne?"

"We used to discuss her disappearance—Catherine, Rachel, and I—but never understood how she could have vanished so utterly. Now it makes sense. She was murdered."

"That's equally hard to understand," Catherine said. "As Rachel told the story, they'd driven all the way from Mackinac, taking turns at the wheel. They were both exhausted, and it was storming. Then they saw the light at the Oaken Bucket Inn.

"The point is," she continued, "they didn't know anyone at the Inn. We assume nobody knew them. It all happened during the time it took Rachel to go down to the dining room—to this very room—and have dinner. How is that possible?"

"The killer buried her body in the garden," I said, "but he couldn't very well have buried her in the rain."

I thought of the suitcase we'd found in the attic. Had the killer kept Cynthia's body there too until the coast was clear? That was the only scenario I could envision. Wouldn't the police have searched the attic, though?

"I'll never understand how it happened," Marsha Anne said. "And poor Rachel died without ever knowing."

I longed to tell Catherine and Marsha that my friend, Annica, and I would try to solve the mystery. Listening to the facts restated, it seemed hopeless. An impossible undertaking. So I simply said, "It's a mystery all right."

But solving mysteries was my specialty. When we'd found the answer, we'd gathered Cynthia's contemporaries together for a grand announcement and hope Rachel would be able to hear it.

~ * ~

I was getting so warm that I was tempted to take the raincoat off. But then I'd be a woman in a plain gray dress suitable for a rainy day at school but not a party. While I was sweltering, Miss Isabel claimed she was cold sitting by the window. Bruce offered to change places with her, but she wanted her cardigan, the white ruffled one, that wouldn't go with her costume. But so what?

"I'm almost too cold to move," she said. "It's the sound of that wind. I hate the wind."

"It isn't really blowing. That's a CD. It's Brent's idea of Halloween sound effects."

She had her arms crossed in front of her chest. Really, I thought, she should have added a shawl to her gypsy costume. "Give me your key, and I'll get it for you."

Brent wanted me to drift through the room in a ghostly fashion, whatever that was. So far I hadn't moved from the table.

Miss Isabel handed me the key. "It's hanging in the armoire. And thank you, Jennet, you're an angel."

"No, I'm a ghost," I said with a wry smile.

As I left the dining room, I wished I had some blue dust to scatter in my wake.

Twenty-five

The sound of the wind was louder on the second floor, and it was colder, but that was to be expected. Grateful for the warmth of my raincoat, I hurried along the hall to Miss Isabel's room.

It dawned on me that I was alone on this level. I might have been the only living person in the Inn in spite of the dozens of partygoers in the dining room below. I certainly felt isolated.

Hurry, I told myself. *Get the cardigan. Rejoin the others.*

For some reason that eluded me, Annica had been in the hall at some time. Or her valentine-spewing wand had been. Tiny hearts formed a trail to one of the rooms. Strange. As far as I knew, Miss Isabel was the only one who lived on the second story. Unless Brent had rented a room for one of his Halloween revelers.

But why were Annica's red hearts glittering up at me from the soft gray carpeting?

As soon as I saw Annica again, I'd asked her.

Here was Miss Isabel's room. Room Three. I fitted her key in the lock and pushed open the door. She'd left a light on in her sitting room. It shone from one of those small Tiffany lamps that use a low-wattage bulb. Casting a modest pool of yellow, it only managed to make the room shadowy. But I saw the armoire in a corner, an intricately carved antique in light wood with one of its doors ajar.

Three white cardigans hung inside, but only one had a ruffled edge. I pulled it from the hanger, threw it over my arm, and left the room, making certain the door was locked.

Now to get back downstairs before… Well, before. I didn't quite know before what.

I didn't like being in this part of the Inn; I felt like an intruder. Why had I volunteered to get Miss Isabel's sweater anyway?

The wind wailed and shrieked and died, only to return stronger than ever. It seemed to break through the walls and bombard me with icy needles. What a strange wind! Miss Isabel must be made of stern stuff to live alone up here.

It's not always like this, I told myself. *It's Brent's sound effects, and wouldn't you think he'd switch to eerie music? Something appropriate for the night like* The Sorcerer's Apprentice?

At the end of the hall, my image in the mirror confronted me. Dark hair swathed in a blue hood, raincoat flapping, eyes luminous. One hand raised to my mouth.

My hands were at my side!

The image stepped out of the mirror and glided toward me.

I froze.

There was no mirror hanging on the wall at the end of the hall. Nothing was there, no window, not even a painting. Just dark wood paneling and the blue thing that had materialized in front of my eyes.

The ghost.

It was moving.

The cold bombarded me again, impossible winds cutting through solid walls, making my hands shake violently.

Dear God! I had seen ghosts before, but this one was different. She was fully formed and looked as real as anyone in the dining room downstairs.

Where had it—or she—come from then?

Rational thought fled. I'd forgotten that I wanted to solve the mystery of Cynthia's murder and find out if Rachel's ghost really haunted the Spirit Lamp Inn. I forgot I was Jennet, solver of mysteries, who took pride in being courageous. I was holding my breath, and my mouth felt as if it were filled with sand.

Close your eyes. Look again. If it's still walking toward you, run.

When I did look again, nothing was there. A blue haze hung in the air. It looked like smoke, but it smelled, faintly, of lilacs.

I ran anyway.

~ * ~

Back downstairs I rushed, unmindful of the need to move with care on the dimly-lit staircase, clutching Miss Isabel's sweater, and looking for Lucy. I had to find her, had to tell her what I'd seen. After I confided in Lucy, maybe I'd tell Brent.

No, I had better wait until the party was over, until all of his guests, except Miss Isabel, had gone home.

I didn't feel that the blue apparition posed a threat to anybody here tonight. After all, what could a ghost do but scare someone to death?

Safely at the entrance to the dining room, I regretted that I'd allowed mindless fear to send me running from her. The next time...

If there was a next time.

Where was Annica with her red heart wand? She would be sorry she'd missed the appearance of Rachel's ghost.

I found Brent and Lucy at the buffet table, filling plates with fried chicken and pasta salad. Lucy had decided not to wear a costume for the Halloween party, but her long black dress and gold jewelry were as striking as any fantastic ensemble; and her shawl was embroidered with sequins.

"Hey, Jennet," Brent said. "How's my favorite ghost?"

Lucy smiled. "You look nice, Jennet, very authentic. Did you powder your face with flour?"

"With Soft Ivory loose powder," I said. "It's lighter than my usual shade."

"If you girls are going to talk make-up..." Brent began.

"Would you please take Miss Isabel her cardigan, Brent," I asked, draping it over his arm. "And maybe you should change the CD before we all freeze."

As he walked away to do my bidding, I said, "Lucy, I have to talk to you. It's important."

"Why, of course. Grab a plate and we'll find a quiet corner."

"Out of this infernal wind," I said with a forced smile.

When we'd found a tiny cafe table in a private nook, I said, "I just saw the ghost. The Lady in the Blue Raincoat."

True to her nature, Lucy didn't seem surprised. "Where?"

"Upstairs. I went up to Miss Isabel's room to get her sweater. Well, that doesn't matter. At first I thought I was seeing a reflection of myself, but..."

Reliving the moment, I found my hands shaking again, my mouth drying up. Lucy took off her shawl and wrapped it around my shoulders. With a shawl over the raincoat, I still felt cold.

"She had her hand over her mouth," I said. "I didn't."

Lucy nodded. "That's interesting, Jennet. She was aware of you."

"I was wearing her raincoat. It couldn't be on both of us at the same time." In a moment I'd be dissolving in hysterical laughter.

"What? Oh, I see. It can't be the same blue raincoat. That's beside the point. Tell me the rest."

I did, playing down my fear because where had it come from? I'd seen spirits before. The murdered girl who lived on after death in the secret room of Eidt House, the ghost of a skater who had tumbled through the ice and drowned while on a winter excursion with her friends, and the three white collies who haunted Lost Lake.

Not one of them had harmed me.

I had immersed myself in Rachel's story, talked to her friends, and read the accounts of previous sightings of the Lady in the Blue Raincoat. I'd hope to see her sometime, preferably with Annica at my side.

There was absolutely, positively no reason for me to be afraid.

But I was.

Twenty-six

"You have to tell Brent about the ghost," Lucy said.

"I will, as soon as the guests leave. He'll be jubilant. It'll translate into more publicity for the Inn. First the bones, now an authenticated ghost sighting. On Halloween night, no less."

"Tell Brent what?"

He was back, without the cardigan.

I searched for another bit of news. The chicken was fried to perfection, the decorated Halloween cookies were the most popular item on the buffet...

He waited, his hunter's instinct alerting him to the presence of a secret. I gave in.

"Just a few minutes ago, I saw the Lady in the Blue Raincoat. She was in the hall upstairs."

He didn't seem shocked. It was as if he'd added her name to the guest list.

"I knew she'd show up. It's Halloween. Her sister is here. The woman with her is Rachel's friend. There's a storm."

"There is?" Lucy asked. "I'd call it a fall shower. Rain changing over to snow by midnight."

"You're carried away by your own wind recording," I said. "But we've strayed from the point. Do you know what this means?"

"That she's real," Brent said. "A real ghost. I want to know where it is now." Brent turned his gaze toward the ceiling.

"Wouldn't it be fantastic if she made an appearance in the dining room?"

I couldn't imagine a spirit appearing in the midst of several dozen Halloween revelers.

"She disappeared in a cloud of blue mist," I said. "She was only there for a second."

"A blue mist. That's how she was described in one of the accounts I read. It's funny. Miss Isabel has lived in a room off that hall for years and has never seen anything out of the ordinary. Just noises. Or so she tells me."

"Nor has anyone else in a long, long time," Lucy said. "At least as far as we know. Maybe all the supernatural experiences weren't shared."

"Jennet is a ghost magnet, but I think this visit ties in with the discovery of Cynthia's remains."

I agreed with his observation. "The spirit—Rachel—was confused because I was wearing a blue raincoat. Catherine just told me that I resemble her."

"Do spirits get confused?" Lucy asked.

"Who's confused?" Annica glided up to us, waving her wand, scattering tiny red hearts on the floor. One landed on the sleeve of Brent's green plaid shirt. He rescued it and put in his shirt pocket.

"The resident ghost," I said. "What were you doing in the second floor hall earlier tonight, Annica?"

"How did you know about that?"

"I saw your trail of valentines."

"Oh, that's right. Well, it's hard to explain. I thought I heard a voice calling my name. Or maybe it was saying Anne."

"Was it someone you knew?"

"I didn't recognize it, and it doesn't matter because there was no one in the hall. Although I thought I heard a sound behind one of the doors. A kind of humming." She looked at Brent. "Didn't you say Miss Isabel was the only one who lived in the Inn?"

"For now," he said. "No one should have been there tonight."

"Well, I would have investigated, but the door was locked. What were *you* doing in the hall, Jennet?"

"A good deed," I said. "Miss Isabel was cold. I volunteered to get her cardigan from her room—and saw a ghost. A lady in a blue raincoat."

"Rachel! Why didn't I see her?"

"You were there at the wrong time."

"Darn it all. Jennet has all the luck. We're supposed to be a team."

"You were playing the Queen of Hearts while I ventured unknowingly into ghost territory."

"I'm hungry," Annica said, eying the cookies. "Suppose you go through the story again while I have a bite to eat. Was she really scary like a zombie? Did she have glowing eyes and bloodstains on her coat?"

I called up Rachel's image, oddly enough remembering luminous eyes. "She looked a little like me, with the same hairdo, and her raincoat was wrinkled."

"The way it would have been in life if she were returning from a vacation," Lucy said.

"Anyone would have thought she was a flesh-and-blood woman until she disintegrated."

"She's still looking for Cynthia," Brent said. "Someone should tell her that her friend has been found."

"What's left of her, you mean," Annica said. "You'd think Rachel would know, being a ghost."

I thought the talk had gone on long enough and recalled that I hadn't tasted anything on my plate, hadn't eaten since a light lunch at home. I picked up a piece of chicken. By now it was cold, but nothing had ever tasted so good.

"Do you think I should make an announcement?" Brent asked. "Tell people you saw Rachel's ghost?"

"Good heavens, no," I said. "People will think it's staged."

"Don't forget that Cynthia's sister and Rachel's friend are here," Lucy added.

"Rachel's friend's name is Marsha Anne," Annica recalled. "Was it Marsha Anne I heard, not Anne? Why would a ghostly voice be calling Marsha Anne?"

No one offered an opinion.

"So we wait till tomorrow to decide what to do about it," Brent said. "I'm going to check out the hall. Maybe I'll see something, even if it's just a trace of blue mist. You coming, Lucy?"

She nodded, and the two of them walked off, arm-in-arm.

"As parties go, this one is on the quiet side," Annica said when we were alone. "It's just sound effects and food."

"And a visiting ghost."

"She didn't visit everybody."

"There's the fortune teller?" I said. "Madame Zara. Did you have her tell your future?"

"Yes, did you?"

"Not yet," I said and added silently "Never." If I wanted a glimpse into the times to come, I'd ask Lucy to read my tea leaves.

"What did she tell you?" I asked.

"Lots of good stuff. I'm going to break hearts right and left until I find my Prince Charming."

"That sounds about right for you."

"Have you tried your hands at the horror movie games?" she asked.

"I don't like games."

So far I'd been occupied with the most Halloween-appropriate diversion of all: seeing the ghost.

"I hope I win the prize for best costume," Annica said brightly.

"You have serious competition."

"Such as?"

"Any one of the three witches."

We stood in the entrance to the dining room, surveying the costumed guests.

"The crowd's thinning out," Annica said. "Catherine's table is empty."

She was right. Belatedly I realized I still had Miss Isabel's room key in my pocket. I didn't see her either.

"People are disappearing," Annica said.

"Don't use that word."

"All right. They're vanishing."

Leaving Annica to study her competition, I set out to find Miss Isabel.

Twenty-seven

Miss Isabel was sitting behind the deserted hostess station, a mug of coffee in her hand. She was bundled up in her ruffled white cardigan, as bundled up as anyone could be in the thin decorative wrap. "It's so cold in here," she said. "I'm freezing."

"I don't think it is."

"You're wearing a coat," she said. "It's snowing out."

"It is?"

I felt detached from the Halloween partyers and what was happening in the outside world but recalled Lucy mentioning rain turning to snow. If it was indeed snowing, my raincoat would hardly be adequate.

For a short walk to my car and another few steps to the house? I'd manage and tomorrow wear my parka and leather gloves.

"I'd like to stay and see who wins the prize for the Best Costume," she said. "It's a hundred dollar gift certificate for the Green House of Antiques."

"I didn't know. That's my favorite shop."

Of course I didn't have a chance to win the prize. I looked too plain, and my costume hadn't garnered the attention Brent had hoped for. In fact, only Catherine had commented on its significance.

"But I might just go up to my room early," she said. "I can't make up my mind. I think the Queen of Hearts will win."

One vote for Annica, but Miss Isabel wasn't on Brent's team of judges.

I pulled her room key out of my pocket. "You won't get very far without this," I said. "Are you coming back to the party?"

"Probably, in a while. When I warm up. If I ever do."

All this talk about cold had a subtle effect on me, even with the warmth generated by the crowd that had thinned out. People wanted to drive home before the roads turned icy. So did I.

I found Brent at the buffet trying to decide which dessert to choose. He added a slice of cheesecake to the chocolate-decorated brownie on his plate.

"Miss Isabel was complaining about the cold," I said. "Could you turn the heat up?"

"I have the thermostat on seventy," he said. "With all these candles burning, I'm roasting."

"I'm just passing on her message. Is all quiet in the hall upstairs?"

"Quiet as a morgue," he said. "I'm going to have to find another permanent guest. I don't like to think of Miss Isabel living up there all alone."

"Maybe she'll see Rachel tonight," I said.

"She isn't there now."

I couldn't resist teasing him. "Not even a trace of blue mist?"

"Just Annica's valentine hearts," he said. "She's a knock-out tonight. That girl is so pretty to begin with, and in that red and white get-up..."

He trailed off, scanning the crowd, no doubt searching for a glimpse of glittering red and white. He didn't have to finish the thought. I knew what it was.

~ * ~

Moonlight illuminated the thin layer of snow on the ground as I left the Spirit Lamp Inn. The walkway was a trifle slippery, and I wished I'd worn boots. Oh, yes. Winter boots with a spring raincoat and white cotton gloves. But I walked slowly and watched where I stepped.

Brent had offered to walk with me to my car. But when I was ready to leave, so ready that I felt I couldn't stay in the Inn another second, I saw him in deep conversation with Annica, newly announced winner of the Best Costume prize. I didn't want to disturb them and saw no need for an escort anyway.

It was still snowing, soft white flakes that drifted down, turning the landscape into a winter wonderland. Well, it was after midnight, the first of November and time for winter weather.

I was alone in the parking lot, alone in the silent white world and, in truth, just a little bit uneasy. Quickly I cleared the snow from the car, anxious to be on my way.

I wasn't thinking about icy roads but about how tired I was. It was a different kind of tired. My experience on the second floor of the Inn had taken a toll on me. I wanted nothing more than to be home with Crane and my collies, to become reacquainted with the familiar, comforting cherished parts of my life.

I brushed the last of the snow off the roof and started the car. Turned on the windshield wipers and lights, slid into the seat, fastened the seat belt—all mechanically, without thinking about what I was doing—and put the car in reverse... And slammed on the brakes as a figure appeared in the rear view mirror.

A woman was crossing behind my car as I was backing up.

Dear Lord, I didn't see her. Didn't look. Thought I was still alone.

Or... My heart pounded, my breath shuddered to a stop.

Did I hit her?

She wasn't there. All I could see through the window was the falling snow.

No, no, you'd know if you hit something.

I got out of the car and took four giant steps to the back. No one was there. Most telling, except for my footprints as I'd walked around the car with the scraper, the snow was undisturbed.

Then I saw a woman walking toward the Inn, back to the gardens where no one in her right mind would venture on a snowy evening. She wore a blue raincoat with a hood. Just like mine.

~ * ~

The second sighting, for I had no doubt I'd seen Rachel's ghost again, unnerved me more than the initial one.

First, although I knew I hadn't harmed anyone, I still hadn't recovered from the fright of thinking I'd almost run over a living person.

She wouldn't have expected anyone to be backing up at the precise moment she walked behind the car. Or knowing she couldn't die again, hadn't cared. For a person, even at a slow back-up speed, a Taurus could do a lot of damage. Break bones, possibly kill...

But that wasn't what happened.

If I had hit her, I would have collided with the frosty night air. A ghost has no substance.

Second, why was Rachel's wandering spirit targeting me? Why not Miss Isabel who lived on the second floor? Or Brent or Lucy or Annica, for that matter?

"Jennet is a ghost magnet," Brent had said.

Was it that simple? Or was there another more sinister reason?

Something else tugged at me. Obviously Rachel didn't confine her appearances to the second floor of the Spirit Lamp Inn. Tonight was she walking toward the site of the grave?

All the way home, the moment when I saw the ghost in the rear window played in my mind.

I didn't worry about the slippery roads. I passed the Haver House without noticing whether there was a light in the window. Once I skidded and veered toward a ditch that ran along a thin line of woods and a sheer drop-off. I regained control of the Taurus just in time to avoid a real disaster.

Thank you God. One more fright to keep my heart pounding.

When I saw the green Victorian farmhouse on Jonquil Lane lit up in welcome for the absent mistress, even though by then it was past midnight, I let the evening's trauma steal away.

The best welcome of the evening came from Crane who had waited up for me with cocoa makings on the counter. Except for Candy and Misty who bounced joyously around me, the collies were asleep, too locked in slumber to do anything more strenuous than lift their pretty heads.

Over hot cocoa, I told Crane about my forays into the other world.

"It may be a cliché to encounter a ghost on Halloween," I said, "but that's what happened. And I was terrified, both times. I still wonder if I ran into someone even though there was nobody there."

"You didn't," Crane said. "Do you think these two so-called sightings were rigged to add excitement to the party?"

"By Brent? I don't see how. I know what I saw both times."

He divided the rest of the cocoa evenly, filling our mugs to the top. "Look on the bright side, honey. Now you can write another chapter for your spirit book."

"Not until I find out why Rachel is walking again," I said.

Twenty-eight

After the drama of Brent's Halloween party, I longed to return to a simpler time in my life before the darkness started to close in on me. I welcomed the sunlight and the frosty November air. I even welcomed my rowdiest class on a Monday morning and the ever-present specter of Denver Armstrong.

He was in a rare quiet mood that bordered on sullen, still drawing his pictures and refusing to participate in class. I suspected he knew that the theft of my grade book hadn't derailed me as he'd hoped, and the knowledge infuriated him. I had no doubt he was planning another assault.

I knew how to deal with Denver. After a fashion. Rachel's ghost was another matter. In one evening she had become real to me. No longer just a name in an old library book, Rachel posed a vague threat. If only I could decipher it and understand why she was appearing to me. Wouldn't her energy be better spent haunting Cynthia's killer?

So I met my everyday challenges, even the ongoing problem of Deanna, Sparrow, and Joyanne Summerton. Sue Appleton and I had left it unresolved, hoping a solution would present itself. That rarely happens.

Sue gave me the latest news in person on Monday evening. "Joyanne Summerton is up in arms again. Sparrow has disappeared, and she's sure Deanna stole her."

There was that word again. Disappear. Was there an epidemic in Foxglove Corners? I sighed, reminding myself that I was going to be grateful for everyday concerns.

"Where was Sparrow when this happened?" I asked.

"In her backyard. It has a fence and a gate with a lock. Joyanne was shopping at the mall. The kids were in school. The father was away. He's a pilot or something. I forget what."

"She left Sparrow alone in a yard with nobody home? Anyone could have taken her."

I felt like adding, "And it's her own fault." I'd never leave one of my dogs unattended in this dangerous world.

I hadn't heard any stories of missing dogs lately, but the dognappers were always lurking in the shadows, waiting for a chance to steal an unwatched pet.

"If Sparrow is gone, Deanna can hardly sue the Rescue League," Sue said.

I wasn't so sure. "She'll find a way. What did Joyanne want you to do?"

"She didn't say. She's going to press charges."

"She can't accuse Deanna of theft without proof," I said.

"I thought you could contact Deanna. Talk to her. See if she has Sparrow."

"And if she does, what could I do?"

"Convince her to give the dog back."

That wasn't going to happen. In many ways, Sue was out of touch with the real world. If Deanna had Sparrow, she'd argue that she'd simply taken back her own property. I understood that. If she was smart, she'd keep Sparrow out of sight until...

Until what? Joyanne Summerton stopped looking for her?

"And what if she doesn't have Sparrow?" I asked.

"Then Sparrow is just one more lost dog."

"I guess I can call Deanna for you," I said. "It would be good to know, but I'm not going to accuse her of anything."

"That's all right. Just see if there's any truth to Joyanne's accusations, if you can."

Her information delivered, the problem resting in my hands, Sue announced that she was late for her riding lesson at her horse farm on Squill Lane.

I jotted 'Call Deanna' down on my calendar, wondering how she would react to an overture from me. Wondering when I could fit a call and a visit into my hectic schedule and, above all, why this was still our problem.

~ * ~

Brent brought a baked ham left over from the party for our dinner that evening, and I told him about Rachel's appearance in the parking lot.

"That lady sure gets around," he said. "But you're the only one who sees her."

"I realize that. Can you tell me why?"

It was a rhetorical question. I put the ham in the oven to keep warm and came back to the living room to find Misty in Brent's lap. No one had told her she was no longer a puppy, but Brent loved dogs, and Misty and Sky were his favorites. The Blue and the White, he called them.

"Now that Halloween is over, let's redouble our efforts to solve the mystery," Brent said.

"What do you propose we do?"

"Annica thinks there's more to find in the attic."

I smiled, well aware of Annica's new obsession. "She's looking for a bloodstained dagger or a vial of poison, anything…so long as it's lethal and gruesome. Instead of focusing on objects, maybe we should think about people."

"How is that possible after so many years?" Crane asked.

"Let's assume that Cynthia's killer is still alive out there somewhere," I said. "We talked to some of her contemporaries at the party. Her sister, Catherine, Marsha Anne, and Miss Isabel."

"Did Miss Isabel know Cynthia too?" Crane asked.

I paused, trying to remember. I was unsure. She hadn't exactly said that.

"She told us she might have stayed at the Inn when Cynthia and Rachel checked in."

"What a coincidence."

"Miss Isabel," Brent said with a groan. "I had no idea she'd be so demanding. She's always complaining about being cold. She wears her winter coat inside and out. The thermostat is set at seventy-two."

"Maybe she's sick," I said.

I recalled Miss Isabel trying to stave off the chill in a thin ruffled cardigan meant to be worn as a light evening wrap. She hadn't looked ill. Only frail and wan.

"I bought a space heater for her room," Brent said, "but I won't turn the temperature up to seventy-five. Nothing's wrong with the furnace. I had it checked."

Crane had built a fire, and its warmth wrapped around me. Our house was never too warm or too cold. I couldn't imagine trying to live in an uncomfortable environment.

"I'll have another tenant soon," Brent said. "Catherine's friend, Bruce Cameron. He wants to join the Hunt Club and be close by for the fox hunting."

"Don't these people have regular homes?" Crane asked.

"The Inn is perfect for a bachelor who can afford the rent. There's no upkeep, meals and laundry are readily available, and it's close to the action."

By action he meant fox hunting.

"That's good," I said. "Not for the fox, for Miss Isabel. You won't have to worry about her being alone on the second floor when the restaurant closes for the night."

"When would you like to go up to the attic again?" he asked.

"It has to be on a weekend. I don't like to drive after dark."

The very thought of Rachel strolling through the Inn's parking lot, walking into the Taurus, turned my blood to ice. But she could also appear in the daylight too. On the Inn's grounds, in the Inn itself. At the site of Cynthia's grave…

Don't think about Rachel or you'll never go to the Inn again.

"Let me check with Annica," I said. "I can never keep up with her schedule."

"I hope you're going to watch out for the girls, Fowler," Crane said. "If the person who killed Cynthia all those years ago is still around, your detective work could be dangerous. And Jennet knows how I feel about danger."

He had been so quiet, sitting with Candy, that I'd almost forgotten he was there. He was right, of course. What killer with a secret to keep likes a snoop?

"Nothing can happen," Brent promised him. "We're just going to go through some old boxes. No one will know what we're doing."

"Jennet tells me the attic floor is unstable."

"It isn't finished. I provide plenty of lighting and we all watch where we step."

"Why don't you come along with us, Crane?" I asked. "We could use a man with a gun."

"I'll be on standby," he said. "As always."

I was going to hold him to that promise.

Twenty-nine

A few minutes into the conversation, I could tell that Deanna was angry. Furthermore, I'd swear she was innocent of stealing Sparrow, which meant Sparrow was lost. Irretrievably? I could only hope she hadn't fallen into the dognappers' clutches.

How much better it would have been if Deanna had been the one to take her.

"This is exactly what I was afraid would happen," Deanna said. "That woman stole my dog and didn't take care of her. Now she's gone."

"Any dog can run away or…"

Deanna interrupted me. "Sparrow was abused. I told you how the Summerton woman choked her. I'm going to find Sparrow, and when I do, she's staying with me. Your Rescue League is out of the picture."

I found it odd that Joyanne Summerton hadn't made a similar vow. It was as I thought. Sparrow's true owner was Deanna, the one who cared enough about her to take action.

"How will you do that?" I asked. "There weren't any clues. Sparrow just vanished from a fenced yard."

"Lost dog posters, ads, calls to shelters, whatever it takes. One of the neighbors might have seen something unusual."

While Joyanne's grand plan was to press charges against Deanna for a crime she couldn't prove. Without thinking the matter through, I said, "Let me know if I can help you."

"Thank you, but the Rescue League has done enough already. If they'd refused to accept Sparrow without proof of ownership, she wouldn't have been given away. She wouldn't be lost now."

That wasn't necessarily true. A man determined to hurt Deanna through her beloved collie would have found another way to do it. And thinking of that man whose name had slipped my mind, I said, "Have you considered your former friend? Maybe he took Sparrow."

"Alex? That's a thought," she said.

"I'm offering my help as a collie lover, not a Rescue League representative," I added.

"In that case, I'll be grateful for whatever you can do," she said.

And there we left the matter. Another mystery to solve, this one as impossible as any of the others in my life.

~ * ~

November brought change to Foxglove Corners. Icy winds, frequent snowfalls, and an imperceptible rush toward the holidays. The most noticeable change took place at the Spirit Lamp Inn.

It was possible to have lunch in the dining room. Louise, the new cook Brent had found, was even more gifted in the culinary arts than the last. Catherine's friend, Bruce, had moved into a spacious room down the hall from the one occupied by Miss Isabel. Brent was talking about bringing his old-fashioned sleigh to the Inn and offering rides in the snow.

All in a week's time.

On Saturday morning, Annica and I donned jeans and warm sweaters and met Brent at the Inn for our secret attic expedition.

How secret it would be remained to be seen as Miss Isabel seemed to be constantly on the move, bundled up in a blue down jacket.

"She's going to coax Rachel out of hiding with that color," Annica said as Miss Isabel stood in the doorway of the dining room surveying the lunch crowd.

Annica was working at the Inn as hostess tonight. She'd brought an overnight case with a change of clothes. The prospect of Brent's company for an entire day had sent a happy glow rushing to her face.

"I'm wearing a red dress with pearl jewelry," she said.

"Continuing the Queen of Hearts theme?"

"Brent says those colors become me." Her sweater was a crimson cowl neck that looked new, hardly attic wear.

"What are you girls up to—dressed like that?" Miss Isabel stopped at our table. She was wearing tall boots and a navy blue scarf that sparkled with sequins.

"Won't you join us?" I asked.

"Not today. I see Bruce over by the window. Just thought I'd say hello."

And ask her question. She waited. I rarely wore jeans and couldn't think of a credible reason for doing so today.

"We're going Christmas shopping at the Green House of Antiques," Annica said.

"But it isn't even Thanksgiving yet."

"Well, I won that gift certificate, and I'm off this morning. Why not have fun with it?"

"Are you still feeling the cold, Miss Isabel?" I asked.

"All the time, especially in the evening. I don't know why. My room is warm enough, unless the thermostat is broken."

"But you've lived here for years, through how many winters? Didn't you ever notice the cold before?"

"Never," she said. "Sometimes I wake up from a dream of snow. I'm being buried alive in a giant snowdrift. It's horrible."

Listening to Miss Isabel's complaint, I could almost feel a chill settle over the table where I'd been sitting with Annica in comfort.

Ghosts bring cold.

I examined the thought while Annica returned the conversation to the Green House and the antique jewelry she hoped to find there on our mythical shopping trip.

Miss Isabel hadn't seen Rachel's ghost, but perhaps her extraordinary sensitivity to the cold was an indication that Rachel was passing by, not only in the hallway outside her room but everywhere. Even here in the toasty dining room.

Because I was so warm, I'd shed my parka. So warm I was thinking of ordering an iced tea with my lunch instead of coffee, which meant I wasn't sensitive to Rachel's passing—yet. No. I just saw her in person. Rather, in spectral form.

Brent materialized at our table rather like a ghost himself, a brawny, boisterous one in jeans and a maroon plaid shirt rolled up to his elbows.

"The day's specials are roast beef sandwiches and vegetable soup," he announced. "Won't you sit down, Miss Isabel? And for God's sake, take off that coat. You'll get overheated."

"If only," she said. "Thank you, Mr. Fowler, but I'm having lunch with Bruce." She winked at Brent. "He doesn't know it yet."

When she was out of earshot, Annica said, "I thought Bruce was Catherine's boyfriend. Or was that Ted?"

Boyfriend? It seemed like an incongruous word for an elegant elderly gentleman. What would you call him then?

"Well, he's Miss Isabel's neighbor now," I said. "And Catherine isn't here."

I stole a glance at Miss Isabel. Bruce had risen at her approach, giving her a polite smile. She sat down—and kept her coat on. Immediately she embarked on an animated one-sided conversation.

"What about it, girls?" Brent asked. "How does the special sound on a cold day?"

"Fantastic," I said.

"Then let's order and eat. I'm anxious to get on with our search."

~ * ~

Welcome back. I've been waiting for you.

Of course the attic didn't say that, and it wasn't my trusty inner voice. It was a feeling, nebulous and slightly frightening. I was glad that my companions were nearby.

The attic of the Spirit Lamp Inn was an unusual place, a repository of memories and secrets. Decades-old boxes waiting to be opened. Antique trunks blanketed with dust. Shadows dancing in the quivering beams of the lantern flashlights.

Annica gasped as the heel of her boot sank between two boards. Brent steadied her. "Watch your step, Annica. You don't want to break anything."

"I'll start with the boxes over by the window," I said. "They look promising."

One after the other, I opened them. Crammed with greeting cards, letters, maps, loose photographs, and certificates of authenticity for assorted prints, here was a motley paper connection that had meant something to somebody once. Packed away, stored out of sight, forgotten in the passage of time, it was overwhelming.

"There's sewing stuff over here," Annica called out. "Patterns and needles. Buttons. Who saves buttons?"

"I have antique Christmas ornaments," Brent said. "They'll come in handy for the Inn's tree."

I rifled through box after box and set them aside. The contents should be burned, but how sad to destroy memories. Still, who would come back to the Inn for them? Certainly not the previous owner who had included them in the sale, sight unseen.

Opening the lid of a candy box that once contained two pounds of Sanders' Fruits and Nuts, I expected more of the same. Fodder for the bonfire. Instead I saw a small brown book sitting on top of a batch of unwritten postcards, and a map of Michigan... 'My Travel Diary.'

Eagerly I opened the book. The owner had printed her name in blue ink on the first page: *Cynthia Lauren.*

Thirty

"Bonanza!" I cried.

"What?" Brent and Annica spoke together.

"I found Cynthia's diary. It was in an old candy box, of all places."

A faint scent of chocolate drifted up into the musty air. Incredible. After all these years, a scent had been trapped in cardboard. Along with what else?

Brent and Annica were at my side even as I turned the first pages. The entries were written in turquoise ink and dated at the top. The pen was there, too, not a ballpoint but the old fashioned kind that you filled from a bottle or, I supposed, an inkwell. Some of the writing was smudged, but overall the text appeared to be readable. At last! A real clue.

This is what you needed to find.

Again the voice that wasn't really a voice made its presence known. I scarcely paid attention to it.

This was even better than a suitcase, which brought up a question. Why wasn't the box in the suitcase, along with the rest of Cynthia's possessions?

Annica voiced the same question.

"Maybe it was an improvised lap desk," I said. "She took it out to make an entry in the diary or to write post cards."

While Rachel went to dinner. But would Cynthia have done that? I thought she stayed behind because of her headache. For whatever reason, the box had been separated from the suitcase.

I read the first entry aloud. Dated July, 1953, it described a trip to the Isle of Capri on a rainy weekend. There were dozens of other entries, half a book full. Cynthia had written the last entry on the day she disappeared.

Rain. Lightning. Flooding. We drove into dangerous weather. I couldn't see the road. We were almost home, but...

"But what?" Brent asked.

"That's all."

I flipped through the rest of the diary. All of the remaining pages were blank.

"Darn," Annica said. "I can't believe it. A cliffhanger in a diary. What happened then?"

"She was interrupted? Who or what made her stop writing in the middle of a sentence?"

"The killer," Brent said.

"Not necessarily. Maybe she was too tired to continue. She lay down and never had a chance to finish the entry."

I could see the scene playing in my mind in full color. Unfortunately there was no way of knowing how true to the facts my imagining was.

Annica assumed her story-telling voice. "Try this. *...but we decided to stop for the night in a gloomy old inn situated in the middle of a dark wood.*"

"Keep going," I said, waiting for the entrance of a dagger-wielding maniac.

"I can't. You need to find something else, Jennet."

"This is the only candy box," I said. "The others are plain nondescript boxes filled with papers and newspaper clippings. I think it's significant that the candy box was stacked with the others.

Maybe it was placed here as an afterthought, found after the suitcase was stashed in the attic."

"After Cynthia was murdered," Annica added.

"We have to give the diary to Catherine," Brent said.

I moved it out of his reach. "Not before we read it."

"Jennet's right," Annica said. "It's her find."

With two against one, Brent capitulated. "I *would* like to know what it says."

"Let's read it then," I said. "In some private place where Miss Isabel isn't likely to turn up. But remember, it's a travel diary. It may not contain thoughts and feelings. Or clues."

"We'll use my office. I'll lock the door. Will that be private enough?"

"Just a suggestion," Annica said. "Make sure Miss Isabel doesn't see us go in."

~ * ~

Brent had put his stamp on a small room near the attic stairway. The walls were forest green, the desk a massive oak antique, and new beige leather chairs invited his visitors to make themselves comfortable. Prints of dogs and horses hung on the walls, interspersed with framed photographs of his own animals.

He turned on the desk lamp. I opened the diary and started reading aloud.

Germany. It's like the fairy tale country I dreamed about all my life. Real castles and enchanting wood carvings. We stayed in Heidelberg for three days, then visited Austria. Perfect weather but cold. On to Paris.

"No clue there," Annica said.

"Well, the Germany trip happened in nineteen fifty-three."

"Find nineteen fifty-five," Brent said. "Start with the trip to northern Michigan. We can fill in the gaps later."

I skimmed the entries, quickly but carefully enough to see that they were similar. A record of the countries Cynthia and Rachel had visited, combined with her impressions. Nineteen fifty-four must have been a quiet year with no travels noted.

Saving for a world cruise, she had written. *I'm learning to speak French. Making good progress. Rachel is studying Italian. We're talking about starting a tourist agency someday.*

"Here's the Michigan trip," I said. "They drove up north in August. We knew that. Bought souvenirs, postcards, took pictures. Routine tourist stuff. If anything unusual happened during that time, Cynthia didn't mention it."

Annica sighed. "I guess this wasn't such a good clue after all."

"It tells us the trouble started when they checked into the Oaken Bucket Inn, as it was known at the time, and ended that night. We ought to concentrate on people. Let's talk to Miss Isabel again. Maybe she's remembered something."

~ * ~

I set the diary on Brent's desk.

"Take it with you, Jennet," Brent said. "Read the rest of it tonight. Just because we didn't find anything pertinent doesn't mean there's nothing there."

"I'll do that." I slipped it in my shoulder bag. A brief glance at my watch told me I should be on my way home. In any event, Miss Isabel had left the Inn. Her vintage automobile was gone.

"That's not unusual," Brent said. "She goes out a few times a week."

"We should talk to Bruce Cameron, too, I said. "Also Catherine and Marsha Anne."

"We can," Brent said, "but if they had any relevant information, wouldn't they have told the police when Cynthia went missing?"

"You'd think so."

"We should talk to Rachel." Annica threw the suggestion out, no doubt hoping it would take wing. It fell flat.

"*You* talk to her," I said. "I hope I never see her again. But think, Annica, if Rachel knew what happened, she'd hardy have kept coming back to the Inn."

"You have a point. We'll concentrate on Miss Isabel, Bruce, Catherine, and Marsha Anne. Oh, and Ted."

Of the five people, I considered only Miss Isabel a good possibility. Only she had mentioned she might have been in the Inn on the night in question.

"We don't want to rouse her suspicions," Annica said.

"I have it! Miss Isabel said that her birthday is on Friday. Let's invite her to a special dinner. I'll have Louise bake a cake. We'll have champagne and reminisce about the good old days. Can you both be there?"

"I'll be here anyway," Annica said. "Remember I'm the Friday night hostess."

"I'll find someone to cover for you so you can join us."

"And I'll check with Crane. Maybe he can come too."

"We have a plan then," Brent said.

It could work. If only Miss Isabel had something to remember.

Thirty-one

While the mystery at the Spirit Lamp Inn took a hopeful turn, life at Marston High School spiraled downward in a melee of rowdy behavior, tardiness, and absences. The reason for the absences was a malady characterized by coughing, sore throats and general aches.

"Every other kid is sick," Leonora said as we dodged snowflakes on our way into the building the next morning. "I hope I don't come down with anything."

"Like nurses and doctors, teachers have to be immune," I said, feeling a pang of guilt because I'd neglected to have my flu shot. "But I wish they'd stay home when they're sick and not spread germs around."

We stopped in the teachers' lounge for hot chocolate which provided a comforting transition from frigid air to noisy classroom.

In American Literature, about half of the students' names appeared on the absence list. One who seemed to have outwitted sickness was Denver Armstrong who sat on the window sill with his ever-present sketch pad.

"Denver," I said.

He ignored me, continuing to move his pencil along the paper in sweeping strokes.

I raised my voice. "Denver Armstrong!"

He looked up and turned a surly gaze on me. "What do *you* want?"

Arrogance dripped from his words. Arrogance, disrespect; annoyance at being interrupted in his chosen pursuit.

"Please take your seat," I said. "Put the art work away. Open your Literature book."

If he followed one of these orders, it would be a miracle.

I glanced at the clock, then at my watch. Could time possibly be moving backward? Whichever direction it chose, I had forty more minutes of Denver Armstrong.

So far, he had a string of zeroes in the new grade book and appeared to have no interest of earning a passing grade today. Meanwhile the class moved into the twentieth century, and the snowflakes grew larger and thicker, commanding more of their attention than the day's poem. For some reason, I thought of the Influenza epidemic that had killed so many people in the early nineteen hundreds. Could we be on the verge of another epidemic? A pandemic?

And what was the difference? I'd look the terms up online and work it into my lesson tomorrow.

November is the cruelest month, I thought. *Not April.*

Not even a holiday could make it more palatable. A long holiday weekend? Well, that was something to look forward to. Crane and I hoped to visit our cabin up north. We'd take all the collies and everything needed to make an intimate Thanksgiving dinner. We needed a romantic time alone with no distractions.

After the day's reading, I assigned a brief essay and walked up and down the aisles checking on each student's progress. Denver was drawing images of the Grim Reaper wielding a scythe. Katrina was coughing. She popped a drop in her mouth and managed to say, "It isn't candy. It's a lozenge." In the front row, Sue Ellen, red faced and overcome with a coughing jag, made a dash for the water fountain outside the room.

I swallowed and detected a sudden scratchiness in my throat.

Oh, no!

Visions of cold medicine, warm beds, and dogs fussing for their walks taunted me. So much for those endearing pictures of the loyal collie lying alongside her mistress's sick bed. Mine hadn't seen them.

I will not get sick!

I looked at the clock again. It was a long time until the last bell of the day. A long week until Friday.

The snow continued to fall. Lovely, lacy flakes making the ground higher and the world whiter. It would be a slow commute home.

~ * ~

During lunch, I told Leonora about the latest developments at the Spirit Lamp Inn. "You're missing out on all the excitement."

"You and Annica left me behind," she said.

"You can join us on Friday for Miss Isabel's birthday dinner."

Leonora struggled to open a pint of milk. "Don't you mean her interrogation?"

"If we're going to solve the mystery of Cynthia Lauren's murder, we need to tap every source, even if it's a memory buried in Miss Isabel's past."

"It's too bad the diary clue fizzled," she said.

It had. Last night I'd read every entry. I now had a good idea of the girls' travels but nothing helpful about Cynthia's last night at the Inn. Except for a handmade bookmark I'd missed when I'd first examined the diary. It appeared to be cut from a travel brochure, a view of Tahquamenon Falls. But that couldn't be a clue.

"Are you planning to search the attic again?" Leonora asked.

"We haven't decided. Brent feels there's nothing more to find."

"What about tapping every source?" Leonora asked.

"There are some boxes we didn't open. Some I only glanced at."
I recalled my excitement on finding the diary. We'd left the attic soon afterward.

"If you decide to look around some more, let me know," she said. "I'd love to see the antiques. Maybe Brent would sell one to me."

"He'll probably give it to you. They came with the Inn. He doesn't particularly want them."

Furniture, lamps, mirrors, paintings—and the belongings of a murdered girl, but those had been removed.

I frowned. "I thought I'd feel better when I ate, but my throat feels like I swallowed a mouthful of thorns."

"Grimsley was complaining about all the subs in the building," Leonora said. "The office is packed with kids who are taking advantage of them. A word to the wise: Don't get sick."

I swallowed again, hoping I was imagining a throat that didn't feel normal. "I'll try."

~*~

Something strange happened that afternoon. Usually my desk, so neat in the morning, became a jumble of papers as the day wore on. Announcements from the office, mail, lecture notes, newspapers—they all came together to create a mess.

As I searched for the phone number of a possible advertiser for the school paper, I discovered a piece torn from a newspaper, not clipped with scissors as Journalism assignments were required to be.

It dealt with the latest school shooting in a small town up north. A teacher, a student, and the boy who tried to disarm the shooter were dead.

Where did that come from?

Perhaps because my nerves were strained to the breaking point with snow outside and coughing inside, I immediately saw it as a warning.

This could happen in Oakpoint. This teacher could be you.
In our violent modern society, it wasn't so far-fetched.
Don't overreact, I warned myself.
I turned the paper over. On the back was an ad for mink coats.
Could that be meant for me? My views on wearing fur were well-known.
Okay. You never saw this.
I dropped the paper in the basket and put the incident from my mind.

~*~

"My aunt thought the best way to fight off a cold was to refuse to acknowledge it."
I drove around a slow moving vehicle cautiously. Another twenty minutes on the freeway, then we'd be traveling a country road with little danger of colliding with another car. The snow was light and fluffy. It made the passing scenery sparkle. Sparkle was welcome after my lackluster day.
"That only works some of the time," Leonora said.
"I don't want to miss a chance to question Miss Isabel on Friday."
"You should be better by then. Or worse."
My thoughts drifted to food. Hot soup, hot tea, cake fresh from the oven. I'd taken a large container of stew out of the freezer for tonight's dinner. Should I have rice or dumplings, or noodles with it? Dumplings, I decided. What was that saying? Feed a cold and starve a fever?
The birthday dinner was to be a surprise for Miss Isabel. I'd bought her a gift, a long red and white scarf that should keep her neck warm. Annica found a vintage teapot decorated with spring flowers at the Green House of Antiques. Brent's present was a surprise, and he was paying for everyone's dinner, of course.
"Our exit's ahead," Leonora said.
"I know."

We were halfway home, halfway to that cup of tea and a quiet refuge where teenaged angst couldn't find me. I persisted in thinking that the green Victorian farmhouse on Jonquil Lane was a safe harbor. No evil could find me there. Nothing undesirable could touch me.

It hadn't always been so in the past, but I held on to the thought.

Thirty-two

Orchestrating a surprise birthday party for a lady who wandered freely throughout the Spirit Lamp Inn proved difficult for Brent but not impossible.

Miss Isabel had seen the cake, a towering chocolate confection, but not in its decorated glory. The gifts were well hidden somewhere on the premises, and the table—three tables moved together—was set aside as 'Reserved" for a special party.

She was therefore truly astonished when she entered the dining room that evening to find Brent and the friends she'd made at Halloween waiting to welcome her. For once Crane was in our group, together with Lucy and Annica.

I'd worn my charm bracelet, and Annica had on her silver bell earrings. Together we jingled whenever we moved. It added a charming magical touch to the occasion. At least I thought so, and wonder of wonders, my sore throat hadn't developed into anything more serious. Occasionally I noticed Bruce eyeing me curiously.

"I can't believe you did all this for me," Miss Isabel said. "And to think you came all this way on such a terrible night." She smiled at Catherine and Marsha Anne.

It wasn't the best night for driving, with snow and frosty air blowing it around. Luckily I had Crane who was a master driver in any weather, and we'd picked up Lucy and Annica. Leonora had decided to stay home. I realized how unusual it was for Crane to be able to accompany me on one of my various jaunts and was grateful that he could be here tonight.

"I haven't had a birthday party since I was a little girl," Miss Isabel said. "That chocolate cake I saw earlier today… Is it for me, by chance?"

Brent beamed with the satisfaction of a job well done. "I had it baked especially for you, Miss Isabel."

"Chocolate is my favorite. How did you know?"

"I think you mentioned it. And there'll be thirty candles on it."

She blushed. "That's about right."

Brent had thought of every detail including a bouquet of red roses and a corsage for Miss Isabel. In a charming fluster, she pinned it to her coat.

"I don't know what it is about this winter," she said. "I just can't get warm."

"It's still fall, Miss Isabel." Brent handed her a large birthday-wrapped package. "Why don't you open this one now? It's from me."

She did. Brent had given her a lovely pink cashmere shawl that had a silver shimmer in the candlelight.

"Oh, it's beautiful." She ran her hand lightly over the fabric. "Exquisite."

"Now you can take your coat off." Brent stood at her chair, ready to relocate the bulky item.

She relinquished it, albeit reluctantly, and wrapped herself in the shawl.

We ordered, and a hush fell on the group. In spite of the trappings of a festive celebration, something was missing.

"The last time Jennet and I were here, we heard a scream," Crane said.

I remembered. It was the night of my own birthday dinner.

"The hostess said it was a kitchen accident," I added. "I thought somebody saw a ghost or had been murdered. But we never heard anything more about it."

"That explains why the wait staff was always changing," Lucy said. "They kept seeing things that frightened them."

"Have you had any trouble with people quitting, Mr. Fowler?" Miss Isabel asked.

"Not really." He glanced at me. Some of my dining companions knew about my Halloween sighting; most didn't. Brent understood that I didn't want it to become general knowledge. "We haven't been up and running very long."

"Any changes you made were superficial," Bruce said. "If the ghost walked before, there's no reason to believe she won't walk again. This is familiar ground for her."

Lucy focused her gaze on the window that cast our reflections back at us. At times I thought she could see things hidden from ordinary people. "Then if we hear a scream tonight, it means our ghost is nearby."

"Come to wish you a Happy Birthday, Isabel."

That was Bruce who didn't appear to notice that Miss Isabel didn't appreciate his observation.

I was again thankful that Crane was present. I didn't think a ghost would dare show its face around my husband. As an added precaution, I didn't intend to leave the well-lit safety of the dining room tonight for any reason.

~ * ~

We had finished a dinner of prime rib, and Miss Isabel was cutting her cake with grace and skill as if she had years of practice when I remembered the purpose that had inspired the evening's get-together. We had hoped to create a non-threatening atmosphere in which Miss Isabel could reminisce about the past and possibly remember a stray bit of information that would shed light on Cynthia Lauren's murder. Even if it was more or less a shot in the dark.

As I searched for a way to introduce the topic into the conversation, Bruce said, "I've been thinking about our sleigh rides at Brandymere Farm. Do you remember, Bella?"

Bella? It sounded as if they had known each other previously and well.

Miss Isabel looked up briefly and down at the half-eaten slice of cake on her plate. "Vaguely. It was ages ago."

"Well, you can't have forgotten that New Year's Eve when my new Dodge got stuck in a snowdrift. We thought we'd freeze to death before another car came along. Marsha Anne had a chocolate bar in her purse. We divided it up."

"I've never heard of Brandymere Farm," I said.

But Brandymere Road. That was a different story. It was the road around which chilling stories had developed over the years. Supposedly it led to the end of the earth. The wayfarer took the risk of falling off the face of the planet if he chose that route of doom.

Ridiculous stories, really. Suitable for telling around the campfire. But in truth that locale had been the site of more than one inexplicable disappearance in Foxglove Corners, which explained the origin of its reputation.

"I heard the family that owned the farm died out years ago," Bruce said. "Those were the best times. You and me, Marsha Anne, and Gavin. He died in Vietnam. Rachel, Cynthia and Catherine. The whole gang. Young people today don't know how to have a good time with their video games and what not."

Crane grasped my hand under the table. "I wouldn't say that."

I cast him a smile. "We're not the young people Bruce is talking about."

"I have a sleigh," Brent said. "In a few more weeks when the real winter sets in, I'm going to offer sleigh rides from the Inn. I have my own horses," he added.

"Reviving the old tradition," Lucy said fondly. "I'm looking forward to it. If I'm invited, that is."

Brent winked at her. "You'll be my first guest."

"And me?" Annica said with a toss of her head that sent the tiny bells jingling. She had been uncharacteristically quiet this evening. But she wasn't about to be left out of any activity that Brent initiated.

"You, of course, Annica. And Jennet. Whoever's game."

"Well it sounds like fun, Mr. Fowler," Miss Isabel said, "But I don't care for cold diversions, as you've probably already surmised."

The pink glow lent to Miss Isabel's face by her new shawl had vanished as quickly as if somebody had turned an off switch. While the flames leapt and crackled in the fireplace near the table, she looked as if she were back in the past, back in the Dodge, trapped in a snowdrift.

I broke off a piece of cake with my fork and studied her demeanor. Why had she never mentioned that she'd known Bruce Cameron before Halloween?

Thirty-three

"I've been admiring your charm bracelet, Jennet," Bruce said. "You don't see them very often."

I exchanged a glance with Catherine who nodded imperceptibly.

"It belonged to Cynthia Lauren," I said. "Catherine kindly said I could keep it."

"I thought I recognized it. But I don't understand. Was it—forgive me, Catherine—buried with the bones?"

"No," I said.

"One of my men found it when he was working on the garden," Brent said. "We didn't know its history until Catherine told us it had belonged to Cynthia."

"What was a bracelet doing in the garden?" Bruce asked.

"We figure Cynthia must have lost it," I said.

"Unlikely." Bruce shook his head. "What a strange story."

"And it's true."

He shook his head. "I think there's another explanation. Cynthia used to wear that bracelet when it had only four or five charms on it. After each one of her trips, there were more. I don't see how she could lose it."

"Let's change the subject," Miss Isabel said. "It's creepy. I don't know how Jennet can wear a dead woman's bracelet."

They were making me feel self-conscious. But I couldn't very well eat my cake without moving my arm. As for wearing the bracelet this evening, it was mine, after all.

Annica leaped to my defense. "It isn't like Jennet robbed a corpse. She wouldn't do that."

Oh, Annica. Leave it to you.

Everyone except Catherine looked uncomfortable. "My sister would have wanted her jewelry to be enjoyed. I'm glad it turned up, whatever the circumstances."

"So leave Jennet alone," Brent said.

Bruce bristled. "I wasn't criticizing her."

Now I felt uncomfortable. A slight tension had crept up on our party. It was a good time to change the subject.

"Did you used to visit the Spirit Lamp Inn when you came up north for the sleigh rides, Miss Isabel?" I asked.

"What?"

Once again, she looked flustered. "I'm not sure what you mean, Jennet."

"You told us you might have been at the Inn the night Cynthia Lauren disappeared."

"Did I? I don't remember."

"Don't remember telling us or don't remember that night?"

"I guess we had dinner here a few times," she said. "It would have been in the wintertime, though. It was so long ago. I can't remember everything I did and everybody I knew."

Clearly I was upsetting her, which hadn't been my intention. She was probably self-conscious about her failing memory. Either that or she was an exceptionally accomplished actress.

"Let's get to the main event and let Miss Isabel open her birthday presents," Crane said.

They were stacked on an empty chair. I reached for our gift and Leonora's.

"Leonora couldn't be here tonight, but she wanted you to have this with her best wishes for many more birthdays," I said.

Soon Miss Isabel sat in the midst of a widening pool of paper and ribbons. Any sign of distress had vanished. She reminded me of a child bubbling with delight and appreciation as she opened each present and set it on the table.

The dainty teapot that Leonora had found at the Green House of Antiques. Gift certificates. A bottle of *Passion* perfume from Marsha Anne. Embroidered handkerchiefs and books. Items carefully selected for an elderly woman who lived in an inn.

By the time she'd unwrapped the last present, the diners who weren't part of our party had finished their meals and left the Inn. The lights had gone out in the kitchen. We were alone at our table, candlelight flickering and tapers melting. It was only ten o'clock, but the dining room had acquired a ghostly midnight ambience. I shivered and felt like pushing my chair closer to Crane's. I didn't, of course.

"This has been the best birthday of my life," Miss Isabel said. "Thank you all. I want everyone to have a big piece of cake to take home."

Marsha reached for the cake server. "I'll cut it, if someone will find the plastic wrap."

"I'm on it," Brent said.

"I've been sitting in one place too long," Miss Isabel said, pulling the edges of her new shawl closer together. "I'm turning into an icicle." She glanced toward the entrance. "Did someone leave that door open? There's a cold draft."

"I don't feel it," Catherine said.

"Do you want me to check?" Ted asked.

"Please," Marsha Anne said. "We don't want to let the heat escape."

He left the table and moments later called, "It's shut. So are the windows."

"I'm so cold," Miss Isabel said. Indeed she looked like a frozen version of herself wrapped in pink, still and wary.

The air *was* a bit cooler than it had been when the dining room had been full, almost as if an invisible ceiling fan had been turned on. The flames in the fireplace still burned, albeit less enthusiastically. The shiver I'd felt when I'd thought of moving closer to Crane was something other than natural.

It was the kind of cold a ghost would leave in her wake as she passed by.

~ * ~

"We didn't learn anything useful tonight," Annica said as Crane steered the Taurus onto Deer Leap Trail. It was a pleasure to let him navigate the snowy road and not even think about waiting hazards.

"We learned that the ghost came to the party," Lucy said.

"You saw her?" Annica demanded. "Where? When?"

"I didn't actually see her," she said. "I felt the sudden drop in temperature. The cold."

"The extreme, unnatural cold," I added. "I think that's why Miss Isabel always complains of being cold. Rachel's ghost is hovering over her."

"That's scary," Annica said. "A stalking spirit."

"Incidentally, we did learn something new tonight," I said. "Miss Isabel and Bruce weren't strangers when they came to Brent's Halloween party. Apparently she was part of the old gang."

"But she didn't say anything then," Annica said. "Did she?"

"I'm sure she didn't. She wouldn't have said anything tonight, but Bruce put her on the spot."

"What do you make of that?" Crane asked.

"Miss Isabel is a woman of mystery. She's someone to keep an eye on. She knows something about Cynthia's disappearance. We'll have to try to draw her out again."

"She already told you she didn't remember," Lucy reminded me. "She'll just say that again."

"I don't believe her. She had no trouble with her memory when we were talking about Cynthia's disappearance before."

"She may be afraid," Crane said.

"That's a thought. Of what, I wonder? Of ghosts? If she was afraid of Rachel's spirit, she wouldn't be living at the Spirit Lamp Inn. No. It's something else. How can I break through her defenses?"

Crane steered the car around a large tree limb that had fallen across the road. "Ask Brent to do it. She likes him, and he has a way with women."

"She's too old for him," Annica said. "Way too old."

"But not immune to attention and flattery," I pointed out.

Crane said, "You have an intriguing mystery to solve this time, Jennet, but I'd like to remind you. There was a murder at the heart of it. Even though it's a cold case, there might still be danger"

As if I'd be likely to forget.

Thirty-four

The snow that was the bane of drivers had its upside. It gave the countryside a fresh, clean look, and, being light and powdery, it was perfect for making snowballs and snowmen. Best of all, Oakpoint and Foxglove Corners school districts declared a snow day in anticipation of ten to twelve inches supposed to start later in the afternoon. Did we dare hope for two free days?

"This is the kind of weather we should be having in January," Leonora said when she called at the ungodly hour of five-thirty.

"Mother Nature is all mixed-up."

"At this rate, we'll have a white Thanksgiving," she said.

"And a spring-like Christmas. Well, it's too early in the morning to have a conversation about the weather. What are you going to do today?"

"I'm going back to bed," she said. "What else?"

I could think of several activities to fill an unplanned day-long vacation.

Later that morning, determined to enjoy the calm before the storm, I leashed Candy, Misty, and Gemmy and set out on a walk to the lake. Snow on the beach and a frozen surface shining under a silvery sky. What was more beautiful than the lake in winter?

We passed Deanna Reid's house. It slumbered beyond an unshoveled walkway. No one stood in the window watching for a tricolor collie to pass by; no paw prints marred the pristine stretch of white that hugged the edifice.

Sparrow was still missing, and Deanna was away.

How would that untenable dilemma ever right itself? All I could be certain of was that the threat of a lawsuit no longer hung over the Rescue League's head.

We walked on, getting colder with every step. Suddenly Candy yelped as a snowball hit her in the chest and disintegrated at her feet. My temper flared, but her tail was wagging.

We were under attack. From the collies' point of view, nothing could enliven our walk more. Misty and Gemmy turned into wild creatures, dragging me forward. If I didn't have three dogs to control, I'd make a snowball of my own.

Ahead, a magnificent snow fort rose in the front yard of a familiar house. In warm layers of red and yellow, Jennifer bounded out from the protection of a slanting snow wall. "Sorry, Candy, I was aiming for Jennet."

Molly, similarly attired but in green, dissolved in giggles.

"Very funny," I said. "Is this how you treat your best customer?"

"No one else went by except old Mrs. Lamb. We couldn't throw snowballs at her."

"I should hope not."

"Have a cup of chocolate," Molly said, offering me a paper container, precariously perched on top of the wall.

"Is it hot?" I asked.

"It's a quarter of a chocolate bar mixed with snow. So, no, it's cold."

A chunk of chocolate lying on top of a serving of snow. It looked quaint but hardly appetizing.

"Thanks, but I don't want to spoil my lunch," I said.

"Do you have a minute to talk?" Molly asked. "We haven't seen you in weeks."

"Just a minute," I said. "It's freezing out. The dogs want their walk."

In truth, they were only too happy for an interruption. Candy sniffed the air, possibly detecting the scent of oatmeal cookie carried on a long ago summer breeze, while Misty reveled in the attention of new two-legged people in her life.

"You're a little snow puppy, Misty, aren't you?" Molly crooned. "Yes, you are."

"It's our mystery," Jennifer said. "We need help with it. We don't know what to do next."

"You didn't tell me what you were investigating."

"Do you see that yellow house with the black shutters and the lamp post in front?"

I nodded. There was only one yellow house in view.

"Look at the table leaning against the side."

I did. It was one of those round tables shaded by an umbrella. Both table and folded umbrella, together with four chairs, had been left out to the mercy of the elements. Naturally they were covered with snow. Behind the house was a one-car garage, painted yellow to match the house.

What homeowner wouldn't store out-of-season furniture in a safe, dry place for the winter?

"We think somebody killed Alicia," Molly said.

"Who's Alicia?" I asked.

"The lady who bought the house."

"Back up," I said. "It's a big leap from a garden table to murder."

But wasn't that the kind of leap I often made myself?

Jennifer said, "We went over the day she moved in with some cookies for a welcome gift. She told us all about herself. How she teaches seventh grade and likes to garden and was buying new furniture for her bedroom. That weekend she set up the table and had some people over for a party. After that we didn't see her."

"She disappeared," Molly added.

"Well, not really." Jennifer, I'd noticed, liked to be precise. "I mean, we don't know that for a fact. She just wasn't there anymore."

Molly continued the story. "We looked through the windows. There's some furniture inside. Not much. There are no curtains, not in any of the windows."

I'd noticed that and something else as well. The house had a dispirited, abandoned look. With its yellow siding framed by the snow, it should have presented a cheerful face to the world. Something was definitely wrong here. But murder?

"Every now and then we see a light come on," Jennifer said. "We think they're on a timer."

"That's likely. Timers come in handy when you want people to think somebody is at home."

"So do you think she moved in and someone killed her?" asked Jennifer.

She was an Annica in the making without the gift for embellishing her sentences with gory images. Give her time.

"No," I said. "It's more likely that your neighbor, Alicia, changed her mind about the house. Maybe something went wrong with the sale. Or she could have found out she needed to have an operation or gone on vacation…"

That last sounded far-fetched to me. No one would schedule a vacation and a move at the same time.

Jennifer nodded gravely, but Molly frowned. "We think she's dead. What if she went into the house and never came out?"

I didn't feel we should pursue that possibility.

"One of these days she'll be back," I said. "You'll see. When she does show up, take her another plate of cookies. Maybe she'll tell you her story. What about the neighbors?"

"They just met her one time like we did. No one knows what happened to her. We're not the only ones who think it's odd."

"Well," I said. "Make a list. Jot down every possibility you can think of. One of them is bound to be right. In the meantime, keep an eye on the house and wait."

"Is that what a real detective would do?" Molly asked.

"I can't think of any other options. I've done a lot of waiting in my time," I added. "I'm waiting right now."

For another chance to question Miss Isabel. For Rachel's ghost to walk again. For an answer to the mystery of Cynthia Lauren's disappearance. For Sparrow to be found. For Denver Armstrong to make his next move. For the big storm due in a matter of hours.

Life was really mostly about waiting.

Cynthia *had* been murdered. As for this new resident in the neighborhood, Alicia, who knew what her story was?

"I'll walk down to the lake again soon," I said. "Maybe next time I see you girls, you'll have some news."

Thirty-five

"You don't need another mystery," Annica said. "You're already on overload."

She set my take-out order on the table. Today's special was pineapple glazed ham with sweet potatoes. My late afternoon pick-me-up was a cup of peppermint tea.

It had been a frenetic day at Marston. The predicted ten to twelve inches of snow had been more like five, which was still impressive for November. With snow and Thanksgiving Recess at the end of the week, no one felt like studying literature, much less writing compositions. I struggled, prevailed, and survived, with visions of a long weekend dancing in my head.

One day down. Two to go.

"It isn't my mystery," I said. "Naturally I'm curious, but there has to be a logical explanation for a new homeowner abandoning her property. I thought the girls were on the trail of something ordinary like missing jewels."

"The most logical reason is that the sale fell through," Annica said.

"If that's the case, why wouldn't the owner move her possessions out? The girls said the bedroom furniture was new."

"Maybe she didn't have any place to put it."

That made sense. "Because she sold her previous house and doesn't have money for storage. You'd think she'd stop by occasionally, though, just to see that everything was all right."

And move that summer table and chairs inside.

"She might have, when the girls weren't looking. See if a 'For Sale' sign goes up at the house. In the meantime, what are we going to do about Miss Isabel? Continue to harass her?"

"That's not what we're doing," I said. "We're encouraging her to reminisce about the past. I expect Brent to visit any night now. I'll see if he can charm her."

"I wish he'd stop by and charm me."

Annica's wistful tone saddened me. At times I thought her feelings for Brent were deeper than I'd imagined. Other times, she was simply Annica, a vivacious redhead with a penchant for flirting and telling gruesome stories.

I couldn't see Annica and Brent in a serious relationship.

"I'm married," I said. "In other words, safe. If Brent started seeing you socially, it would look like he was courting you."

Annica's merry laugh rang out, attracting the attention of diners at the nearby tables. One of her customers beckoned to her.

"Courting? Really, Jennet, join us in the twenty-first century. No one does that anymore."

"Whatever you young people call it then. Brent enjoys being a bachelor. Forget about him."

"I guess I have no choice."

"Between working part-time at Clovers and at the Inn, you have plenty of opportunities to meet nice young men," I said.

"Don't forget classes, though there aren't a lot of men in Poets of the British Isles."

I nodded in agreement. "It's a dilemma."

I had been lucky to find Crane practically on my doorstep after I moved to Foxglove Corners. Before that, when I lived in Oakpoint, my prospects were limited.

It was all a matter of chance. Who meets whom. What happens afterward. Even a bright, pretty girl like Annica might find it difficult to find her soul mate in today's world.

I smiled. Was 'soul mate' another outdated word? I'd better compile a lexicon of modern usage.

Annica's customer beckoned to her again.

"Well," she said, "I have to go back to work. See you at the Inn."

"Did I miss something?"

"On Saturday, to continue our search," she said. "You'll see Brent by then, won't you?"

"I hope so. Crane and I are going to have a quiet Thanksgiving. We thought about going away, but it won't work out. I suppose Brent has plans, but he never misses a holiday visit."

"It's a date then." She bounced up, menu in hand.

I sipped my tea slowly. It was cooling off. Time to finish and do battle with the elements again. Fortunately, at battle's end, I had a ready-made dinner for two.

~ * ~

No matter how busy the world around me grew, home was a refuge. Crane, turning the pages of the *Banner*, a fire burning, the dining room table cleared of dishes, and six healthy collies recuperating from their walks and dreaming about the next meal's leftovers. This was the American dream.

Who could ask for more?

I leaned back in the rocking chair, savoring the warmth of the blaze and the scent of apple wood. The world beyond the house was far away.

Suddenly Candy and Misty woke and rushed to the front door while Halley lifted her head and followed their progress with sleepy eyes.

"Did you hear a car?" I asked, raising my voice to be heard above the barking.

"No, but I see one." Crane had moved to the bay window where the last of the day's light lingered. "It's Brent. He's carrying a package."

"He missed dinner," I said, thinking like a hostess taken unaware. We'd finished the pound cake, but I had chocolate chip muffins that could pass for a dessert and a banana nut bread in the freezer.

Crane told Candy and Misty to Sit and Stay and opened the door. All of the dogs were on their feet by then, gathered in a tail-wagging pack. Brent blundered in, stamping snow from his boots. To the collies' delight, it flew in all directions.

"Cold out there," he said by way of greeting.

"What's in the box?" I asked as Crane hung his snowy jacket.

"Attic treasures," he said.

"You went exploring without us? Annica won't be happy."

Curiosity warred with consternation. Naturally I wanted to know what Brent had found, but I didn't have a lot of storage room. This box was large.

"Bring it into the kitchen," I said.

He set it down on the oak table and opened it. It was crammed with old linens, thin and fragile. I touched one. As fragile as air. There were scarves, doilies, pillow slips, and an ivory tablecloth with matching napkins. They were edged with lace or embroidered in fanciful floral patterns. A faint scent of lavender drifted up from the bundle.

I unfolded a long white scarf crocheted in the graceful pineapple pattern.

"I thought you could use these," Brent said. "They're too nice to be hidden away in an old box."

"You could have kept them for the Inn," I said. "They'll go with the vintage look."

"There's plenty of stuff on the other floors. Think of these as surplus."

"Well if you're sure, thank you. We already had dinner, but I have fresh muffins. How about some coffee and chocolate to ward off the cold?"

"It sounds good, if you two will keep me company."

He settled himself in the living room. Misty leapt into his lap.

"Down!" I said. "Now."

She tilted her head and looked at me, trying to see how serious I was.

"Let her stay," he said, stroking her head. Encouraged, Sky padded up to him and rested her head on his foot.

In the kitchen I put the percolator on for coffee and arranged muffins on a tray. As I passed them to Brent and Crane, Misty eyed them longingly and licked her chops.

"No chocolate for dogs," I reminded Brent.

"Are you keeping the Inn open for Thanksgiving?" Crane asked.

"Not this year. Next year maybe. It's making me crazy. I'm taking Lucy to the Hunt Club Inn for a turkey dinner."

"A restaurant?" I said.

"Not just a restaurant, Jennet. The Hunt Club Inn."

The establishment catered to the Hunt culture. The food was excellent, but the stuffed fox's head on the wall could take away my appetite, unless I ignored it, which was difficult to do. I knew it was there, wearing a wreath decorated for the current season. On Thanksgiving it would be adorned with autumn leaves, miniature gourds, or winterberries.

"Crane and I will be alone," I said. "I have a big turkey. Why don't you join us?"

"I'll have to ask Lucy."

"Ask her then."

I couldn't imagine Lucy vetoing a change of plans that involved getting together with Crane and me.

"Now please explain why the Inn is making you crazy," I said.

Thirty-six

"It isn't the Inn," Brent said. "It's the people in it. My three tenants."

Three? "Miss Isabel, Bruce, and...?"

"Ted," he said. "He's renting a room for the holidays. If Catherine and Marsha Anne come on board, we'll have the whole gang together again. Except for Cynthia and Rachel."

"Rachel will be there," Crane said. "You just won't be able to see her."

"There's something odd about that," I said. "Everybody leaving their homes to move into an Inn."

Occasionally Crane liked to play the Devil's Advocate. "It could be old friends reuniting, trying to revisit their youth in a country setting."

"I wonder."

"Miss Isabel is the real problem," Brent said. "She asked me if she could move to another room, and yesterday she took off all day without a word to anyone. Then she goes around wearing coats all the time, checking the thermostat. She's got me thinking I'm keeping the place too cold. I'm not," he added.

"Lucy and I have a theory about that," I said. "We think Rachel's ghost is staying close to Miss Isabel."

"Why?" Brent asked. "She says she never saw the ghost."

"I can think of two reasons. Miss Isabel killed Cynthia..."

Brent interrupted me. "Not that sweet lady."

I frowned at him. "Sweetness can be superficial. Being a man, you're easily fooled. Or the ghost wants Miss Isabel to catch the killer."

"Then why doesn't Rachel show herself to Miss Isabel? You're the only one who sees her. Remember, Miss Isabel has been living in the Inn for ages."

That dealt a blow to my theory. Neither Crane nor Brent appeared to be impressed by my speculation.

Crane helped himself to another muffin. "You're getting carried away, Jennet. Maybe it's simply that Miss Isabel has a low tolerance for cold. For all we know, she's coming down with something."

"I don't keep the Inn uncomfortable," Brent reminded us. "Some would find seventy-two degrees too warm."

"Don't dismiss the lady," I said. "Has she talked to you about the good old days?"

"Just about how movies and television shows were better when she was young, but she claims the present is more interesting for her. You can't argue with that."

"It's a dodge," I said. "I think Miss Isabel is at the heart of the mystery—somehow. And Rachel's ghost is right behind her."

"I heard from the previous owner the other day," Brent said. "She didn't know anything about a missing charm bracelet but tells me she's long believed the Inn is evil. She wanted to cut all ties to it."

"By evil, I assume she means haunted. Well, that's true."

I left the men alone while I went to the kitchen to make coffee. No matter how what they thought of my theory, I felt I was on the right track. Of course I didn't have any evidence that Miss Isabel even knew Cynthia Lauren. There was only her remark that she might have stayed at the Inn on the night of Cynthia's disappearance. She probably regretted saying that.

But Bruce had talked as if Miss Isabel were part of the old gang. Why the need for mystery?

Then consider her prior acquaintance with Bruce, who *had* known Cynthia. For some reason she'd intended to keep that information to herself.

Miss Isabel was a secretive person, but I couldn't see her as a killer any more than Brent could.

Back in the living room, I poured coffee. The muffins were rapidly disappearing. Thank heavens I had six more in the kitchen.

"Did Miss Isabel give you a reason for wanting a different room?" I asked.

"Only that she found a spider in the closet and was afraid there were more."

"How about yesterday? Where was she?"

"Visiting her niece. I don't have to know my tenants' private business, but I do worry about her. She took that old Plymouth out on the icy roads. Something could have happened to her."

"Annica and I are going to be at the Inn on Saturday," I said. "Could we have lunch with her?"

"I'll invite her and have Louise cook up something special."

Without exception, Brent's staff was competent and exceptionally friendly, and Louise was a special treasure. So far no one had screamed or claimed to see an inexplicable drift of blue mist in the hallway. As far as I knew, I was the only one who had seen an apparition, and very few people knew about it, since of course I hadn't screamed.

A person needed nerves of steel to deal with whatever was going on at the Spirit Lamp Inn. I prided myself that I qualified.

~ * ~

For different reasons, a teacher needed steel nerves to deal with a classroom filled with restless adolescents on the last day before Thanksgiving vacation.

To begin with, almost half of my illustrious fourth hour students were absent. According to those in attendance, this warranted a free day. Too many kids would miss the day's story and notes, they argued. In World History, they'd played a game involving foreign words and holiday customs. In the classroom separated from mine by a thin divider, Leonora was showing a movie.

"So why do we have to do work?" That was Katrina who, in anticipation of a day off, had come to class without her Literature textbook.

Examining their arguments fairly, I shelved my lesson plan and decided to read Truman Capote's *A Christmas Memory* to them. We were still in the realm of American Literature, just several years ahead of our chronological survey.

Midway through the story, the door opened. A young man in a brown sweater with an armload of books and a paper in his hand stood on the threshold, shifting from one foot to the other.

"I'm in your class," he mumbled and added, "Name's Joel Carstairs."

He showed me his schedule. Fourth Period: Ferguson—American Literature Survey.

Just what I needed in this overloaded, boisterous class. I'd have to requisition another desk, one more textbook... The office doled both out as if they were rare and costly artifacts.

"I'm from Lake Orion," he volunteered.

A transfer student in the middle of the semester could indicate a move or trouble. With my luck, Joel Carstairs was going to be trouble. On the other hand, he might be studious and well-behaved, a good influence. Time would tell. It always did. It certainly was strange to enter a new school on the day before a holiday recess, though.

That was neither here nor there. I found a welcome smile. "Well, Joel, for today, find any empty seat. I'll assign you to a permanent one on Monday."

He slid into a desk in the front of the room. Unloading his books, he leaned his arms on them.

This interruption, lasting only seconds, had resulted in a suspension of attention. Whispers, snatches of conversation, a discreet cough and its mocking echo. While I hadn't been looking, Katrina had moved to a chair next to Denver Armstrong who was drawing as usual. From his covert glances at me, I figured I was once again his model, probably clad in a witch's robe and peaked hat.

"Class—settle down," I said, and continued reading, suppressing an urge to cough. I wished I had a drink of water. Soon the bell would ring for lunch, and Leonora would bring me a soft drink from the machine in the lounge.

At the story's conclusion, I said, "Now write a Christmas memory of your own. One and a half pages."

Amidst the requisite grumbling and snapping of notebooks being opened and the rustle of paper, about half the students began the assignment. Denver continued his drawing. Katrina appeared to give up her attempt to snare his interest, and Joel stared at the bulletin board on the front of the room with its pictures of American authors framed by student-made snowflakes.

Through the divider wall between my classroom and Leonora's drifted a snatch of "Good Christian Men, Rejoice."

Outside, real snow began to fall.

Thirty-seven

"Miss Isabel is out again," Brent said. "I didn't see her leave."

"In this weather?" Annica unwound her scarf and patted snow from her red-gold hair. She seemed to sparkle, diamond dust in her bangs, crystal snowflake earrings, sequins on the scarf.

"*We* came out," I said.

After a long and trying day at school. Through blustery winds, over ice-slicked roads, fortified by Clovers' hot chocolate and a desire to solve the mysteries at the Spirit Lamp Inn.

"We're on a mission," Annica added.

"Miss Isabel said something about early Christmas shopping, and she isn't back yet," Brent said. "She's always on the go. I had the impression she was a recluse."

He led the way to the dining room which was already half full although it was only four-thirty. "Louise made her famous chicken pot pies."

"Yum." Annica wasn't disappointed in Miss Isabel's absence. I was the one who wanted to talk to her. That is, to question her. Annica had her sights on the attic and on Brent, of course. Always on Brent.

Over lunch, Brent said, "If Miss Isabel didn't consider the Inn her home, I'd close up the second floor and keep it as a sort of Exhibit A. I had no desire to be a landlord. I just wanted the Inn."

"Are your tenants causing problems?" I asked.

He paused, cutting into the flaky crust with relish. "Not exactly, but something's off. I don't know how to describe it. The feeling around here has changed."

"You're talking about ambience?"

"I guess. I'm not sure what that is. But take Bruce. He suddenly lost his interest in fox hunting. I don't believe it was real. Just an excuse."

"For what?" I asked.

"To be here at the Inn. Turns out he never even rode a horse. Now there's Ted, but I'll have to say he isn't here much. He's out every day taking pictures of the scenery. He gave me a nice photo of the Inn in a fresh snowfall. I'm going to have it framed."

Annica had finished her pie and was dismantling the salad, a Jell-O confection in four flavors.

"This is a spectacular lunch," she said. "Miss Isabel doesn't know what she's missing."

"Louise saved a pie for her. She can have it on a tray when she comes back."

"Do your tenants socialize with one another?" I asked.

"Miss Isabel and Bruce did, a little, at first, but not now. The men hang out together, and she goes shopping or visiting or whatever."

"That sounds natural," I said.

"Well eat up, girls. Let's see what secrets the attic holds. We'll be alone on the second floor today. No one to spy on us."

Now why did he say that? I wished he hadn't because almost as soon as the words were uttered, I became aware of a prickly sensation at the back of my head. I felt as if an unseen presence were watching us.

~ * ~

Annica said, "Brent, if we find any more doilies in the attic, may I have them?"

I paused on the top step, wondering if I'd heard correctly. "Doilies, Annica? You?"

She smiled slyly. "For my hope chest."

Now who was using outdated terminology? I might be wrong, but I didn't think Annica had a hope chest. I wondered if they still existed outside an antique shop.

"Let's not forget what we hope to find," I said.

Annica took the bait. "The murder weapon. Another diary, incriminating old photographs, a coffin... All the good stuff."

"A coffin?" Brent scoffed. "Don't be silly. There was only one body, and it wasn't buried inside the Inn."

He set the lantern flashlight on a stack of boxes marked 'Candleholders /old candles' and helped us up to the attic floor, such as it was.

"I'm only humoring you, Annica," he said. "We're not going to find anything pertaining to the case up here. 'But there's all kinds of stuff."

"Some of it is valuable," I said. "And all of it's interesting."

I'd ironed the linens Brent had given me and stored them in my closet with bars of lavender soap. For my next dinner party, perhaps for Christmas, I planned to use the tablecloth and matching napkins.

Annica stood beside Brent, moving her flashlight slowly from one side of the attic to the other. "We don't want to cover old territory. Where shall we start?"

"How about over here?" Brent walked to the west side of the attic, stepping heavily but with care on the boards. "This is where I found the linens."

I followed. "Here's a steamer trunk, Annica. Should I check to see if there's a body in it?"

"It's empty," Brent said. "At least it was when I checked it the other day."

"Just to be sure..." Annica opened the lid. "Ugh. Cobwebs. This is funny. It's lined with Christmas wrapping paper."

I looked over her shoulder at miniature Currier and Ives scenes in ovals against a green background.

"What's funny about that?" I asked. "It's prettier than white shelf paper."

A faint sound crackled through the attic as Annica lifted a sheet. "The trunk isn't empty. Look what I found."

She held up a silver chain.

"Whoever owned the trunk must have kept her jewelry in here. For some reason, this piece was left behind."

The trunk was too big for a jewelry case. More likely, a traveler had kept an entire wardrobe for an overseas trip inside. In unpacking, she had overlooked the chain.

"Could I see it?" I asked.

Annica handed it to me and moved on to the boxes behind the trunk. I let it rest in my palm and with my free hand shone the flashlight on it.

And felt a cold draft swooshing across the expanse of boxes and shadows. So intense it was that I looked toward the ventilation slats, wondering if the outside temperature had dropped.

Brent had spoken of something being off. I knew what he meant. The ambience in the attic was different.

Cold equals ghost.

Again I felt unseen eyes boring into the back of my head. Someone was in the attic with us, observing our every move. Watching me as I examined the chain.

"Rachel?" I whispered.

"What did you say, Jennet?"

With an effort, I forced myself to return to the real world. There were only three people in the attic, all of us corporeal.

"For a necklace, this is rather plain," I said. "That silver heart charm you found, Brent… I wonder if it went with this chain?"

"Anything's possible," he said. "I could have it attached, but don't you remember? I lost the charm."

"You never found it?"

"Never looked for it."

"Well, if you ever do…"

A heavy thump, accompanied by a jingling, interrupted me in mid-sentence.

I glanced in the direction of the noise and saw Annica crumpled on the floor, her head resting on a wood crate.

Thirty-eight

"Annica!"

Who had spoken? Brent or I—or someone else? Strangely, I wasn't sure. All I knew was that my friend lay motionless on a treacherous, cold attic floor.

Brent reached her first. "Did you trip, Annica? I told you to watch your step." His slightly hectoring tone echoed around us.

Annica didn't answer, didn't spring up with a light-hearted quip. Panic surged through me. "She fainted," I said.

Or died.

What inspired that morbid thought? She was only stunned from the fall.

At that moment, her eyelids fluttered open. "No…"

Brent surveyed her prone figure for a second, then scooped her up in his arms. Her bangs fell back, revealing a red mark—a gash—on the left side of her forehead where she had come into contact with the crate. Drops of bright red blood fell into the sweep of blue eye shadow above her lids.

"She hit her head on that crate," I said and reached into my pocket for a tissue. None there. Never when you need one.

"Take the lanterns, Jennet," Brent barked. "Let's get out of this damned attic."

Annica was shaking. "S-so cold."

"We better call nine-one-one," I said.

She tried to touch her wound, pulled back her finger and stared at it. "No."

"ER then," Brent said. "Be quiet, Annica. Don't waste breath arguing."

Warm air engulfed us as we descended to the second floor, quiet and deserted, and made our way down the staircase, Brent with Annica, I struggling not to drop the lanterns.

Sounds of conversation drifted in from the dining room, signs of normalcy and bursts of soft laughter.

I hurried around Brent and opened the door to his office. Since my last visit, he had added a beige sofa. Gently he lowered Annica down on it and hovered over her, tall and, I'd guess, intimidating.

"I'm all right. Just bleeding." She'd closed her eyes, but her voice was a little stronger. "But my head hurts."

Brent, apparently used to emergencies of all kinds, produced a first aid kit from his desk drawer and set to work cleaning and bandaging the wound.

"It could be worse," he said.

He eased her shoes off and frowned at them. "High heels in an attic, Annica? I thought you had better sense."

"They're not that high," she said. "And I didn't faint. I never fainted in my life. That's what girls do in those old Gothic novels. Tell him, Jennet."

I breathed more easily. Annica sounded like herself again.

"I'm not sure what happened to you. One minute we were looking at the chain, the next I heard you fall."

And I felt the cold draft. I'd forgotten that.

"I'll get you a cup of tea from the kitchen," I said.

"And something for pain. I have a headache."

"That isn't a good idea," Brent said. "You need to be checked out by a doctor first. He can write you a prescription."

I left them alone, arguing half-heartedly. Annica insisted she didn't need medical attention, although her pale face told a different story. Brent claimed responsibility for the accident since it had happened on his property.

"I just don't want you to sue me," he said.

"I won't," she promised.

When I came back, they had fallen silent. I swished the teabag around in the cup, tossed it into Brent's basket, and thought of Lucy and her tea leaves. I wanted to talk to Lucy. Needed to talk to her.

Annica was sitting up with Brent's support. It seemed that some of her color had returned. She touched the bandage gingerly and combed her bangs over it with her fingers. "I must look awful. No one wants to see a hostess with a bandage above her eye."

"You look pretty," Brent said. "Bandage or no."

She managed a smile. She must be feeling better And from her point of view, weren't a gash on the forehead and a few drops of her life's blood worth Brent's fussing over her?

"Here," I said, handing her the cup. "Drink this while it's hot."

"Nobody except me goes up in that attic again," Brent was saying. "It's dangerous…"

It's haunted, I thought. *A haunted attic, that glorious staple, that cliche of mystery writers worldwide.*

"There's no real floor," Brent said, "and I'm not going to have one put in. There's no reason for anyone to go snooping around anyway. I'm going to get rid of everything in the spring. Have a big bonfire."

He couldn't do that. "Not without knowing what you're burning."

Annica was fussing with her hair again. "Oh…"

"What's wrong?" I asked.

To my amazement, tears glittered in her eyes. They rolled down her cheeks.

"I lost my earring," she said. "My crystal snowflake."

"It must have fallen off when you fell."

Frantically she felt her other ear. The earring's mate was still in place. "I took her necklace. She took my earring."

"What are you saying?"

I thought I knew; still I asked. "She? Who are you talking about?"

"The ghost."

"Oh, that silver chain you found in the trunk. I have it. I think…"

Desperately I searched my pockets. Suddenly it was important that I find it. I remembered holding it… But it wasn't there.

"It must be in the attic too," I said.

"Don't cry, Annica," Brent said. "I'll find your earring and that chain too. Jennet, can you come with us to Emergency?"

"I don't need to go there," Annica's voice was unsteady. She was sobbing in earnest.

Not, I felt, because of the lost earring. It was more a matter of delayed shock.

"It's not necessary," she insisted. "I want to work at the Inn tonight."

"No," Brent said. "Not tonight."

"We'll all feel better knowing you're really all right," I said. "You don't want to have a scar," I added, knowing that would get her attention.

"Let's be off, then," Brent said.

Not for the first time I could hardly wait to leave the Spirit Lamp Inn.

~ * ~

The Emergency Room was crowded. Periodically Annica threatened to leave, convinced that other patients were more in need of care. An hour passed.

I glanced at my watch. I'd been away from home longer than planned. Crane wouldn't be home yet, and Camille and Gilbert were in Tennessee for Thanksgiving week.

"You don't have to stay, Jennet," Annica said. "I'll be fine."

"I'm staying," Brent said.

"Well, then…"

"Don't neglect your dogs," Annica said.

I touched her shoulder. "I'll call you tonight."

"We need to talk about what happened," she added quietly.

"I thought you didn't remember."

"I don't. That's what frightens me."

I summoned a hearty tone. "You never get frightened, Annica. Just like you never faint."

"Something happened up there," she said. "It must have."

"You slipped between two boards and lost your balance," Brent said. "You fell and hurt your head."

"Whatever you say." She smiled faintly. "My headache is worse. Don't you have aspirin in your purse, Jennet?"

Brent said rather loudly. "Wait a little longer, Annica. Hang in there."

He walked me to the revolving door. "I'll call you after I take her home," he said. "She's rambling, letting her imagination run wild. I wonder if she has a concussion."

He looked so uneasy, so unsure, that I said, "But you think there's something wrong in the attic, don't you?"

"It's an unhealthy place. Annica could have been seriously hurt. Maybe she is. But it isn't an evil place, if that's what you're thinking."

"I don't know what I'm thinking," I said.

Which was only half-true.

Thirty-nine

Annica was going to be all right. I'd never doubted it. All the same, I was happy to hear her assurances on the phone. Still, she sounded a little unlike herself. An uneasy note had crept into her voice.

It troubled me.

"All I remember before I fell was that crate," she said. "I was going to open it."

"Instead you hit your head on it."

"My face looks terrible, and I still have a headache."

"You will, for a while, but it'll go away. You need to take your pills and rest."

I carried my cell phone into the living room and sank into the rocker. Misty trailed after me, carrying her treasured white goat. I could use a little rest myself. Yesterday had taken a sizeable chunk of energy from me, although once I arrived home, took care of my dogs, and started dinner, I seemed to unwind.

Telling Crane about our latest adventure in the attic completed the process, but that night my dreams brought disturbing images of moving boxes and pouncing shadows. There was no way to edit dreams.

"That crate," Annica said. "It didn't want me to open it."

Suddenly the cold was back with me, invading my cozy living room through frosted panes of glass and substantial window coverings.

"A wood crate doesn't have will," I said.

"The ghost of Rachel Carroll then. What if she was guarding the crate? There has to be a reason. Maybe there's a clue in it. Some evidence..."

"Take a step back and think about what you're saying, Annica. Rachel wanted to find her friend. Now that Cynthia's grave has been discovered, she must want the killer brought to justice."

I should pay attention to what *I* was saying. Talking about the ghost of the Spirit Lamp Inn as if she were a living, breathing entity. Well, that was how I thought of her.

The crate, though. That was real. Did it contain something pertinent to the case?

"So she'd want me to open the crate," Annica said.

"That would be my guess."

"And not cause me to faint—er—lose consciousness."

Annica appeared to have forgotten her strange fancy that Rachel had stolen her crystal earring because she'd taken Rachel's silver necklace. That made no sense at all.

"We have to open that crate," Annica said.

"You heard what Brent said. He's not going to let us search in the attic anymore."

"We'll have to figure out a way to bypass him, then."

Perhaps Annica's thought processes had been damaged. Brent would never allow himself to be bypassed, whatever that entailed. It was expedient to change the subject.

"Tomorrow's Thanksgiving," I said. "Are you going to have dinner with your family?"

"My mom and aunt are on a cruise. I'm going to catch up on my reading for school."

"On a holiday?"

"I have four long Victorian novels to read."

"Is there any other kind? Why don't you join us for dinner? Lucy and Brent will be here. You can go home early and read afterwards."

"Thanks, but I need the whole day," she said.

Annica didn't want to be a fifth wheel. She didn't have to say that. I knew how she thought.

"I'll set aside some turkey and pumpkin pie for you and take it over tomorrow," I said. "We can talk more. Maybe by then you'll remember something."

That she accepted. "I don't think that'll happen. Except I dreamed about that crate last night. I was just about to open it when I woke up."

One way or another, Annica was going to find a way to return to the attic. That surprised me. After her experience, with the after effects still troubling her, I thought she'd never want to see it again.

~ * ~

Lucy spooned cranberry sauce from the pan to a bowl decorated with pumpkins and gourds. "The Spirit Lamp Inn is a hotbed of psychic activity," she said.

"It could be, but what I felt there yesterday was cold. That isn't unusual. Attics are cold."

"So are ghosts."

I glanced around the kitchen and into the dining room, table set with the candles flickering softly in the heirloom candlesticks.

Everything was ready except the rolls. I took them out of the oven and transferred them to another bowl. A whole home cooked Thanksgiving dinner planned and cooked without a single stumble. I was improving. The turkey, the star of the show, was already on the table.

"I've seen the ghost in the second floor hall, then in the parking lot," I said. "Not the attic."

"That doesn't mean she wasn't there."

Lucy was right. Rachel could be anywhere. Just because no one had seen her lately... I remembered the great cold. I'd felt her.

"After a single discovery, Annica has decided there was more evidence hidden there. She's determined to keep looking."

Brent stepped around Candy who insisted on lying in any doorway she could find while the other dogs maintained a polite distance from the turkey, well aware of the tasty rewards to come.

"What?" he demanded, reaching for a roll as I passed by with the bowl. "What did you say about Annica?"

"I think you heard me," I said.

"Do I have to padlock the attic to keep you girls out of it?"

"Not 'you girls'," I said. "I'm never darkening your attic door again. Instead I'm going to concentrate on solving Cynthia Lauren's murder. Just this once, I'll let the ghost hunt go."

"How unlike you," Lucy said.

How to explain my abrupt about face? This apparition frightened me. That made no sense either. The ghost Spirit Lamp Inn was on a mission of good will. Why should I have anything to fear from her?

What I did fear was the sudden all-encompassing cold. Lucy would understand, but it wasn't a tale for Thanksgiving Day.

"How do you plan to solve that old, cold case?" Brent asked.

"Easy. You may have the suspects living under your roof."

"Under the Inn's roof," he corrected. "And that's a stretch."

"Maybe, but it's a coincidence that three people who knew Rachel and Cynthia long ago are back at the Inn where the murder happened—soon after your workers discover the grave."

"They're returning to the scene of the crime," Lucy added. "But Jennet, the murder and the ghost are connected. In trying to solve the case, you'll invariably have to deal with both of them."

I was sorry I'd let the conversation wander in this direction. The candles were beckoning us to the table, signaling the end of ghost and murder talk. Crane stood at the head of the table, brandishing the carving knife. Candy had sneaked in from the doorway and lay in his shadow, no doubt thinking herself invisible.

I did a last-minute inspection. Every side dish was on the table, and the pies were stashed safely out of reach of canine mouths.

"We're ready," I announced.

"Before I carve the turkey," Crane said, "let's everyone remember what day it is. I'm thankful for the best wife in the world. What are you thankful for, Jennet?"

"For you, of course," I said.

Lucy smiled. "I'm thankful for my good friends and my new book, finished just this morning."

"Brent?" I said.

"My horses, my dogs, my life, and the people in it."

He laid his hand on Lucy's wrist. I pretended not to notice.

"And most of all," he added, "for this big turkey Jennet cooked. Can we eat now?"

"After grace," Lucy said.

Behind Crane, Candy forgot herself and gave a discrete woof.

"I love Thanksgiving," I said.

Forty

The day after a holiday can be anti-climactic, depressing even. The silver is back in the chest, leftovers are stashed in the refrigerator, and the husband for whom I was thankful was somewhere in Foxglove Corners keeping the peace under a cold, sunless sky.

Fortunately my day was too full to encompass a post-holiday letdown. After the dogs' walk, the first item on my agenda was to visit Annica with a Thanksgiving dinner in a picnic basket. All the trimmings and two pieces of pie, one pumpkin and one pecan, should cheer her up.

I found her looking like a pale copy of herself with bangs combed low and straight to cover the angry red mark on her forehead. She wore a black maxi dress and no earrings. I hardly recognized her.

Halfway through *Jane Eyre* and a bowl of popcorn, she brightened considerably at the sight of the basket.

"I'm so hungry," she said. "I just had a hamburger last night."

"What other novels are you reading?" I asked as she deserted Victoriana to unpack her holiday dinner.

"*Wuthering Heights*, *Vanity Fair*, and *Bleak House*."

"Three great ones," I said, remembering my own study of the Victorian novel. "And *Jane Eyre* is my all-time favorite."

As she filled the teakettle, I said, "Did you remember anything else from your fall?"

"Just that I was wondering if the silver heart was part of the chain from the trunk, or the charm bracelet."

"There's nothing helpful about that."

"Like I said yesterday, I was going to open the crate, then Brent was scolding me for falling. The in-between part is a blank."

"Brent was concerned," I said. "Very concerned."

"He took me to Emergency and stayed with me. Don't you think that's a good sign?"

"That he cares about you? Yes, I do."

Still, I remembered Brent laying his hand on Lucy's wrist. In retrospect, that hadn't been a romantic gesture. He was expressing thanks for the people in his life. I was sure that included Annica. Which didn't change the fact that Brent was a perennial bachelor.

"Do you think Brent found my crystal earring?" she asked.

"If he remembered to look for it. I'll remind him."

Annica set slices of turkey on a paper plate, along with a serving from every container.

"Don't you want to warm it up?" I asked with a glance at the microwave.

"I'll eat it cold."

"Even the gravy?"

"I'll heat it tomorrow for a hot turkey sandwich." With that, she tucked into her dinner with relish.

As the teakettle began its piercing whistle, I found tea bags in a flowery canister and made tea for us.

"Brent doesn't want me to work this weekend," Annica said. "He's going to pay me anyway."

"He's the soul of generosity."

She helped herself to another heaping spoonful of stuffing. "This is my favorite part of the meal," she said. "Are you going to go to the mall today?"

"Not on your life."

I'd seen pictures on television of people lining up in the pre-dawn hours to save incredible amounts on electronics and other selected items. Some enjoyed the crowds and chaos. I considered them torture.

"This Christmas I'm going to make my own gifts," I said, wondering what I could give Annica.

"If Brent is going to ban us from the attic, will you ask him to open the crate?" she asked. "I have to know what's inside."

That crate. We couldn't get away from it.

"I suspect it's empty," I said.

"It can't be. Who'd keep an empty crate in an attic? Besides all the boxes had something in them."

"I'll ask him to check it out when he looks for your earring."

"The earrings belonged to my mother," she said. "She gave them to me on my eighteenth birthday."

"We'll have to find the missing one then."

Somewhat mollified, Annica turned all her attention to finishing her dinner.

I took a sip of tea and wished that it had been made from loose leaves. And I wished that Lucy were here to interpret the symbols in my cup.

I wanted to know if I was going to solve the mystery of Cynthia Lauren's murder—and do so with no risk to life and limb.

~ * ~

With my time and energy focused on the Spirit Lamp Inn, I hadn't spared a single thought for Deanna Reid and the search for her missing collie.

That changed when she called me later that afternoon. She came right to the point with no small talk of the 'Did you have a nice Thanksgiving?' variety.

"I wanted you to know I found Sparrow in a shelter in Ellentown," she said. "She's home with me to stay."

"My goodness. You must have looked for her all over the state."

"Pretty much. I visited dozens of shelters."

"Do you have any idea how she ended up in Ellentown?"

"A very good idea. My ex-boyfriend took her to the shelter there. He told them he found her in the road."

"Then he *did* steal her," I said.

"And dumped her in a high-kill shelter. I suppose he was going to let me know when it was too late."

"It's a shame you can't prove it."

"I don't have to prove it," she said, "and I'm not involving the law. He's going to pay for tangling with me and hurting Sparrow."

Her calm, icy tone boded ill for the ex-boyfriend.

"How is Sparrow?" I asked.

"Thinner. Traumatized. She doesn't want to leave my side. But we'll be all right."

She didn't mention the Summerton family. For all practical purposes, they were out of the picture.

I wished her and Sparrow well and said goodbye. But I couldn't stop thinking about the ex-boyfriend whose name I could never remember, whose name, come to think of it, Deanna hadn't mentioned. What form would her revenge take and would it result in more trouble for her and Sparrow?

I had a suspicion that the story wasn't over yet.

~ * ~

Still later, when I had a turkey casserole in the oven and the dogs were recuperating from a long winter walk, I rummaged through my desk until I found my mystery notebook. Once it had been my constant companion. I'd started new pages for each mystery that came my way and painstakingly recorded clues.

It was a good system but had unfortunately fallen by the wayside, along with old half-filled diaries and garden journals. The mysteries of the Spirit Lamp Inn were complicated. I needed to see the facts of the case set down in ink.

Finding a blank page, I began writing:

August, 1955—Cynthia Lauren vanishes from the Spirit Lamp Inn while returning from a vacation on Mackinac Island with her friend, Rachel Carroll.

Subsequent investigations prove fruitless.

Over the years several people report the appearance of an apparition that became known as the 'Lady in the Blue Raincoat'.

The previous owner sells the Inn, as is, to Brent Fowler who sets about to repaint and refurbish it. A permanent guest is Miss Isabel Bryte, who says she might have stayed at the Inn when Cynthia went missing.

Brent's landscapers discover a charm bracelet buried on the property.

They also discover a grave in the garden. There's a high probability that the remains are those of Cynthia Lauren who is now a murder victim. Brent pays for her burial.

Brent's painter finds a silver heart charm in the closet.

Cynthia's suitcase is discovered in the attic and is ultimately returned to her sister, Catherine.

Brent's Halloween party brings together Catherine, Marsha Anne, Ted, and Bruce. Bruce reveals that he knew Cynthia and Isabel.

I see Rachel Carroll's ghost in the hallway of the Inn and also in the parking lot.

Bruce moves into the Inn, ostensibly for the fox-hunting. Ted follows soon after.

Further exploration of the attic reveals a silver chain meant to be worn as a necklace.

I paused. Should I add Annica's fall?

Probably not until Brent opens the crate.

So… I looked over what I had written. It read like a story with scattered bits like the silver heart that defied connection. Of course, I was missing whole chunks of it, but I had a feeling the answer was in front of my eyes. If I could just find the missing pieces.

Forty-one

I needed to learn more about Miss Isabel and Bruce—and Ted, Catherine, and Marsha Anne, too. How to accomplish this eluded me. Miss Isabel, Ted and Bruce, living at the Inn, would be easier to contact. I'd have to lure the women to Foxglove Corners.

But what then? I'd have to ask Brent to help me. Perhaps he could arrange another get-together. We'd celebrated Halloween and Miss Isabel's birthday. What could we do next?

I had to remind him about Annica's missing earring and ask him to open the crate anyway.

No one was going to confess to murdering Cynthia and tell me what had happened on that long ago stormy night. I had to be cleverer than any killer, approach him or her by stealth and pounce.

On the other hand, what if my prime suspects didn't know anything about the crime? Suppose they were innocent. Where did that leave me?

Back in Square One with a "now you see her; now you don't" ghost. I supposed I should forget about all of it, but unanswered questions refused to let me do so.

For example, why did Miss Isabel really want to be moved to another room, and had Brent humored her? I loathed spiders and their kind myself, but the sight of one wouldn't send me scurrying for a new home.

Of course not. A green Victorian farmhouse on ten acres was a far cry from a rented room in an inn.

And I was rambling while the roast might well be burning. I hurried to the kitchen, dodging collie paws.

It wasn't burning, only done. All was well in the kitchen; all was well with my collie family. I still had to make biscuits and a salad. Dessert was covered. When Crane came home from his long day patrolling the roads and by-roads of Foxglove Corners, he'd have a good dinner waiting for him, together with a loving wife and six adoring collies.

How truly blessed we were to have one another. Before I dissolved into a sentimental puddle on the floor, I gathered the biscuit makings and shooed Candy away from the counter on which the pie was perhaps an inch too close to the edge.

I'd returned to the kitchen just in time.

Just in time…

As a random thought slid into my mind, Candy made a dash for the kitchen door. Outside I heard a door slam. Crane's Jeep. I'd know that sound anywhere. I wiped my hands on the dishtowel and let the thought slide away.

~ * ~

Crane kissed me and divested himself of his gun in that order.

"It smells like Thanksgiving again," he said, eying the stove.

"We're having pot roast. I hope you're hungry."

Thinking that last was meant for her, Candy sidled up to me, sniffing the air.

"I'm starved," he said. "I skipped lunch."

That wasn't good. "Why?"

"Accidents," he said vaguely. "Road rage."

Knowing he liked to leave the problems he'd encountered during his shift outside the house, I didn't question him further. Instead I told him the day's good news. Annica was recovering, immersed in nineteenth century literature, and Deanna Reid had found her stolen Sparrow in an Ellentown shelter.

"A high-kill shelter," I added. "Fortunately Deanna found her in time."

"Won't Sparrow have to go back to the family that adopted her?" he asked.

"According to Deanna, that isn't an issue. I haven't heard that Mrs. Summerton wants her back. Deanna is talking about getting even with her former boyfriend, though."

"In other words, expect more drama."

"I wish she'd just be grateful she found her dog and make sure she keeps her safe," I said.

Then I remembered that I didn't really know Deanna Reid and I had never even seen her thieving boyfriend. Maybe the *status quo* wasn't possible for her.

In the meantime, my life went on in its usual comforting way. Crane went upstairs to shower; I fed the dogs and put the finishing touches on my dinner. As I lit the candles in on the dining room table, mayhem and murder couldn't have seemed farther away.

~ * ~

I woke in the hours before dawn in the grip of a nightmare. Images swirled through my mind.

Attic, crate, shadows, bats flying out from behind towering boxes and a glass window that turned on its own volition, changing colors and patterns with each evolution. A kaleidoscope.

The images were receding, too frightening to be remembered. But the Imp of the Perverse had taken possession of me. I lay still and tried to call them back, give them substance.

We were in the forbidden attic, Annica and I, dodging trailing cobwebs and stepping carefully from board to board. Then as often happens in a dream, I lost Annica. In front of me was a plain wooden crate large enough to contain two dozen grapefruits.

Open it!

The whisper came from behind me. The voice wasn't Annica's.

213

I lifted the lid and recoiled in horror. Tried to scream but couldn't. Wanted to run away but couldn't move.

Inside the crate lay a jumble of bones and a disintegrating blue raincoat.

~ * ~

"I have one more question," I said to Leonora as we drove to school the next morning. "How did Rachel Carroll die? Was she murdered too?"

Leonora turned onto the southbound ramp of the freeway. "That should be easy to find out. She certainly wasn't interred in a crate in the Inn's attic."

"Now I'm as anxious as Annica to have Brent open the crate."

"Remember, a dream isn't real," Leonora said. "It isn't a vehicle for transporting messages from beyond."

I didn't believe that was always true, but it was too early in the morning to debate the issue. After my conscious effort to remember the dream, I hadn't gone back to sleep until it was time to get up and consequently felt ill equipped to face my students on the Monday after a holiday recess.

"If Rachel was murdered, don't you think it would have been part of her story?" Leonora said. "According to all the accounts, she returned to the Inn year after year to search for Cynthia."

"You're right," I said. "But why would I dream about a second set of bones in the Spirit Lamp Inn attic?"

"Who knows? What did you eat last night?"

"Pot roast and pecan pie."

"That's it, then. Pecan pie. It can have that effect."

I responded with the required laugh, and we lapsed into a companionable silence. The lanes were clear, a vast improvement over the slick country roads with their dangerous drops, and the landscape that sailed by glittered with snow cover.

December was a happy month, trimmed with excitement, good will, and the promise of another holiday. It was time to count days, make plans, be merry.

214

What bothered me then, aside from a mystery that didn't want to be solved? Because something troublesome lingered on the fringe of my consciousness. I'd just become aware of it in the stillness inside the car.

Some less-than-pleasant situation or task waiting for me? A hurdle to overcome? A deed left undone? What?

I couldn't figure it out and gradually set it out of my mind. Whatever it was, it would eventually make itself known.

Forty-two

The bell rang, and my fourth period American Literature class trooped or sauntered or stormed into the classroom as noisily as I knew they would.

And I knew—don't ask me how—that this class was the cause of the unease I'd felt in the car a little while ago. They were the unpleasant situation and the hurdle and the deed left undone all rolled into one.

I knew this as surely as Mr. John Oakhurst, gambler, knew that killer snow was on the way.

Discordant notes lurked behind the familiar chaos of thirty-three—make that thirty-four—teen agers. Was I the only one who heard it?

I opened my grade book and glanced from my seating chart to the class. Katrina was out of her assigned seat again. She'd pushed the desk that should have been occupied by Kent Douglas as close to Denver Armstrong as possible. I didn't see Kent.

Nothing annoyed me more than students switching seats, unless it was desks that undid the symmetry of my rows, meticulously straightened by me between every class.

"Katrina!" I said. "Move that desk back in the row and return to your assigned seat."

"What difference does it make?" she asked with an unbecoming pout.

I chose not to answer, having explained the need for a seating chart several times already.

"You ought to know our names by now," she added.

I glared at her.

She unleashed a stream of invective too indistinct to be heard clearly, but her tone conveyed her sheer defiance. She moved the desk, contrived to kick it, and finally moved herself.

Insolent brat.

Principal Grimsley would decry this uneven start to the day's lesson, as I did myself. I hoped he wasn't passing by in the hall outside my room as he liked to do during fourth hour.

The new student had settled himself in Katrina's desk. What was his name again? Joel Carstairs. Neatly dressed in jeans and a gray sweater, he had a knack for blending into the scenery. He seemed detached. No obvious problem.

"What about me?" he asked, rising quickly before Katrina could plop into his lap.

I scanned the room. The desk I'd requisitioned was nowhere in sight. Nor did I see an extra textbook. Marston had a unique way of making a new student feel welcome. And the fault would appear to lie with me.

"For today, take the desk Katrina just left," I said. "Tomorrow I'll make sure you have one of your own."

Before I forgot, I wrote Kent Douglas' name on the absence slip.

Denver had already begun his fourth period art project. Did I want to tangle with him today?

No, but I couldn't keep ignoring the fact that he never brought his book to class, never turned in an assignment, and was on a fast track to fail a course required for graduation for the third time.

You can't reach every student, I told myself. *This one doesn't want to be taught, and he won't be.*

Denver made me feel like a failure every time I looked his way and saw his pencil flying across the sheet of paper on his desk. What was he drawing now? Another dragon named Jennet?

He's not the one you should worry about.

How did I know that? An inner voice born of the discordant notes? Or a foreboding?

I'd been associating with Lucy Hazen too long.

It was a seasoned teacher's hunch. I surveyed the class again, seeing no sign of disorder, no likely source of future mayhem.

Just be on guard, I told myself.

I *was* on guard every time this wild class convened.

Be extra vigilant then.

That intuitive voice told me that whatever was going to happen in this classroom wouldn't happen today. It added that it would involve Denver Armstrong. Naturally.

"What are we going to do today?"

The voice was challenging, strident. I couldn't tell who had spoken, but it called me back to the present. I'd left my class to their own dark devices while I pondered future calamities. It was my job to lead—or be dragged down.

I initialed the attendance slip and said, "We're continuing our survey of local color with a new Bret Harte story, *The Luck of Roaring Camp.* Page one hundred eighty-nine. I think you'll enjoy it."

At least I hoped they would.

~ * ~

"Something bad is going to happen in my fourth hour class," I said to Leonora as we tucked into our semi-appetizing cafeteria lunches. A patty made from unidentified meat, mashed potatoes, a vegetable, followed by milk and a jumbo cookie. Uninspired.

"What brought this on?" she asked.

"Something in the air."

"Mmm. Your group is rowdy, and there's a lot of them, but it's been like that since September."

"It's been building up," I said. "When I was in college, a professor told our Methods class that if we kept students busy and interested, we wouldn't have discipline problems."

She smiled. "And you believed him?"

"Sure. Right up until I had my first classes."

"Seriously," Leonora said. "What could happen?"

"A class in rebellion. A Grimsley intervention. Don't forget. I already had my grade book stolen."

She nodded. "But that turned out all right."

"Thanks to a student informer. I can't count on that happening again."

"Overall, I think our kids are good." Leonora grimaced at the meat patty on her plate and pushed the gravy off its top. "We have a few bad apples, every school does, but I never worry about what could happen. If I did, I'd be too nervous to teach."

"You should."

We were both aware of violence in the classroom and, rarely, of teachers who had lost their lives at the hands of a disturbed student. Teaching had become a dangerous profession. We were the public's scapegoat, enjoying long summer vacations, a short work day, and disproportionately high pay. I could foresee the day when we'd all be replaced by robots.

How do you kill a robot?

"I considered Denver Armstrong a bad apple," I said.

I couldn't seem to keep myself from focusing on him. Denver, trouble with a capital *T* from day one. He made no secret of his dislike for me.

"I just have this feeling," I added, eying my peas and corn with distaste. Either peas or corn would have been fine. Mixed together, they made a ghastly side dish.

A problem easily solved. I set out to eat only the corn.

Would that all problems could be so efficiently dealt with.

My thoughts shifted to the Spirit Lamp Inn. With all its secrets and dangers, I wished I were there. Perversity again.

~ * ~

Teaching could be difficult. Solving a mystery, on the other hand, was a virtual piece of cake. Even a cold case without a single viable clue, or a real suspect? Yes.

Well, compared to kindling excitement for an antiquated short story.

"I'd rather investigate mysteries than teach school," I announced to Crane and Brent that evening.

Brent had joined us for a simple dinner of steak and salad, sparing me the need to track him down.

"I'd like to see you out of that school," Crane said.

"But how many mysteries do you expect to come your way?" Brent asked.

"Since I moved to Foxglove Corners, they've come in droves. One after another."

"We're in a mysterious part of the state," Brent said. "Speaking of mysteries, I brought you the silver chain we found. It was on the floor."

"You mean the one Annica found."

"So she did. Should I give it to her instead, do you think?"

"She'd like that."

"I found her earring, too."

"Annica wants you to open the crate she fell on," I said.

"I'm fast losing interest in that attic."

"She thinks there may be a clue inside. Or something important."

An image from my dream formed in my mind. Old bones. The remains of a blue raincoat. Nightmare stuff. Strange. I should have forgotten that dream by now.

"I guess it's worth a look," he said. "I'll do it."

That matter taken care of, I moved on to the next one. "What do you know about Bruce?"

"Just that he's no fox hunter."

"So he lied. He has something to hide. I'd like to know everything about the people who might have been involved with Cynthia and Rachel. If they had a family, what they did for a living... Well, everything."

"Why?"

"To help me solve the mystery. So far Miss Isabel, Ted, and Bruce are just names and faces. How can I uncover a secret motive unless I really know them?"

"That won't be easy," he said. "They're private people."

"Can you think of a way to get us together at the Inn again?" I asked.

"Not offhand."

"Well, work on it."

"You have your orders, Fowler," Crane said. "But whatever you do, keep my wife out of your attic."

"Don't worry," I said. "It's a horrible, scary place. I never intend to go up there again."

Forty-three

Brent came up with two ideas for another get-together at the Inn. First, to mark the completion of Lucy's new book, *Trapped in the Mist*, and second, to celebrate his birthday. That he had been born in February was irrelevant.

"No one has to know that," he said.

He described his plan to us the next evening. "I'll invite the whole gang. The champagne will flow freely. You'll encourage them to reminisce about the good old days. Maybe Rachel will make another appearance."

Still clear in my mind was our last party. Leaving the table to fetch Miss Isabel's cardigan, seeing Rachel's ghost in the second floor hall and a drift of blue mist in her wake. Once again, I remembered my nightmare. Bones in a crate, cradled in disintegrating blue cloth.

A dream isn't real, I reminded myself.

"I certainly hope Rachel won't be there," I said. "Don't invite her. Don't even think about her."

I wanted to conduct my interrogations without any interference, ghostly or otherwise.

"I'll have Louise bake a couple of her coconut cakes, one for each end of the table," Brent said. "Annica will take pictures. No one will realize it's a set-up. We'll do it on Friday, if that's okay with everybody."

The mention of Annica reminded me to ask Brent about the crate in the attic. "Did you open it?"

"Yes. It was stuffed with maps and postcards, the kind you collect for souvenirs but don't send, lists of places to visit, and..." He paused for dramatic effect. "Something really weird. You remember the silver heart charm I misplaced? It was in the crate under a stack of maps."

"How on earth did that happen?" I asked.

"Don't ask me. I sure didn't climb up to the attic and put it there."

"Someone did."

Jewelry disappearing and turning up in unlikely places. It had to tie in with Cynthia's murder. But how?

"Somebody is having fun at our expense. Playing musical charms."

"Whoever did this might have done other things," Crane said. "Past and present."

I nodded. "Good observation. Or the Supernatural may be at work. Where's the charm now?"

"In my desk drawer. It's not going to vanish from there."

"If it does, you can blame the ghost," Crane said.

Noting the gleam of humor in his gray eyes, I reminded him that Rachel was real. A real ghost, that is.

I wouldn't hesitate to blame her for the wandering charm, but in this case I felt we were dealing with a living trickster. Or maybe hiding the charm wasn't a trick. It occurred to me that whoever took the silver heart and relocated it to a crate in the attic couldn't know that Annica would fall on that particular crate and be curious about what was inside. In ordinary circumstances, the charm might never have been found.

Who had hidden it? And why?

"I'm going to start making calls tonight," Brent said. "The weather looks okay for the Oakpoint ladies."

"If you plan on inviting me, I'll be free," Crane said.

I smiled at him. His presence would turn the gathering into a date night. We had so few of them.

"Be extra persuasive," I said to Brent. "We want them all to show up."

~ * ~

The night of Brent's make-believe birthday party was cold and windy with a few snowflakes that proved no impediment to those traveling a long distance.

Strangely, the only person who didn't show up was Miss Isabel. She stayed in her new room on the second story of the Inn, claiming to suffer from a headache and refusing Brent's personal entreaties to join the party.

"Miss Isabel said she wasn't hungry," Brent said with a shrug. "Didn't even want a cup of tea sent up to her. Just wanted to be left alone. What could I do?"

"Nothing. But this is a disappointment. She's the one I really wanted to talk to, but I guess I can do that another time. Oh, well, everyone else is here."

Ted looking dapper in a tweed jacket, Bruce in a plaid flannel shirt, and the ladies wearing sequin-sprinkled tops with black pants. The whole gang minus Miss Isabel and the ones who were dead.

"I'll make do with what we have," I said.

"Hey, you two! What are you whispering about?"

Marsha Anne sidled up to us, her blue eyes bright with curiosity. The sequins on her top looked like a three-strand choker, and long ruby earrings sparkled between wisps of silvery curls.

"Cake," I said.

Brent winked at her. "Yeah, cake."

"Your twin cakes are wonderful, Mr. Fowler," she said. "Coconut is my favorite. Before I forget, Happy Birthday. How odd to throw a party for yourself."

Brent remained nonplussed. "If I don't, who will? I'm just a lonely bachelor whose friends think he's too old for candles and cakes."

I resisted the impulse to cough. A bachelor Brent might be. Lonely? Never. He had even collected a few presents stacked at one end of the table.

"Anyhow, I'm sharing the spotlight with Miss Lucy Hazen tonight. She's a famous horror story writer who just finished her latest book." He glanced over Marsha Anne's shoulder. "There she is now. Excuse me."

I didn't see Lucy but welcomed the chance for a few private words with Marsha Anne.

Now which words would be most effective?"

She spoke first. "Mr. Fowler is such a nice man. If he doesn't have a wife or a significant other, I'd like him to meet my friend, Sara. She's single too."

I let that pass. Brent didn't need introductions to eligible women. He had plenty of female admirers. Besides, what if Marsha Anne's friend belonged to her own generation?

She couldn't be that clueless.

"It must bring back memories for you, being here at the Inn with your old friends," I said.

"Oh, it does." She gave the small crowd a cursory glance. "I don't see Isabel, though. Isn't she coming?"

"I heard she wasn't feeling well. Brent says she's in her room, just upstairs."

"I'll go up and see if she needs anything. Oh, I know. I'll take her a piece of cake. Isabel always loved cake. Eating it, baking them, it didn't make any difference. She used to make the most fabulous layer cakes. Everybody wanted one."

Cake, I thought. Interesting, but how could Isabel's penchant for creating memorable cakes help in my investigation?

"I guess they didn't have all those mixes in your day," I said.

"Of course you could buy box cakes then, but Isabel always made her cakes from scratch. Goodness, how old do you think I am anyway?"

Uh oh. That was a good question to sidestep.

"I thought they just had mixes for chocolate and white cakes. Maybe strawberry. Whereas today..."

I drifted off. We'd covered the subject of cake thoroughly. I was ready to move on. Across the room, Crane was smiling at me. I should have rehearsed my questions with him.

"I think the party's starting," I said. With a nod for her, I walked over to join Crane.

~ * ~

Throughout dinner, strangers kept stopping by our table to wish Brent a Happy Birthday and compliment him on the improvements he'd made in the Inn.

If they only knew what was going on behind the scenes.

At some point, it occurred to me that Miss Isabel might not be ill at all. Was her absence suspicious? Could there be someone here tonight she didn't want to see?

It was worth investigating, but I didn't have time to pursue that avenue of thought. I still had three people to question, rather, to talk to, and the party was at the coffee-and-cake stage. I didn't have much time left.

Crane sat on one side of me, Bruce on the other. Bruce seemed intent on his dessert, disinclined to talk. But surely he couldn't ignore me.

"Have you gone on any fox hunts yet? I asked Bruce, feigning innocence.

"Not yet. Fowler's looking for a horse for me."

"Isn't it too cold to a—er—ride to the hounds?"

"They hunt in all weather," he said. "We consider a day like this bracing, not cold."

"You've been hunting for a long time then?" I asked.

"When I was young. Not in recent years."

Should I believe him? Brent didn't.

"I like all outdoor sports," he added. "Especially winter sports. When I was in my prime, I used to ski…"

"Smile," Annica said and snapped a picture. She'd aimed her camera at Bruce and me instead of Crane and me.

"Excuse me." Bruce pushed his empty dessert plate to the side and rose.

Darn. I'd lost him. Just when he was speaking of his prime.

Annica slid into the chair he'd vacated. "I got everybody except Miss Isabel. What are we going to use these pictures for?"

I shrugged. "It was Brent's idea.

"He's going to open his presents soon," she said. "Presents for the man who has everything!"

Catherine and Marsha Anne had left the table, no doubt in search of the rest room.

"Take some more pictures, Annica," I said. "I'm going to keep Ted company."

Forty-four

Ted was demolishing an enormous slice of coconut cake. It looked like two slices, one on top of the other.

"Jennet?" he said as I sat beside him and set my coffee cup on the table.

"The cake is good, isn't it?" I asked, hoping I could move from cake to murder without arousing his suspicion.

"It's excellent. I haven't been to a birthday party in ages," he said.

"Since you were all young?"

"Not that long ago." He scooped up a piece of frosting with his fork, breaking the 'BR' away from the 'ENT.' "I have three nephews and five nieces."

"It must be nice to reconnect with old friends," I said.

"Marsha Anne and I have kept in touch through the years, and I've seen Cathy on occasion. Isabel, not at all until the Halloween party."

"Poor Cynthia met her fate right here in the Inn, and Rachel... How did Rachel die?"

The question, meant to be subtle, was probably the worst segue in history.

Ted paused, a forkful of cake halfway to his mouth. "What?"

"I just wondered. Cynthia was murdered. Did her traveling companion, Rachel, die violently too?"

"In a way," he said. "Rachel was driving home one winter night and skidded into the path of an oncoming truck. It was a quick death, I understand."

So there was no way Rachel's bones could have ended up in a crate in the Inn's attic. Abruptly I reined in my imagination. That was in a dream. The real crate contained travel material and a silver heart charm, which was just as mysterious as bones and much less ghastly.

"Why are you interested in how Rachel died?" Ted asked.

I didn't care to explain about my dream and certainly couldn't mention the attic. Our forays in the uppermost level of the Spirit Lamp Inn were supposed to be a secret.

Suspending his cake demolition, Ted waited for my answer.

"It's just that the story captured my imagination," I said. "Two young women who dreamed of traveling around the world coming to such sad ends."

"They both died a long time ago."

"But one of the stories is unfinished," I pointed out.

He shoved a piece of cake into his mouth. There was only a little left on his plate.

"Dead is dead," he said. "You can't get more finished than that."

"You can when no one knows who the killer is," I pointed out.

"After all these years, nobody is going to know. It was a fluke, discovering that grave. The killer must be long since dead."

"Maybe not."

"Would you like to put your money where your mouth is?"

I was saved from replying to this crude challenge by the appearance of a flustered Marsha Anne at my side. Her lipstick had worn off, and her silver curls looked a trifle disarranged.

"Jennet, could I talk to you? Privately?" She cast an apologetic glance at Ted. "Girl talk," she said.

"Of course."

Leaving my coffee cup on the table, I followed her out of the dining room to the hostess' station, deserted at this hour.

Marsha Anne lowered her voice. "It's Isabel. She isn't in her room. Didn't you say she had a headache?"

"That's what I heard."

"Where else would Isabel be but in her room then, or here with us?"

"Are you sure?" I asked. "Maybe she's sleeping or just not coming to her door."

"I knocked, but the door was unlocked, so I went in. She isn't there. Not anywhere. I left her cake and tea on the table. Where could she be?"

The first thought that came to me was the attic. Miss Isabel, feeling quite well, taking advantage of her chance to conduct her own surreptitious search. Navigating the treacherous boards that served as flooring with unsteady steps. Braving the shadows. Watched by the ghost.

She might have fallen like Annica, might be lying in the attic now.

No. At least I hoped not.

"Is her car gone, too?" I asked. "She drives a vintage yellow Plymouth with those long fins. Maybe she went to the store for headache pills or something."

"I didn't look," she admitted. "I hoped she might have come down to the dining room and I missed her somehow."

"I haven't seen her."

Just to be certain, I checked out our group and the strangers who sat at their tables absorbed in their own affairs. Miss Isabel wasn't among them.

"I'm afraid for her," Marsha Anne said. "Isabel is really very frail, although she'd never admit it. What'll we do?"

Lose no time, I thought. "Tell Brent and my husband. Crane is a deputy sheriff."

Marsha Anne paled. "You don't think something happened to her, do you?"

Instead of answering, I said, "Where is Catherine?"

"In Isabel's room, in case she comes back."

"Brent can see if Miss Isabel's car is still here. The others don't have to know yet."

The others being Bruce and Ted, Lucy and Annica.

Brent was in the midst of opening the presents he didn't need under the watchful eyes of Lucy, Annica, and Annica's camera. And Crane? I didn't see him but he couldn't have gone far.

I left Marsha Anne pacing in the doorway, whispered the news to Brent, and watched his expression change from feigned delight to instant alarm.

"I'm on it," he said as Lucy and Annica leaned forward expectantly.

Did I really think I could keep this new development from them?

I had a bad feeling about Miss Isabel disappearing. It brought back memories of that other disappearance. Cynthia vanishing into thin air, only to be found in skeletal form decades later.

They say history repeats itself.

I'd hoped to solve a mystery tonight, not add another one to the list. But the Spirit Lamp Inn had a mind of its own. Or its resident spirit did.

~ * ~

By the time Brent returned to report that the vintage Plymouth was parked in its usual place, Crane wandered back to the dining room. Quickly I apprised him of Miss Isabel's disappearance and the need for discretion.

"We don't want to alarm her friends if she's okay," I said.

At this point the only two who didn't know that Miss Isabel was missing were Ted and Bruce.

"But where is she?" Annica wanted to know.

"She has to be in the Inn," Crane said. "People don't disappear from inside a building."

"They do in Foxglove Corners," I said.

"I checked the attic," Brent added. "There's nothing there. Nothing living, I should say."

"Why would you check the attic?" Marsha Anne asked.

Catherine had joined us, barely concealed panic in her aspect. "She didn't come back."

"Who didn't?" asked Bruce from his seat at the table.

Ted looked up from his coffee. "What are you talking about?"

Brent explained.

"Why are you all so worked up?" he asked. "Isabel probably went out with a friend. If her car is here, the friend picked her up."

If it were only that simple. How wonderful it would be if Miss Isabel would come waltzing in right now, surprised by all the fuss we were making when she'd simply gone to a movie.

"What about her headache?" Marsha Anne asked.

"That was an excuse," Ted said. "She didn't want to come to Fowler's party."

"We'd better notify the police." Catherine pulled her cell phone out of her purse.

Ted shook his head. "Don't. You'll look like a fool when we find out it was all a misunderstanding."

"What do you think, Crane?" I asked.

"If your friend isn't in the Inn, she has to be outside it."

In her best gloom-and-doom voice, Lucy said, "I think she slipped away from us. But maybe it isn't too late to bring her back."

Forty-five

Lucy sounded as if she believed that Miss Isabel was dead. Of course it was just her way of talking, that horror genre mindset, but her words left a discernible chill in the air.

Catherine sank into a chair, still holding her cell phone. "I don't like this. It isn't going to turn out well."

"Another woman disappears from this accursed Inn," added Marsha Anne.

"I tell you it's all a mistake," Ted said. "She'll turn up safe and sound."

Crane, already dressed for the outdoors, was holding my coat for me. He knew I'd never stay behind if I had a chance to join in the search.

Brent said, "You ladies wait here and try not to worry. If we don't find Miss Isabel, we'll call the police."

Annica made a dash for her own coat. "Wait up. I'm coming with you."

I wrapped my scarf around my neck and pulled my gloves out of my pocket. Calling the police was well and good, but what would they do? Miss Isabel was an adult and hadn't been missing long. Brent had spoken to her before the party, around seven o'clock, when she'd told him about her headache. Most people wouldn't sound the alarm for an absence of a little over two hours.

But Miss Isabel was elderly and frail and, according to Brent, nowhere inside the Inn. Therefore she must be outside on one of the coldest nights of the year.

The police wouldn't help unless we had a body to show them.

Good grief! What a ghoulish thought, one worthy of Lucy Hazen. Unfortunately it was an accurate one.

"Coming, girls?" Crane said.

Annica and I caught up with the men at the hostess' station, and together we went out into the night.

The wind had picked up. It blew snow from their neatly shoveled mounds across the driveway, giving the ground a powdered-sugar sheen. A stunning sight, but the wind's feral howl chilled my blood.

Beside me, Annica shivered and pulled the hood of her parka close around her head. Brent said, "I'll go check out the Plymouth again."

Annica was looking over her shoulder at the lights in the windows. They seemed to beckon us back inside, and indeed we couldn't stay out in the extreme cold much longer. The tips of my fingers were already tingling painfully.

Crane was studying the ground. What he was seeing I couldn't imagine. There wasn't much hope of any kind of print lasting in the constantly blowing snow.

I left them and ventured into the semi-darkness on the side of the Inn that would be a newly designed garden—if spring ever came. Faint light streamed out through a single window, providing meager illumination.

A small, slender figure in a long black coat stood staring at the ground. The ends of the scarf tied loosely around her head flapped wildly in the wind.

Until recently this section of the property had been enclosed with yellow crime scene tape. It was the gravesite, and the figure had to be Miss Isabel as motionless as a graveside statue.

"Crane!" I shouted. "Over here." He appeared instantly at my side as I went up to Miss Isabel and touched her arm gently.

"Miss Isabel," I said loudly, "come inside. It's too cold for you out here."

Her reply, if indeed she responded, blew away in the wind.

I was close enough to see that she had been crying. Teardrops glistened on her pale face. They looked as if they'd frozen to her skin.

In the most forceful tone in his repertoire, Crane said. "It's no night to be outside. This weather can kill."

Responding to his voice, she moved, a statue slowly coming to life, becoming aware of her surroundings.

"You need to go back inside the Inn," Crane said. "We all do."

"All?" she murmured.

"And warm up," I added. "Have a hot drink. Coffee or tea. Whatever you want."

Annica rushed to join us. "What on earth is she doing out here?"

I shook my head. She ignored my not-so-subtle hint to be silent.

"Well, really, Miss Isabel," she said, "if you didn't want to come to the party, why didn't you just say so?"

Crane guided Miss Isabel around the side of the Inn, steadying her when she stumbled on one of Brent's decorative boulders.

Brent waited for us at the front door. "You found her. Good work! I was just going to call the cops. Where the hell were you, Miss Isabel?"

"Shouldn't we take her to the hospital? Annica asked.

At that prospect, Miss Isabel spoke her first word. "No!"

Brent ushered us inside to the blessed warmth, and Crane slammed the door shut behind us. Brent led her to a table at the front of the dining room.

"Here, sit down," he said. "You look terrible."

Miss Isabel collapsed in a chair and pulled the scarf off. She proceeded to twist it and shake it loose, only to twist it again. She seemed unaware of the curious stares of the few customers who remained in the dining room, unmindful of her friends who gathered around her, all talking at once.

"I'm all right," she said. "Just cold."

"About the hospital, Miss Isabel, I think you'd better go," Brent said. "I'll drive you. You're my responsibility."

"Wherever did you ever get that idea, Mr. Fowler? I'm responsible for myself, and there's no cause for alarm. I was just…" She trailed off.

"Just what?" I asked.

"Just visiting Cynthia's grave. I'm allowed to do that, aren't I?"

"She isn't there," I said.

"In the dead of night?" Annica demanded. "In the dead of winter? Who does that?"

"There's no season in death," Miss Isabel said.

~ * ~

Brent was still talking about a visit to the Emergency Room, but Miss Isabel was adamant. She was just chilled. Chilled to the bone, maybe, but rapidly thawing out. She told Catherine and Marsha Anne to stop fussing over her, and announced her intention of going straight to bed.

From the fringe of the crowd, Lucy watched her silently. She hadn't said a word since we'd brought Miss Isabel back inside the Inn. I wished I knew what she was thinking.

"See," Ted said to no one in particular. "Isabel is safe and sound. No need to call in the cavalry."

"There's tea and cake in your room," Marsha Anne said, "but the tea will be cold. Let me get you a fresh cup."

"Thanks, but that's all right." Miss Isabel gave her scarf one final shake, and made her escape.

As soon as she was out of earshot, Bruce said, "Now what do you make of that?"

"It's crazy," Annica said. "You'd better check on her in the morning, Brent. If she lives through the night."

"Don't say that," Marsha Anne admonished.

Bruce said, "Isabel always was a bit unusual. Or should I say unique?"

"Now that everything is okay, let's head on home," Catherine said. "It was a pleasant party, Mr. Fowler."

"With a bit of excitement at the end." Bruce yawned. "I think I'll turn in. It's times like this I'm glad I live in the Inn."

"Jennet and I will be leaving, too," Crane said. "Ready, honey?"

"Wait!" Lucy's voice startled me. "Wait just a minute, Crane. Jennet?" She beckoned me to her side.

"What is it?" I asked.

She lowered her voice. "I suggest you look a little more closely at Isabel Bryte. I'm not a hundred percent sure, but I have a feeling you may have found Cynthia's killer."

"Miss Isabel?"

"Not so loud."

"What she did tonight was strange, I'll admit. But Miss Isabel a killer? I can't believe that."

"I said 'may have,' Jennet. But this I know. She's involved."

A premonition or foreboding too clear to be denied? A rare glimpse into the future, or, in this case, into the past?

I didn't ask Lucy to explain. She wouldn't. Or couldn't. But she'd been right more often than wrong, and I wasn't averse to accepting help from the Supernatural.

Whatever worked.

Forty-six

The band of white that was Deer Leap Trail wound its way through farmland and forest, taking us home. It looked as if we were trapped in a snow squall, but it was only an illusion—wind blowing existing snow, creating a massive white-out.

Neither wind nor blowing snow fazed Crane, and because he remained calm and in control, I could relax and rehash the events that had turned Brent's birthday party into a near disaster.

If Marsha Anne hadn't decided to take a tray to Miss Isabel's room... If we'd wasted precious time calling the police and waiting for them...

In my mind I saw Miss Isabel, silent and still, staring at the gravesite, tears in imminent danger of freezing on her face. I'd tried to push the image away, but it kept returning.

If we hadn't found her when we did... How long does it take to die of hypothermia?

"What Miss Isabel did tonight was certainly strange, but it wasn't the action of a killer," I said, breaking the companionable silence in the car. "Still, Lucy wouldn't have said anything if she wasn't sure."

"Bruce said Isabel had always been unusual," Crane reminded me.

"Yes, unusual and unique. For all we know, she might have made it a habit to visit the gravesite, but no one noticed her obsession until tonight."

I should stop referring to it as a gravesite. The place where Cynthia's remains had lain until their discovery was a more accurate description. All that was left of Cynthia lay in a proper cemetery now, the yellow tape on Brent's property gone, the crime still unsolved.

"Standing outside in the bitter cold isn't the act of a rational person," Crane said. "She could have frozen to death."

"I don't entirely believe Lucy is right this time, but I'm going to keep an eye on Miss Isabel. I sure didn't learn much from the others tonight."

"If one of them is the killer, he or she wouldn't be happy to answer your questions."

That was true, but I'd hoped to trick them into revealing their secrets. As if aware of my ploy, they had avoided it.

"I'll stop by the Inn in a day or two and take Miss Isabel a gift," I said.

With Christmas fast approaching, I'd seen assortments of teas in fancy seasonal tins for sale at Zoller's General Store. Eggnog and fruitcake-flavored winter teas. She might like that.

As we drove through the swirling snow, I created a heartwarming scene out of nothing more substantial than wishful thinking. Miss Isabel resting in a recliner, opening an early Christmas present.

"How wonderful, Jennet," she would say. "After Christmas I can use this pretty tin for my stationery and stamps. And while we're here, let me tell you what really happened on the night Cynthia Lauren disappeared..."

We had left Deer Leap Trail but not the wind. The *Farmer's Almanac* had predicted a colder than average winter with record-breaking snow. It seemed as if someone were always predicting a harsh winter. Maybe this time the doomsayers were right.

~ * ~

It was a cold morning, but not cold enough to cancel school in Oakpoint. That decision, originating with the district's superintendent, gave rise to endless grumbling in my classes. A fair number of students declared their own personal 'Cold Day' and flooded the attendance office with requests to sign out.

I sympathized with them, but it was only December. If we started using our snow days this month, we'd be in trouble come spring.

Suppressing a shiver, I glanced at the snow-draped woods outside the classroom. It was a day of frosted panes, shrieking wind, and blowing snow, a day to remember past years when the main concern was whether we'd have a white Christmas.

In Journalism class, the editors were putting the finishing touches on copy for the Valentine's issue of the school newspaper. Because of the holidays and semester break, we didn't publish a paper in January. Consequently the bulletin boards were decorated in red hearts and Cupids. They gave the room a rosy glow that did nothing to raise the temperature. They also elicited many a comment about my not knowing what month it was.

In American Literature, Denver Armstrong was drawing snowmen with grotesque expressions, a fairly innocuous project but not one to help him pass the course.

I was glad I'd worn a new knit dress, cobalt blue with long sleeves and a soft turtleneck. New outfits were a 'must have' for cold winter days, especially dresses that fell below the knees.

"I like your outfit, Mrs. Ferguson," Katrina said with a simper that made me doubt her sincerity.

"Teacher's pet," someone shouted.

Katrina, my pet? Hardly. But a burst of confidence or energy, some good thing, inspired me to say, "Put the drawing away, Mister Armstrong. I have a pop quiz for you today."

To shouts of 'No way!' and 'No fair! You didn't warn us!' Denver added his comment. "Just for me? Gosh, thanks, Teach."

"For everyone," I said, reminding myself to think before I spoke, especially in this class. Some of my students waited for an opportunity to throw a wisecrack into the mix.

I consulted the wall clock in the front of the room. Ten forty-five. The quiz shouldn't take more than fifteen minutes. That left ten orphaned minutes before the bell rang for lunch.

Principal Grimsley had a penchant for materializing at a door when time was in danger of being wasted.

What to do with those leftover minutes?

Inspiration struck. I'd have them exchange papers and read the answers while they corrected their neighbor's quiz. What meticulous principal could object to that? It was reinforcing the lesson and saving time (for me).

Undaunted by the previous taunt, Katrina popped up and followed me to my desk. "I'll help you pass them out, Mrs. Ferguson."

As I turned around to pick up the stack of quizzes on my desk, I heard a scream. Screaming. A firecracker noise that sounded like a gunshot. Another one.

Gunshots?

I whirled around on instant alert and registered a scene straight from Dante's hell. Chaos. Kids hitting the floor, rushing the door. Overturned desks, Denver on his feet, his papers flying, and the new boy…

He had a gun!

I shoved Katrina behind me. She slammed into the blackboard.

"He's got a gun!"

A gun, a gun, came the echo.

Dear God! Was that blood on the floor? A girl with blood pouring out of her shoulder onto her long blonde hair?

Do something!

Denver vaulted over a desk and flung himself at the shooter. "Drop it!" Denver's voice. "You don't want to do this."

My mind went blank. I couldn't remember his name. The new boy...

That isn't important.

Denver twisted the boy's arms behind his back. The gun fell from his grip and flew across the room like a predatory bird.

Time lost any semblance of chronological order. It rushed forward and stalled, fell backward and broke into fragments, each piece swirling madly through the air. Like the windblown snow.

A tall bulky form darkened the doorway. Jeff Lasenby from the math room across the hall.

"Call nine-one-one," I cried.

"I did. Are they...?" He pointed to the fallen students. The girl was moaning; a boy lay still.

I shook my head. "I don't know."

A distant siren wailed its message: Help on the way. The police station was less than a mile from the school.

Leonora shoved her way through the crowd, her eyes wide with horror. The young faces in my room were unfamiliar to me. Most of my class had fled into the hall; curious unknowns had taken their places.

I was dimly aware of a voice in the hall shouting at everybody to go back to their classrooms. Someone was saying, 'Here comes Grimsley!' A girl was sobbing. 'Let me through. That's my sister in there.'

I was aware of something else. Nothing at Marston High School would ever be the same again.

Forty-seven

An eerie silence descended on the halls of Marston High School. The school had first been on lockdown, then dismissed. The shooter was gone, in police custody. Denver Armstrong, hailed as a teenaged hero, was gone, too. The ambulance had taken Jessica Spencer to the hospital, and Danny Ellis was dead, felled by the first shot. I supposed they'd taken him to the morgue. The new boy, whose name I finally remembered, Joel Carstairs, wasn't talking.

One word threaded through my jumbled thoughts. *Why?*

I longed for home where no evil thing could find me. At least that's what I often told myself. I yearned for the comfort of Crane's strong arms around me and the dogs offering their canine caring.

I'd called Crane to assure him that I was unharmed, then started crying, which is what I didn't want to do.

Now it was over—in a sense. Statements and first aid had been given. We'd had to attend a very brief staff meeting in the library. The smell of the gunshot lingered in the room. Even if the windows were left open throughout the night, I suspected the smell would still be there when we returned to school.

Leonora pressed a cup of coffee into my hands. "From Grimsley's private cappuccino machine, with his blessing. He says we can leave anytime. He's going to be the last one out."

"Down with his ship," I said.

She frowned. "That doesn't apply."

"I guess it doesn't. My brain is scrambled."

I was cold, could never remember being so cold in my life, not even when Leonora and I had been stranded in a snowstorm near the infamous dive, the Cauldron.

"Danny," I said. "He was one of the good kids. Always interested in class. Always polite. He wanted to be on the honor roll. He would have been. Will be."

"And the girl? Jessica?"

"She was good, too. Quiet and very smart. They were all good, even Denver," I said, marveling that I had been thinking of American Literature as my bad class since September. Well, they were loud and on occasion obnoxious. But bad? No.

"He had the gun in his backpack," I said. "There wasn't a sign, not a single sign he was going to open fire. I turned around to pass out quizzes."

Katrina, dissolving in tears, had cried that I'd saved her life by pushing her behind me. It wasn't true. Joel had been facing the other direction, but he could have turned, so I didn't argue.

"It just happened," I said. "No warning."

But there had been a sign. Call it a foreboding, the feeling I'd had that something bad was going to happen in this class. Something involving Denver Armstrong. My incomplete, unspecific foreboding.

"Isn't it lucky that Denver didn't cut class today?" Leonora said.

I took a sip of coffee and discovered I didn't want it. It had an unpleasant after taste. But it was warm; I wrapped my hands around the cup, not to warm them but to stop them from shaking.

Jeff looked in the door. "If you ladies are ready, I'll walk you to your cars."

I hadn't realized he was still in the building.

"To Leonora's car," I said, thankful that it was her week to drive. I didn't trust myself behind the wheel. My hands were still shaking.

I got my coat out of the closet, slipped my plan book and grade book into a tote, and locked the door.

"Hell of a note," Jeff said as we walked through the silent halls. "Shootings like this happen in other schools. In other states. Not at Marston High School in Oakpoint, Michigan."

"They're too frequent," Leonora said. "It seems like you read about one every week."

"The shooter was new in the school," I added. "It didn't seem like he had a particular target. He just shot into the class."

Leonora shuddered. "He just wanted to kill somebody."

"And if I'd been facing the class instead of turning around, just at that moment... I was going to hand out quizzes."

"What do you think you could have done?" she asked.

"I might have seen him pull the weapon out of his backpack."

"And?" That was Jeff. "Do you think you could have disarmed him? He's bigger than you. Stronger too, I'll bet."

"Don't think about that," Leonora said. "It happened the way it happened."

We'd reached the cafeteria without encountering a single person. The kitchen lights were out, chairs were in disarray, and trays with half-eaten lunches scattered on the tables—or on the floor. Word of the shooting had spread rapidly through the building and activities were summarily abandoned. There'd been no clean-up, no return to order.

"Thank God you weren't killed, Jen," Leonora added. "I mean that as a prayer, not an expression."

"But Danny is dead. Jessica may be dying..."

As Jeff opened the door, I felt a blast of cold wind and a gust that all but swept me off my feet.

"I was the teacher," I said. "The adult. I should have been able to do something."

The winds swept my words away, along with any answer Jeff or Leonora might have made. Maybe it was just as well.

~ * ~

Marston High School was closed the next day. Jessica's condition had been upgraded to critical; Joel Carstairs refused to reveal his motive. His mother, newly moved to Michigan from Vermont, refused to believe that her son had gunned down two classmates. The gun was hers, purchased for protection. She thought she'd had it hidden.

Early the next morning, I broke eggs for an omelet.

"There's been too much drama in my life," I said. "First Miss Isabel hovers over the place where Cynthia's bones were buried. Now this."

Crane drank his coffee slowly and quietly, watching the creation of the enormous omelet we were going to share.

"Your semester ends next month, doesn't it?" he asked.

"In January. The twenty-first, I think."

"That would be a good time for you to hand in your resignation."

I spilled the beaten eggs into the frying pan. "I don't think I want to do that," I said.

After any bad day, I usually toyed with the idea of parting company with the Marston family. Family was the operative word. I'd been teaching at Marston for so many years my fellow teachers were indeed like my family. As for my students, they needed me. Denver had only a matter of weeks to turn his dismal record around. And Journalism... We all looked forward to our February issue and the Valentine heart to be given to one lucky winner.

"You don't have to work at all," Crane said. "You could have been killed yesterday," he added.

"Crane, you run that risk every day."

"That's my job," he said. "I'm trained to deal with violence. You're not."

"But teaching is my job too," I said. "This may never happen again, and that boy wasn't from Oakpoint or even the state. He was only in my class for a few weeks."

Crane smiled for the first time since I'd told him the story in detail. "You're implying that Oakpoint kids don't commit violent acts?"

"Yes. They fly paper airplanes, litter the floors, start fights with another, talk back to their teachers, and use appalling language. They're kids, annoying at times but generally good. They're the next generation."

"Okay. That's Oakpoint kids. Another student could transfer to your class from another district at any time."

He was right. Any time.

"I'll give resigning some thought," I said. "But it won't be next month."

He was silent.

I cut the omelet in half, passed him the plate of toast, and took my place opposite him at the table, petting Candy before starting to eat.

Silence wasn't necessarily good.

Forty-eight

With no classes to teach and no desire to while away the day reliving the tumultuous hours at Marston High School, I took the dogs for a walk in the snow, then set out for the Corners.

The stately old buildings were still drowsing, draped in snow. Clear Christmas lights twinkled in the branches of the trees. The old white Victorian that housed the Foxglove Corners Public Library had its own Christmas tree in the front yard, a tall blue spruce decorated with red and green ornaments.

One day soon I intended to pay a visit to the town's beloved librarian, Miss Eidt, and stock up on new mysteries to read over Christmas vacation, but today my destination was the Spirit Lamp Inn. I planned to take an early present to Miss Isabel. Brent had informed me by phone this morning that she refused to leave her room.

"Is she sick?" I asked.

"Doesn't seem to be. She says she's just feeling depressed and wants to have a quiet week in bed."

"A whole week? That *is* depression. Maybe I can cheer her up."

"Good idea. She likes you. I'll be at the Inn around noon myself. We can have lunch if you like."

"I would."

"The sheriff filled me in on the shooting," Brent said. "You know what I think?"

"That I should resign?"

"No doubt about it."

Sometimes Brent tended to agree with Crane, which annoyed me as Brent had been my friend first.

"But if you decide to stay, you teachers should insist on being armed. You could have nipped that shooting in the bud if you'd had a gun. Maybe saved two lives."

"Two?" My heart skipped several beats.

"Okay, one. Last I heard the girl was holding on."

"Arming the teachers would cause more problems than it would solve," I said.

"How so?"

"Because..." I hesitated. "For so many reasons."

Items had a way of disappearing even from desk drawers. Pens were especially mobile, but the tape dispenser and stapler were always wandering, then turning up after class on a windowsill or the floor. The articles on and in the teachers' desks were universally regarded as public property, paid for by the parents' tax money.

"Explain it to me, if you can," he said.

"What's going to stop the teacher's gun from getting into the wrong hands?" I asked.

"Keep it locked up."

"Then you couldn't get to it in time."

He stalled, apparently out of ideas. "As long as you're safe, Jennet, that's all that matters."

"Everyone needs to be safe. I'm all right."

Only traumatized. Dreading going back to school tomorrow. Knowing I have to go back and carry on. There's no opting out.

Leonora would understand, as would Jeff and Grimsley. Crane, too, no matter what he said about my leaving Marston.

"Well, that's what I'd do if I made the laws." He said goodbye and rang off.

In Zoller's General Store, I found the assorted teas I wanted for Miss Isabel. The most appealing tin depicted a snowball fight involving four cherubic children and a tricolor collie. I added a decorative shopping bag with jingle bells attached to the handles and drove on to the Spirit Lamp Inn.

Deer Leap Trail looked different on a weekday morning. More desolate and colder.

I should be in school. Teaching my classes, gossiping with Leonora over lunch, fretting about ice on the freeway for the commute home, and complaining about the principal.

Once begun, the images marched on. Denver's drawings, the Christmas concert, the Valentine issue of the school newspaper, the Art Club's holiday decorations, dates made in the hallway and flirtations carried on in the classroom... All shadowed by tragedy, all spoiled because a disgruntled transfer student had brought a gun to class and for no discernible reason killed one of his classmates and wounded another.

Ah, Marston! I could have wept for all we had lost.

~ * ~

By the time I reached the Spirit Lamp Inn, I was depressed myself. That wouldn't do. My mission was to bring Miss Isabel a figurative cup of good cheer. Taking her present out of the back seat, I made my way around snow banks to the front door.

The Inn opened at noon. At eleven thirty, it had a sad, dispirited look even with the freshly painted façade glowing in the morning light. It might have said, *"I may have a bright new look, but don't forget, for many years I had a grave in my back yard."*

Inside were signs of activity: clanging and banging in the kitchen and the hum of a vacuum on the second floor. Nonetheless, the muted sounds couldn't dispel the air of gloom that hung over the Inn like a low snow-filled cloud.

A ghost walks here.

Our quest was the same. Uncover the identity of Cynthia Lauren's killer. Bring him or her to a belated justice. How strange to be working hand and hand with a spirit!

I walked up the stairs to the second floor and rapped softly on Miss Isabel's door. After a few silent moments, she said, "Come in, but I don't want any breakfast."

The bells on the shopping bag jingled as I came through the door. "That's good because I didn't bring you any."

"Oh, Jennet, hello." She made a valiant attempt to banish the look of annoyance from her face. "Come in. Sit down. Mr. Fowler told me about the shooting at your school yesterday. You must be so upset."

"I am. It happened in my classroom."

"Do they know why that boy did it?" she asked.

"Not yet."

"There has to be a motive."

I remembered Leonora's theory. He just wanted to kill somebody. All right. That was a motive.

"As of now, there isn't much to know. The shooter, Joel Carstairs, transferred into my class before Thanksgiving. I didn't know him well. I wonder if he made any friends."

"It was like that with Cynthia all those years ago," Miss Isabel said.

She was gazing out the window. Or gazing into the past?

"What do you mean?" I asked.

"No one ever knew why Cynthia was murdered. Just like with your student."

"Let's talk about something more cheerful," I said. "I brought you a Christmas present."

Her entire countenance brightened. "How lovely!" She took the tin out of the bag and exclaimed over the illustration on the lid. "All these different teas! How wonderful! Eggnog is my favorite. The stuff they serve here tastes like medicine."

I didn't agree, but what would be the point in saying so?

"Well, I hope you enjoy these." I watched as she examined each packet of tea. "Tell me, did you have any ill effects after what happened the night of the party?"

"Nothing worth mentioning. That meddling Marsha Anne. She was always one to raise a fuss."

"We were all worried about you when you weren't in your room," I said.

"I'm not used to having people watch my every move."

I sat back in a soft cream wing chair and surveyed the room. Fresh mint green paint and rugs with purple flowers that looked like pansies. Pastel accents created a restful garden-like retreat. Ivory drapes were half-open to reveal the snow-covered woods across from the Inn. You could have both summer and winter in this room.

There was no television or radio in sight, not even a CD player. Only an electric teakettle on a white console table by the window, sitting next to a silver tea service. I could only hope no spiders lurked in the closet.

Best of all, Miss Isabel wasn't alone up here.

"Do you see much of Ted and Bruce?" I asked.

"Not at all. They usually go out."

It wasn't always that way. I remembered her seeking Bruce out in the dining room. It seemed so long ago. "Would you like to go out now and catch a breath of air?" I asked.

She shuddered. "It's too cold."

It had been colder last night, but I didn't mention it.

"Then I could make you a cup of tea," I said. "Eggnog, if you like."

"I'll have some later."

It was difficult to carry on a conversation with someone who turned every answer into a dead end.

Was she doing it deliberately? Being evasive? I couldn't tell, but it did seem as if she would be happier when I left. Perhaps she was truly depressed and only wanted to be left alone.

She had been willing to talk about the Marston shooting, though, and about Cynthia. Just not about herself. Or was I being overly imaginative again?

I rose, glad I'd kept my coat on. It made leaving more efficient.

"Then I'll come back some weekend when it's warmer and take you out to lunch," I said. "I know a restaurant where the home cooking is beyond belief. Clovers."

"That'll be nice," she said. "Another time. Thank you for the present."

She didn't rise. With the tin of teas opened on her lap, she watched in silence as I walked out of the room.

I had an odd feeling that I'd never see her again.

Forty-nine

Brent was waiting for me in the dining room at a table with a view of the future garden, in other words, the place where Cynthia Lauren's bones had lain for so many decades. He pulled out a chair for me.

"Every time I see this section of the yard, I think about Cynthia," I said. "I wonder if we'll ever know what happened to her."

"In the spring I'm going to have an arbor planted with climbing rose bushes. It'll be a memorial to Cynthia. I think I'll have a stone laid down there, too."

"It won't look so desolate then," I said. "When all the snow is gone and flowers are in bloom."

"What did you think about Miss Isabel?" he asked as he hung my coat on a peg.

Where to start? How much to include?

"She does seem depressed. I asked her to go outside with me for some fresh air, but she said it was too cold."

"That's true enough. Did she say anything on the weird side?"

"She talked about the shooting, then about Cynthia. She seems to be fixated on motives. I consider that natural, given the circumstances."

The room was slowly filling up with diners whose food choices, judging from the contents on passing trays, leaned heavily toward steaming soups, stews, and hot drinks.

We ordered stew, and within minutes a waitress brought water, salads, and rolls to our table.

"As boss, I get special treatment," he said. "You, too, when you're with me."

"About Miss Isabel, what do you consider weird?" I asked.

"Yesterday she was wondering if she could have killed Cynthia and forgotten about it."

I let my fork fall back on the plate. "Good grief."

Not that I hadn't momentarily entertained the idea that Miss Isabel could be guilty of the old crime. Someone else had suggested it. Leonora? Lucy?

It wasn't so far-fetched, now that I thought about it. Many an accused killer claimed he didn't remember pulling the trigger, or spiking the drink with arsenic, or shoving the victim off the cliff.

But if Miss Isabel had killed Cynthia, why had she moved into the Inn? In her place, I'd have stayed as far away as possible. And surely she couldn't have buried the body without help.

"Did she say why she did it?" I asked.

"She couldn't remember that either."

"I wonder what put that idea in her head," I said.

"She's a nutcake?"

"She *does* seem to be disturbed, but thinking you might have killed someone... That's extreme. And why would she confide in you?"

"People trust me," he said. "Maybe she shouldn't be living at the Inn. There's no telling what a crazy woman will do."

"What do her friends think? Bruce, for instance?"

"You're the only person I've told," Brent said. "She told me this in confidence. I guess I shouldn't have said anything, but, hell, it's been bothering me."

"It could be the result of being cooped up inside with this wintry weather we've been having. A severe case of cabin fever. I never heard of it making people think they committed murder, though."

"She should get out more, and I'm not talking about night visits to a grave."

"Former grave, you mean." I picked up my fork and speared a grape tomato. "Miss Isabel appears to be obsessed with Cynthia Lauren's murder. In a sense we all are."

"Speak for yourself, Jennet."

"I think you should talk to Bruce or one of her other friends," I said. "Not Marsha Anne, though. She doesn't seem to like her. See what you can find out about Miss Isabel's past and her relationship with Cynthia."

"You're the detective," he reminded me.

"I hardly know Bruce. He's living in your inn."

"Okay," he said. "I'll do it, next time I see him. But I'm not going to tell him what Miss Isabel said."

"Of course not. There's no point in broadcasting the lady's secret fear. Besides, she told you that in confidence."

"Enough weird talk," Brent said. "Louise makes good stew, doesn't she?"

"Even better than mine."

"I wouldn't go that far."

I fell silent and concentrated on my lunch, occasionally sparing a thought for Miss Isabel. She would be sitting in her room, staring out at the snow scene beyond the window and thinking about an old crime that had taken place on the premises. Alone, which was her choice. Take alone, mix in a touch of cabin fever, and you end up with an unhealthy fantasy.

Could the shooting at my school have sent her mind careening back into the past, changing events to create an imaginary drama around an old mystery?

Possibly. At this point, who could know?

Still, I simply couldn't imagine Miss Isabel as a killer. To me she seemed like a lonely, unhappy woman who needed protection—from herself, perhaps. But I could be wrong.

I wondered if she'd made herself a cup of eggnog tea yet, then wondered what inspired the thought that I might never see her again. Whatever her situation, I was glad I'd taken her a Christmas present.

~ * ~

"School is going to be strange today," Leonora said as we neared the Oakpoint exit the next morning.

Our commute had been relatively easy. There was no snow to turn the freeway into a danger zone, and it was Friday. We'd been discussing the shooting practically non-stop for the past hour and agreed that the District should have closed the school for one more day.

Everything was going to be different, to say nothing of difficult. We were heading to school a half hour early for a brief staff meeting. Then—what should it be? Classes as usual? Grief counselors in the building? A message from the principal with an update on Jessica's condition?

"I imagine a lot of the students will stay home," I said.

"If they want to talk about the shooting, we should let them," Leonora said.

"I agree. Especially in my class. And if they don't?"

"Then we play it by ear."

"Emphasize the good news," I said. "Jessica is improving. We can encourage the kids to write to her. I'll bring in a get well card tomorrow for everyone to sign."

"What if they want to talk about that boy, the shooter?" Leonora said.

"Let them, but discourage speculation. He's in the hands of the law now."

We left the freeway, drove through a small residential area, and passed the local ice cream shop, closed and boarded for the season. All too soon the school came into view, its flag flying at half-mast.

257

Among the many questions vying for attention in my mind, one stood out. Would my fourth period American Literature class still be rowdy?

I found that it didn't matter anymore.

~ * ~

I'd assumed that with our plan in place, we'd be able to cope with the first day back after the shooting. It wasn't to be. The first clue was the parking lot, filled with unfamiliar cars and news vans—and police cruisers. Reporters were interviewing kids and adults. I recognized Coach Adam Barrett talking to a blonde reporter from Channel Four.

Inside, nothing could break through the somber mood that permeated the building. The familiar halls were silent. Footfalls and voices were hushed. Even lockers seemed to close more quietly than usual. But not the bell. It shrieked as I walked to the teachers' lounge after the meeting. Rudely, it pierced the doomsday atmosphere.

We should have a tolling bell, with one ring for each day of Danny's young life.

At the meeting, which was still dispersing, Grimsley had informed us that Jessica was holding her own, that there'd be a candlelight vigil for Danny on Monday and a memorial service on Tuesday. Grief counselors would be at the school all day. A retired police officer, Tim, had joined the staff as a second hall monitor, and visitors would be issued passes. Grimsley planned to address the student body during homeroom.

Effective immediately, Leonora and I were to be moved out of our classrooms, separated by only a sliding partition, to a new location at the west end of the building. This, of course, would result in additional disruption, but we agreed it was for the best.

The first classes were going to be the most awkward. The worst would be American Literature. Once that was over, I hoped the rest of the day would be better.

When the bell rang to begin fourth period, the class entered the new room in a relatively civilized manner with a minimum of comment. Entered. When had I ever used so sedate a verb to describe them? There were some stragglers who claimed they hadn't been able to find the new room, which was probably true.

"Can we sit anywhere we want?" Dale asked, eyeing the different arrangement of rows.

"Anywhere," I said.

They had never been so subdued, not even on the first day of the semester when surroundings and teacher and classmates were new.

I opened my grade book and slowly began listing names on the attendance slip. There was some small comfort in routine.

I'd guessed right about the day's poor attendance. Who could blame anyone for needing more time to mourn?

Katrina's eyes were swollen with tears. Some of the other girls had been crying, seemingly uncaring that tears streaked their make-up.

How could it be business as usual today? Should I continue with the story we'd been about to read when Joel fired his shots? Encourage the class to talk about the incident? Start a new selection, consigning Bret Harte and *The Luck of Roaring Camp* to oblivion?

No, no, and no.

As I looked out on the class and the empty desks, the answer came to me. Writing. I'd remind them of our study of Henry David Thoreau and the journals they had kept for two weeks; then I'd assign a composition. They could record their thoughts on Danny, on violence, on guns—whatever they wanted.

Satisfied that I'd found the perfect plan for the day, I closed the grade book just as Denver sauntered in with an irreverent, "Hi, Teach. Sorry I'm late. My bud, Grimsley, stopped me in the hall."

He dropped an excused pass signed by the principal on my desk. I nearly dropped my pen. In his hand he carried the heavy blue American Literature anthology we used in the course.

Unable to think of a rejoinder, I didn't make any.

Fifty

Days passed, and suddenly it had been a week since the shooting at Marston. Grief counselors, police, reporters, and anxious parents contributed to the continued unreality that permeated the school. I found myself longing for my old classroom with its view of the wooded area and the school life I'd known before. But from the beginning I'd realized that Marston would never be the same again. We all had to adapt.

With the trauma and surprises in my life, I had almost forgotten about the raincoat-clad ghost who wandered the halls of the Spirit Lamp Inn. I supposed ghosts didn't suffer from the cold like we mortals do. Most likely because they were already cold.

I was halfway home from grocery shopping one day when I realized that the last time we spoke, neither Brent nor I had mentioned Rachel, who should have been part of our conversation. If, by chance, Miss Isabel had murdered Cynthia, wouldn't Rachel haunt her instead of me?

Did this mean that Rachel was confused or Miss Isabel was innocent? Or had Miss Isabel seen the ghost and neglected to tell anyone? That was possible. Looking back, I realized that Miss Isabel had changed since I'd met her. The charming elderly tenant of the Inn had become reclusive and strange. What had caused this transformation? And when did it begin?

With the sighting of an apparition?

I moved smoothly from Miss Isabel to motives. Why had Cynthia been killed? Why did anyone kill? Take Joel Carstairs, for example, shooting into the class without an apparent target. If Denver Armstrong hadn't overpowered him, would Marston have had more victims to mourn?

Would I be one of them?

Possibly Carstairs had hoped to gain a reputation for himself, but I noticed people either didn't want to say his name, or they couldn't remember it. They usually called him "that boy" or "the shooter."

As for Denver...he was a true enigma. An insolent ne'er-do-well turned hero. He had handed in his first paper, his composition on the shooting. Not forsaking art work entirely, he had sketched a weeping snowman on top of the page.

At the end of that first class, he'd hurled a parting request at me. "Tell us when we don't need our book, Teach. It weighs a ton."

"We'll use it tomorrow," I said.

On that day I'd returned to our survey of American Literature. I dared to look into the future. Eventually the student body would begin to heal. Jessica's condition would be further upgraded. Everything in my world would be reasonably well again.

Taking note of my location, I saw that I was alone on the road and the lanes were clear, enabling me to return to a contemplation of murder and motives and ghosts.

Joel Carstairs wasn't my problem anymore. He had passed into the care of his lawyer and the court. Cynthia Lauren, however, was my concern because I'd undertaken to solve the old case and also wanted to help Miss Isabel attain peace of mind—unless she really was Cynthia's killer. Even then. If Miss Isabel were guilty, there must have been extenuating circumstances.

Then there was Rachel, the ghost. I hoped one day she'd finally rest in peace, for as pleasant a place as the Spirit Lamp Inn was, I was sure no one wanted to spend eternity walking up and down its halls.

My mind raced ahead to spring and the rose garden Brent planned as a memorial for Cynthia. How lovely it would be. How much better to think of dreams than bones when wandering in the garden. I could almost see it. A commemorative stone glistening in the shade of the arbor, the rich fragrance of roses carried on the breeze, the blessed warmth of spring sunshine.

Sunlight and tranquility and... What was that? Snowflakes hitting the windshield, snow powdering the lane. We had a long wait for that glorious season, but at the moment I was about to turn onto Jonquil Lane.

~ * ~

Crane and Brent and I sat around the fire the next evening rehashing the cold case and talking about Miss Isabel. Misty, her toy goat in her mouth and a hopeful look in her eye. had settled herself happily near Brent while Sky and Halley lay at his feet lost in contented slumber.

"Bruce says Miss Isabel always was a bit unusual, even as a young girl," Brent said.

Crane leaned forward in his chair. "In what ways?"

"She liked to travel alone. She was quiet, and she had a crush on him. He never gave her the time of day."

I bristled at the arrogance of the man. "Bruce said that? What a jerk!"

I stared into the flames leaping to life in the fireplace, scenting the air with apple wood. The collies loved to lie by the fire, too close, in my view. But coax them away and before long they were back again. Well, they'd learn if they singed their fur.

I pulled my mind back to the conversation. Miss Isabel as a young girl. In my mind she looked the same as she did today, except her hair was brown and glossy.

"That doesn't sound strange to me," I said.

Before my marriage, I liked to travel alone. Some people would consider me quiet, but not those who knew me well. I was only too happy to share my thoughts, especially about mysteries. As to crushes? I suppose you could say I'd had a crush on Crane, but it had quickly turned into a serious relationship. Before Crane? That handsome blond star on a television western, long since departed, both the show and the actor. What was his name again?

"The way Miss Isabel's acting lately just isn't normal," Brent said.

"What did you find out about Miss Isabel and Cynthia?" I asked.

"They were friends in Oakpoint years ago. Bruce doesn't know how they met. He doesn't think they were particularly close. It was always Cynthia and Rachel—and Marsha Anne. Miss Isabel was a hanger-on."

"And yet she pretended not to know them at the Halloween party," I said. "I thought she was meeting them for the first time that night."

Brent nodded. "Like Bruce said, she's a strange woman."

"Has Miss Isabel done anything else odd?" I asked.

"As far as I know, she hasn't left her room. God knows what she does all day without any electronics. She doesn't order breakfast and just nibbles at lunch and dinner. She complains that all the food is cold. Well, the trays have to travel up from the kitchen. Stuff is bound to cool off."

"It sounds to me like she's hiding," Crane said.

"That's likely." I thought of ghosts and cold again. Did even food lose its warmth when it came into contact with Miss Isabel? "Hiding from what, I wonder?"

"The ghost," Brent suggested.

"Maybe from Bruce," I said. "For two old acquaintances living in the same inn, they don't seem especially chummy."

"Remember I said he wasn't interested in her when she was young. Why would he be now that she's old?"

"He's old too, for heavens' sake."

"She could be hiding from the winter weather?" That was Crane again. "Lots of winter people hibernate when it's this cold. Or they fly south."

"I don't like it," Brent said.

"Well…" I didn't either. "Keep an eye on her, Brent."

He promised to do so. "I have a funny feeling about Miss Isabel," he said. "It's like one of those premonitions Lucy's always talking about. Something bad is going to happen, and it's going to involve her."

He couldn't possibly have surprised me more. I'm sure some men had premonitions, but Brent had usually scoffed at even the hint of the supernatural. That is until the haunted painting had slammed his life off course.

I for one intended to take his feeling seriously.

~ * ~

The next day after school, I settled back with a cup of hot chocolate and the paper. The current edition of the *Banner* was filled with tales of violence. Senseless rage, reckless acts, ghastly accidents, and murder. All had transpired during the night or early this morning.

A carjacking, a middle school boy who'd brought a gun to school, possibly in imitation of Joel Carstairs, a motorist driving the wrong way on a freeway, and a man shot to death in his own back yard in Oakpoint. Alex Blaine. Something about his name tugged at me. Was he someone I knew or had known? A board member or parent perhaps?

I tried to make a connection as I flipped to the *Home & Life* section, tried and failed and almost gave up. Then it surfaced from the deepest recesses of my mind. Alex Blaine was Deanna Reid's former boyfriend, the man who had surrendered her collie, Sparrow, to the Rescue League without Deanna's knowledge.

Now he was dead, shot once and left to freeze in the plummeting night temperatures.

The police were investigating the shooting as a homicide, but at present they had no witnesses, no clues. They were asking for help from anybody who had information about the crime.

She wouldn't.

But she had stated in clear bell tones that Blaine was going to pay for hurting Sparrow. After all, revenge was a time-honored motive for murder, and Deanna, too, was a little strange, unwilling to be content with having found Sparrow and brought her home.

Maybe she would.

Now, what should I do with this information?

Fifty-one

"Nothing," Annica said.

That was the conclusion I'd reached after discussing the matter with Crane, but I wanted Annica's opinion as well.

She unloaded the tray, two cups of coffee and two pieces of chocolate meringue pie, my favorite. So what if I spoiled my appetite for the dinner I hadn't cooked yet? 'Live dangerously' was my new motto.

"It isn't like she told you she was going to shoot the guy," Annica said. "Lots of people talk about revenge. If they meant it, there'd be millions of corpses cluttering up the landscape."

The picture of those dead bodies stacked from ground to sky made me smile. Not that there was anything humorous about mass murder. It was just Annica's way, expressing herself in the most gruesome manner possible.

"You can't accuse her of murder," she added.

"I never intended to."

"Or set the cops on her trail, not with what you have. She might have been talking about Karma—the harm you do to others coming back to you."

"You're right, and the police may find their way to her on their own. If I were in charge of the investigation, I'd want to know if the victim had any enemies. A vengeful angry ex-girlfriend would be a red flag. Sooner or later they'll find out what he did to Sparrow."

"So you don't have to do anything. Don't you have enough on your plate already with a crazy student and Miss Isabel?"

"I have pie on my plate, and it's delicious." Amazing how a fantastic dessert could make the day seem brighter.

"The school is almost back to normal," I said. "The Christmas activities help, and for some reason the boy who disarmed the shooter has turned over a new leaf. He's handing in assignments. The class he's in is acting almost civilized."

"Then all we have to worry about is Miss Isabel. Do you really think she killed Cynthia?"

"I didn't say that. Brent does."

"But you don't?"

"No, and I can't figure out why she told him she might have done it."

"Because deep down she wanted to?"

A figurative light came on.

"That could explain it. Hidden hostility emerging. An unthinkable act blocked out. But how could she manage to dispatch Cynthia in so short a time with other people at the Inn coming and going? And could a woman have buried the body without help?"

"It's a mystery, all right. The killer was very lucky."

I paused to ponder the unanswerable. "If only we could hear the story from someone who was on the scene."

"Go back in time! Yeah!"

That brought us back to Miss Isabel. She might have the truth buried in her head with the secret hostility.

I'd have to arrange to visit her again.

~ * ~

A plain white envelope without a return address was waiting for me at home. At first I thought it was deceptive advertising, the kind that seems to be a card from a friend but is really an announcement of a sale or a request for money. I didn't recognize the handwriting.

I tore it open, prepared to toss it in the wastepaper basket with the other discards. But it was a personal note, an invitation from Miss Isabel:

Please come to tea tomorrow afternoon at 4:00 o'clock. I'll order pastries from the kitchen, and we'll break into the Christmas tin you so kindly gave me. I'll be looking forward to seeing you.

I set the note down, wondering if I should go. Tomorrow was a school day, after which I had dogs to walk, dinner to cook, and at least a dozen household chores I should do. Afternoon teas were for the leisurely, not a busy teacher. They went along with floaty party dresses and hats and three-tier plates of delicacies.

Besides, I found the wording of the invitation confusing. It sounded like a summons, as if Miss Isabel had no doubt I would accept.

Or she could simply want to express her gratitude for the Christmas present. Still there was that wording. *Please come...* Well, she *did* say please.

I did a bit of quick planning. I'd have to check with Crane, but I had a casserole in the freezer, and I'd make it a brief visit, perhaps an hour and a half, including travel time.

In a sense the invitation was fortuitous, if slightly inconvenient and imperious. I'd wanted to see Miss Isabel again. Perhaps she was ready to talk about the past.

~ * ~

Against a backdrop of dark evergreens and drifted snow, the Spirit Lamp Inn sparkled in the late afternoon sunshine. It reminded me of a fairy tale castle with its graceful lines and Victorian embellishments. Brent had chosen his color well: creamy white with green accents.

It was indeed a newly-envisioned place, one that had left its dark history behind.

Almost.

As I made my way cautiously over the ice-patched surface of the parking lot, my gaze shifted to the section of yard in which Cynthia Lauren's bones had been discovered.

I wished I hadn't looked. I wished I could have walked blithely up to the Inn with never a thought of death.

On the porch, I pushed open the door. The hostess' station was empty. In the dining room, every table in my view was set with snowy linens and shining table wares. Low conversational murmurs from unseen diners drifted through the door.

It was still early, not quite four. I didn't encounter a single soul as I walked down the hall to the stairway. Would Brent come to the Inn this evening, I wondered? Sometimes he liked to have his dinner in his own Inn, so enamored was he of Louise's cooking.

I'd probably see him on my way out.

I climbed the stairs, leaving what little sound there was behind. When I reached the second level, I stopped and surveyed the hall, every inch of it, just to assure myself that no blue mist lurked in the corners.

I couldn't imagine how Miss Isabel could live happily in the semi-solitude of an inn. It would be different if all the rooms on this floor were tenanted, if she shared the space with cordial companions, if a ghost had never haunted the Inn. Then living here might even be fun with all the comforts of home and none of the work.

Coming to her room, I rapped softly on the door and waited, suddenly becoming aware of the deep silence. I didn't hear a sound on the other side. I waited a few minutes, then knocked again louder.

Surely she was expecting me. Four o'clock today. It had been her idea, the date and time of her choosing.

Finally I raised my voice. "Miss Isabel? It's Jennet. Are you there?"

More silence.

Could she have meant our tea to take place in the dining room? I couldn't remember the exact wording of her note.

Maybe.

Maybe I had assumed we'd meet in her room since, according to Brent, she hadn't left it in days.

I knocked again.

It was no use. It was also ten minutes past the hour.

Better check the dining room, I told myself and descended the stairs a little more rapidly than I'd moved on the way up.

The hostess had arrived at her station. She was another redhead clad in black, pretty but without Annica's sparkle. She looked a little flustered as if she had just walked in the door.

"Table for one?" she asked with a distracted smile, looking over my shoulder.

"I'm not sure," I said. "That is, I was supposed to meet a friend here. Maybe she's in the dining room."

"A lady alone? I don't think so. We have a few family parties."

Nevertheless I peered inside. Miss Isabel wasn't there. Neither was Brent. A faint sense of wrongness flickered to life like a newly-lit candle.

Could she have gone out on some errand? Lost track of time?

I glanced at my watch. Ten more minutes had passed. Was it time to worry about her?

If it were anyone but Miss Isabel, I would be thinking of an unavoidable delay. I could check to see if her car, that vintage yellow and white Plymouth, was in the special parking area behind the Inn.

You're too late, my trusted inner voice said. *She's gone.*

But Miss Isabel was expecting me. She wouldn't have left the Inn. The water in the electric teakettle should be boiling, the pastries ordered from the kitchen, set out on a tray alongside the tin opened with its enticing variety of teas on display.

Eggnog was her favorite.

It was four-thirty.

Something must have happened to detain her. I was afraid to think what it could be.

Fifty-two

"Do you know if Mister Fowler is coming to the Inn for dinner tonight?" I asked.

The red-haired hostess glanced into the dining room which had filled up in the last half hour. "Mr. Fowler doesn't let us know his plans. Did you find your friend?"

"Not yet," I said.

I couldn't stay at the Inn much longer, but how could I leave, without knowing where Miss Isabel had gone?

I'd simply have to find her.

"I'll check his office," I said and left before she could raise an objection.

Once again I stood in a silent, deserted hall knocking at a closed door. Once again a door remained closed, guarding its secrets. Apparently this was one of the nights when Brent was dining at Clovers or the Hunt Club Inn, his two favorite haunts.

What now?

See if Miss Isabel's vintage Plymouth was in the lot and alert Brent to her absence. Especially if the car was still there. Because if it was, that meant she had never left the Inn.

Another woman goes missing at the Spirit Lamp Inn. Ironically, she was acquainted with the woman who disappeared from the same establishment several decades ago. That woman met with a tragic end.

I could almost see the story splashed across the front page of the *Banner*.

No. That was taking irony too far. Nonetheless, an eerie sense of *déjà vu* tugged at me.

Déjà vu is always eerie.

I left a message on Brent's voice mail and felt a little better about leaving the Inn. Driving in the dark on country roads that might be growing slick as the temperatures dropped was taking a chance. Crane and the collies depended on me. Still, I wasn't ready to go home yet.

I realized I'd been looking forward to a cup of hot tea and Louise's homemade pastries, not to mention the chance to have a private visit with Miss Isabel.

I'd have to leave with my curiosity unsatisfied. Why had Miss Isabel issued that strangely-worded invitation? More important, what happened to her? Where was she now?

I remembered the last time Miss Isabel had vanished on the night of Brent's birthday celebration. We'd found her shivering at the site of the former grave.

History repeats itself.

Look outside, I told myself.

I backtracked to the Inn's front door. From the shelter of the porch, I peered around the side of the Inn. The erstwhile gravesite glistened in the fading light with nothing to distinguish it from the rest of the property. No dark figure kept a lonely vigil in the snow. I walked to the other side of the porch and saw her car lightly dusted in white.

She was still here then; she had to be.

But where?

All right. There was something else about that night. Marsha Anne and Catherine had found the door to Miss Isabel's room unlocked. Maybe she was in the habit of going out without locking the door.

It was worth a try.

Back inside, I nodded to the hostess and ascended the stairs once more, hurried to Miss Isabel's room, and rapped on the door.

There was no answer; I didn't expect one. Holding my breath, I turned the doorknob. The door opened easily.

A quick look told me that Miss Isabel had indeed planned to invite me to tea: the electric tea kettle on the small table, tarts arranged on a silver tray, and the silver service with a newly-acquired shine in the light of a Tiffany table lamp. The tin was open. Several missing packets told me that she had already sampled the tea.

"Miss Isabel?"

I thought I was speaking loudly. My voice was a croak, strange and unfamiliar in the silent room and my throat was dry. Oh, for a cup of tea!

As there was no answer, I set about making a thorough search of the entire suite of rooms, including the closet and the enormous armoire, half dreading to find her body crammed into an out-of-sight hiding place.

She wasn't there, and that was good, but on the nightstand a glint of silver caught my attention. It was jewelry, a small silver heart. Wait a minute! It was *the* heart, the one that Brent's painter found in a closet, the one suspected of being part of the charm bracelet.

The traveling heart.

Brent had misplaced it, found it again, and put it in his desk drawer where, presumably, no one would find it.

What was it doing on Miss Isabel's nightstand?

Don't jump to conclusions, I told myself. *The world is full of hearts—silver, gold, crystal, plain, encrusted with precious stones.*

I had a crystal heart myself.

Was this the same one that Brent's painter had found? It seemed a trifle larger than the other. It was impossible to tell without having the two of them together.

Assuming it was the same heart, though, it opened the door to a range of possibilities, none of them palatable.

Dear Lord, maybe she *was* the killer? Or, almost as bad, out of her mind?

Without thinking, I slipped the charm into my pocket. It wasn't stealing, not exactly. This was evidence. And when I found Miss Isabel, I'd give it back to her, together with an explanation.

None of this answered the crucial question. Where was she now?

As I passed the silver tray, I succumbed to temptation, helping myself to one of the tiny strawberry tarts that had been set out for our tea. Surprisingly in spite of my angst, it tasted good.

Quietly I closed the door and went back downstairs, thinking and planning my next step.

Could someone other than Miss Isabel have penned the invitation as a lure? Someone who wanted me to walk into a trap? I'd never seen her handwriting.

The thought stopped me cold, but on closer examination, it didn't hold up. I'd showed up at the Inn, gone twice to Miss Isabel's room, stayed there for perhaps fifteen minutes, and nothing had happened.

It's something else then. Something sinister.

I remembered my inexplicable feeling that I might never see Miss Isabel again. At the same time I recalled Brent's unusual premonition of disaster involving Miss Isabel.

Why didn't he answer his phone?

More to the point, why was I still here?

~ * ~

It was five o'clock. Time to be heading home or Crane would worry about me. The darkness would fall rapidly; the roads would be iced-over. If I didn't leave soon, I'd have a nerve-wracking drive home.

Again I descended the stairs and walked into a hub of activity. A couple with three noisy young children in tow was leaving the dining room. Others waited to be seated, chatting loudly. Although I knew it would be fruitless, I surveyed the tables once again. Nowhere did I see Miss Isabel or any lady dining alone.

How about a man and woman sitting together at a table? Isabel and Bruce?

No. But Bruce? Suppose Miss Isabel was in his room?

I couldn't imagine why she would be there on a day when she was expecting company, but that too was worth a try. I wished I'd thought of it when I was on the second floor. Anyone would think I was demented, going up and down the stairs.

I remembered hearing that Bruce's room was at the end of the hall, on the right, close enough to Miss Isabel's suite to offer the illusion of company, but not near enough to be intrusive.

Holding fast to the certainty that Miss Isabel had to be someplace in the Inn, I reached the top of the staircase and started down the second story hall.

Fifty-three

The air was different on the second story. I could have sworn it was thinner and colder, perhaps charged with electricity or something similar. Although I couldn't describe it adequately, I felt it. I took a deep breath. Yes, it was definitely different.

Strange not to have noticed the disturbance in the air when I was up here before since it had only been about fifteen minutes ago.

Maybe not so strange.

This was a new difference, as was the sensation that this time I wasn't alone in the hall. From behind one of the closed doors came a barely perceptible hum. Somebody was running a vacuum cleaner or some other kind of machine. To my knowledge, Brent only had three permanent tenants, Miss Isabel, Ted, and Bruce.

Bruce might be in his room then, perhaps with Miss Isabel. My spirits soared. I had only to knock on his door to find Miss Isabel and hear my elusive explanation for her absence.

Or was this another dead end?

Now that I thought of it, it didn't sound as if the hum originated in one of the rooms. It was all around me and so muted that I wondered if it was in my mind. There was another possibility.

The ghost is near. Any minute the blue mist will form and Rachel will materialize.

I waited.

I could almost see her, buttoned into her blue raincoat, the hood covering straight dark hair. She seemed unaware of the mist that swirled around her feet and lower body. She looked as if she had just come inside after walking a long distance in the rain.

Did she walk up and down this hall forever, except for the times she haunted the area outside the Inn? What a grim way to spend eternity! How unbearably boring! Being confined in death to one small space was more hellish than anything I could ever have imagined.

A minute ticked by. I stared down the hall—at nothing. The ghost wasn't there. Either she had never appeared or she had come and gone in the blink of the proverbial eye.

I *did* have a penchant for seeing ghosts, especially when I expected to see one.

Abruptly I reined in my fanciful flight. Almost isn't seeing. In actuality, I was alone. There wasn't so much as a wisp of mist forming and certainly no nebulous lady in a blue raincoat.

But what about the hum?

I listened. There was no hum now, only the sound of my footfalls and breathing, but the air still wasn't right. It was as if somebody had turned on an air conditioner, and I was receiving its full blast. I was thoroughly chilled and only vaguely aware of why I was walking down the hall in the Spirit Lamp Inn in the first place.

All in the space of five minutes.

~ * ~

Back in the real world, I started walking again. I was glad I hadn't seen the ghost. Good heavens. With Miss Isabel missing, I had enough going on without adding a visitor from beyond to the mix.

What about the other times?

They were different. Real. Today I had been treated to the prelude but the actual materialization had never happened. That didn't mean the ghost wasn't near.

Impatient with my roving imagination, I noted the brass numbers on the doors; they looked new and shiny. Bruce, I recalled, was staying in Suite Seven. I knocked, not really expecting to find him in his room and probably not Miss Isabel either. This was one stone, however, that I couldn't leave unturned.

I wasn't surprised when the door didn't open.

Now leave, I told myself.

But first, knock again to be absolutely sure. Go back down the stairs one last time before you find yourself in a horror story, trapped in the Inn, doomed to travel up and down the stairs for all eternity.

Like a ghost.

As I walked to the top of the staircase, a perverse imp threw a thought my way. There was another last stone, one place left to look. The most likely place to find Miss Isabel alive or dead was the attic.

I'd purposely avoided thinking of the attic for obvious reasons. In that way danger lay. The treacherous floor that had tripped Annica. The stacks of boxes casting grotesquely shaped and restless shadows. The sensation of an invisible watcher waiting for an interloper to take one false step. Possibly causing it.

Stay out of the attic!

This was Brent's property. He could explore every square inch of every level of it to his heart's content. He could bring in the police to help him, if he liked.

For once in my life, I was going to do the smart thing. Go home.

~ * ~

If there was any hum in the Inn, it originated in the dining room where all the tables appeared to be filled and every guest seemed to be talking at once. I glanced in, hoping against hope to see Miss Isabel in a bright pink dress sitting at a table with Bruce.

They weren't there.

Out on the porch, the cold air tried its best to shove me back to the relative security of the heavy door. Dislodged by the wind, a smattering of icy snowflakes tumbled from the overhang. Icicles hung low to the ground, gigantic thick cones with pointed ends, powerful enough to take a victim out of this world.

Behind me a voice shrilled into the wind.

"Oh, Mrs. Ferguson? Jennet?"

I whirled around. The hostess had followed me outside. Shivering in the thin folds of her long black dress, she waved a paper at me.

"Are you Mrs. Ferguson?" she asked, catching her breath.

I nodded.

"I almost forgot to give you this. A message."

She thrust a sheet of fine stationery at me. It had a floral fragrance that managed to be unpleasant. She beckoned me back through the doorway, and we stood together in a wash of air, heat combined with cold in an uneasy mix.

"It's from the friend you were looking for, I think. She said to be sure and give it to you as soon as I saw you."

Miss Isabel! At last!

"When?" I asked.

"Just a few minutes ago."

I unfolded it eagerly, recognizing the handwriting. It read:

Sorry to have been detained, Jennet. It was unavoidable. I'll explain later. I hope you're still at the Inn and we can finally have our tea."

I recognized the imperious tone, too.

"Did she say anything else?" I asked.

"Just that she'd be in Room Three, waiting."

"Did she seem all right?"

"Near as I could tell."

"Well..." I pushed my jacket sleeve up and glanced at my watch. It was almost six o'clock. Should I obey the summons or ignore it, pretend I'd never received it? It was, after all, two hours later than our agreed-on time.

I didn't want to go back up to that spooky second floor again. On the other hand, I wanted to know the reason for the great runaround I'd just lived through. I could spare a few minutes for an explanation, an apology, and a sip of hot tea. Then I'd be on my way, late but moving in the right direction.

I shoved the note into my pocket and hurried back to the staircase.

Fifty-four

The door to Room Three was slightly ajar. Soft light streamed out into the hall, making the space seem less daunting. I rapped and gave the door a gentle push.

"Miss Isabel?"

The table came into view, glowing in lamplight, the strawberry tarts—minus one—neatly arranged on the silver tray. All inviting, all welcoming.

I stood just inside the door, scanning the room. "Miss Isabel? Where are you? It's Jennet."

Something slammed into my back, pitching me forward onto the hardwood floor.

In the instant before the world turned black, I saw a splash of hot pink that could have been Miss Isabel's favorite silk blouse.

She wasn't wearing it.

~ * ~

I lay in a cold, dark place, with my head on a hard object. Wood? A board? My head... I tried to raise it. Oh, no. What happened? My head felt as if it were coming apart. I'd been hit by a door?

Not likely. A great pounding at the top of my skull and behind my eyes forced me down again. I felt sick and broken.

Somebody had hit me. Not the door. Somebody. Miss Isabel. She must have been waiting for me in the shadows of the hall or in the room beyond the door.

I closed my eyes.

Maybe this is a dream.

Pain followed me, a relentless pursuer.

~ * ~

I was conscious again, cold and still in pain but able to think more clearly. Had I fallen on my head or had my assailant struck me after the fall? Both?

My fleeting vision of a pink blouse swam into my mind.

Miss Isabel. She set her trap with strawberry tarts and I walked right into it. Stupid, stupid, stupid, stupid!

But why? She liked me. Brent had told me so. I'd given her a Christmas present. It didn't make sense.

Why bother to search for a motive? Miss Isabel was crazy. Brent had said that, too.

Even a crazy person has a motive.

Facts tumbled around in my head, the obvious mixing with the maybes and the unknowns.

Miss Isabel was Cynthia's killer. She had as good as confessed the crime to Brent. And forget that nonsense about not being sure she'd done it.

I had made excuses for her, sympathized with her, accepted her invitation to tea when it would have been so easy to decline. Good lord! I'd believed that note, too!

What a fool I was!

I was still at the Inn then. In the attic, I'd guess, from the cold air and the musty odor. It was night time. After six o'clock, anyway. The dining room would still be open. I felt along my wrist until I reached my watch. Seeing the time in the dark was hopeless.

But I detected a grain of hope.

Crane would miss me. He'd know where I'd gone and be on my trail with reinforcements.

The red-haired hostess would remember giving me the message. She had watched me walk to the staircase, presumably en route to Room Three.

Unless she was in on it.

But I wouldn't be there. I wondered if Miss Isabel was sitting in her chair with the water boiling in the tea kettle. She'd claim I'd never arrived. *"I can't imagine what happened to her,"* she would say. *"One just doesn't disappear between floors.'*

Cynthia Lauren did.

Crane would never accept that as an answer. He knew Brent's opinion of Miss Isabel's mental state. He knew everything I did.

Brent would check his messages. Sooner or later. It depended on what he was doing tonight.

Tonight. My heart sank.

When the last customer paid his bill and left the dining room, when the hostess and wait staff and Louise went home, I'd be alone in the Inn. Except for Ted and Bruce, possibly, and Miss Isabel, killer.

With no cell phone, no food... I should have grabbed a handful of tarts.

I didn't have my purse. Where was it now? I had a pen that doubled as a flashlight. With my cell phone I could have dialed nine-one-one.

I couldn't stop berating myself. I'd made all the wrong choices. Now...

Now was an endless expanse of uncertainty, bound to end badly. I would be like Rachel who was doomed to haunt the second floor hall of the Spirit Lamp Inn for all time. My haunt would be the attic.

If only the pain would stop. I pushed my hair back and touched my forehead gently, willed the pain away. That never worked. If only I had a pill and a glass of water to help it along...

I had nothing except my wool coat to protect me against the attic's deadly chill and a watch. But no light. The pain was quickly draining my strength and my will to fight.

I was going to die in the attic of the Spirit Lamp Inn without ever knowing why.

~ * ~

The dream came, a happy dream painted in pastel colors. It was full of light. A golden sun shone high in a pale blue sky. Clouds, the puffy white kind, floated lazily from east to west, and green grass went on forever in a rolling meadow starred with wildflowers.

Halley came bounding across the rolling fields. Her black fur blew in the gentlest of breezes, her ears lay flat against the side of her head, and the famous collie smile radiated on her face. With a joyous yelp, she threw herself into my arms.

I hugged her, crushed her head to my breast, breathed in the familiar scent of her. My dog.

Hold fast to her, and it'll be all right.

The dream was so enchanting, so comforting, I never wanted to leave. Not only because it was my own vision of Paradise but because the pain couldn't touch me there.

~ * ~

It was waiting for me when I opened my eyes.

Something had awakened me, some muffled sound I was certain hadn't been part of the dream.

It was quiet in the attic now. Dark and silent. Like a tomb.

Don't create morbid comparisons, I told myself.

I was in the attic of the Spirit Lamp Inn, not yet a tomb, and the faintest sliver of light made its way through the ventilation slats, cast by the lamppost, I imagined, or the moon.

There was the sound again. A moan. Close. Dear Lord, I wasn't alone.

I tried again to raise my head and found that it was possible. Now to sit up. Now off the floor.

I stood shakily, tried to ignore the pain in my head, and moved my hand gingerly into the darkness.

It encountered a gritty surface. A box wrapped in brown paper, and the coarse thread that tied it. No surprise. The attic was crammed with boxes.

Encouraged I took a careful step forward, remembering the unfinished floor.

Where was I? Near the attic's entrance? If so, there was more than a grain of hope. I could be my own savior.

It wasn't locked. I could raise the panel that blocked off the attic from the rest of the Inn.

From the inside? Could I? If so, I could lift it and walk down the stairs to the second floor, past the dangerous Room Three, past the dining room, and out the door.

But my missing purse... My cell phone. My car keys.

The Inn must have a land-line phone unless Brent had had it removed.

I walked forward, colliding with more boxes, and stepped into a depression between the boards.

You'll never find the way out.

It wouldn't be easy, but I'd keep trying. Anything was better than lying on the floor, drifting in and out of consciousness.

Turning, I stumbled over an object where I didn't expect anything to be. Flailing wildly, I caught myself before tumbling forward.

Curious, I knelt to see what had almost sent me falling for a second time. My hand closed on a hard cold object with a boxy shape.

Could it be...?

One of the lantern flashlights that Brent had supplied for our attic explorations. One of us had left it behind!

Thank God! With light I had a chance. I pressed the *on* button and winked as the attic burst into brightness.

Fifty-five

I shone the lantern on my watch. It was eight-thirty. How could that be? It felt as if long hours had passed since I'd set out to answer Miss Isabel's second summons.

My situation wasn't as dire as I'd thought. It wasn't the middle of the night. People in the dining room still lingered over their meals, with no idea of the drama that had played out on the floor above, no inkling that I was a prisoner in the attic.

I moved the lantern flashlight slowly back and forth. Its beam illuminated stacks of boxes and more stacks. I might have been miniaturized and trapped in a forest of boxes with a wood sky pressing down on me.

A barely audible moan followed by a sinister creaking almost stopped my heart. I'd forgotten about the noise, proof that I wasn't alone in the attic. Possibly the person who moaned was in a similar shape, wounded but still able to function to a degree.

Someone who moans doesn't pose a threat.

Over a makeshift aisle between towering boxes, I stepped carefully, praying that I wouldn't trip in the treacherous spaces between the boards. Past lamps without shades, broken chairs, a hall mirror whose glass was cracked, an ironing board, steamer trunks...

She lay on her side on the jagged floor, one arm bent under her head for a pillow. Her blouse, an incongruous hot pink color, sprang to life beneath my flashlight beam. The luxuriant material was wrinkled and streaked with dirt and cobwebs. She was as still as any object carted up to the attic to hide away out of sight.

Dead?

Dead people don't moan.

I wasn't alone! I came closer.

Miss Isabel wasn't my assailant. An elderly, frail woman couldn't have carried me up the stairs to the attic. A man could have done it with ease. I should have realized that earlier. The fall or the blow on the head must have scrambled my brains.

That left Ted or Bruce, or some unknown lurking in the Inn, perhaps even in the dining room, in plain view.

Bruce. I preferred to deal with the devil I knew. But how well did I know him? Not at all.

As for Miss Isabel, she was a victim too. With two of us, we had a double chance of escaping our prison in one piece.

Setting the lantern on the floor, I knelt beside her. Her pulse was strong, but her wrist was cold. If she'd been assaulted, she bore no apparent sign of it. But then I supposed I didn't either.

I kept my hand on her wrist, although I longed to pull it away. It was like touching an ice cube.

"Miss Isabel?" I waited and said her name again.

Minutes passed. Weak light washed across her face, highlighting every fine line and her faded pink lipstick. Finally her eyes fluttered open.

"Jennet? You *did* come. I was beginning to worry about you. I had the strangest dream. I dreamed I was a girl again..."

"That must have been pleasant."

I wanted to help her up, support her as we made our way to the panel that served as the attic's entrance and exit, as we went back down the stairs... Just as I'd envisioned it before I knew I wasn't alone. Freedom was at hand.

My trusted inner voice whispered that we had to hurry.

Miss Isabel was shivering. "I'm so cold. Why is it always so cold in this room? "

In her mind she was back in her suite. She had a way to go before she reached lucidity.

"Because the ghost is near," I said.

"What ghost?"

She struggled to sit up, as I had, and lay back down.

"The Lady in the Blue Raincoat."

"Oh, her. Yes, I think she is. Jennet, would you be a dear and make the tea? The water's boiling. I should have had the tea ready, but I was waiting for you."

"Soon," I said. "We have to get out of here, Miss Isabel. There'll be time for tea later."

She appeared to hear me, but her response wasn't what I expected.

"I'm so cold," she said. "So cold."

Well, so was I, but I was younger than Miss Isabel by several decades, and wearing a turtleneck sweater. I shrugged out of my coat.

"Here, this should help," I said. "What happened to you?"

"Happened? I saw what happened. I remembered. After all these years. How could I forget?"

"What did you see?"

"Cynthia. He killed her. He put his hands around her neck and strangled her."

"Who did this?"

"Bruce," she said.

I knew it! He was the enemy, and chances were he was still in the Inn.

"Or Ted," she added. "What does it matter who did it? She was dead. Jennet, can't we have our tea now? The tarts are still warm. Louise made them with fresh strawberries. I don't know where she found them at this time of year."

Miss Isabel's eyes were focused on something or someone behind me. Alarmed, although I hadn't heard a sound, I followed her gaze.

She was looking at a motley collection of lamps and clocks pushed together on top of a small dresser.

Hurry! You can't afford to linger in her fantasy.

"Do you think you can stand?" I asked.

"No, not yet. My back hurts so. It's this freezing temperature. Mr. Fowler keeps the Inn too cold. It's fine for him. He's young and healthy. But when you're old like I am... I'd feel better if I had a cup of tea."

"All right," I said.

It seemed I didn't have a confederate after all.

~ * ~

If my brains were scrambled, Miss Isabel's were pureed.

How much faith should I place in her revelation? Assuming there were threads of truth woven into her story, she'd seen Cynthia strangled, subsequently forgotten about it, then suddenly remembered everything—while unaware that she had been dumped in the attic.

Miss Isabel saw an electric tea kettle filled with boiling water and strawberry tarts. I saw danger and the probable reason for our dilemma. Presumably she could identify Cynthia's killer, and the killer assumed she'd confided in me. Well, he was right. She'd done that. Bruce—or Ted. She and I were both obstacles to be removed.

What was his plan? To come back and kill us? Keep our bodies in the attic until he could dispose of them? Why hadn't he killed us already? That would have been more efficient.

Just be glad he didn't. And hurry.

The hour hand was racing up to nine. Once the dining room closed... I didn't want to complete the thought.

"Where's the land-line phone in the Inn, Miss Isabel?" I asked.

"In the kitchen. Why?"

"Can you stay alone for just a little while?"

I didn't like to leave her, but she wouldn't be able to come with me. That was okay. I had a better chance to escape and get help for us both if I went alone.

"I can," she said. "I've been here before, looking. Always looking…"

So now she knew where she was.

"I'll bring help," I said. "You rest here. I'll leave the lantern on for you and bring back a cup of tea," I added.

She didn't answer. Her eyes were closed. The warmth of my wool coat had relaxed her. I took up the lantern and lit a precarious path to the attic exit.

Please God, don't let it be blocked. Let Bruce or Ted be far away. Let Brent check his messages. And let Crane be downstairs questioning the hostess at this very minute.

I felt cold myself.

Because I'd given Miss Isabel my coat or because Rachel, the ghost, was near, cheering me on?

I'd be everlastingly grateful for a little help. Natural or supernatural, it didn't matter as long as I could carry out my plan.

I had no sense of Rachel's presence, but strangely it seemed that Halley had bounded out of the dream to my side. I could almost feel the soft brush of her fur.

Hold fast to her and you'll be all right.

Leaving the lantern on the floor near the exit, I found a leather loop on the panel's surface and lifted it.

Fifty-six

I let the panel fall shut behind me and stepped into a rush of warm air and light. After the dimly-lit attic, my eyes struggled to make out the stairs. They were there, where they should be, and I didn't see anyone waiting to pounce. The coast was clear. At least this part of it.

So far so good. Quietly now. Quickly.

Down to the second floor.

The door to Room Three was closed as were all the others. Bruce and Ted must be elsewhere. The bulb in the hall's overhead light fixture cast a pale blue light on the floor. Rachel's mist?

Most likely my vision. I blinked it away.

Keep moving. Don't stop to think.

Down more stairs into semi-darkness on the ground floor.

Lights encased in brass sconces burned above the deserted hostess' desk. The dining room was dark and empty.

If I had my car keys, I could dash out to the parking lot and drive to the nearest police station. Since I didn't, I had only one option: to find the land-line phone.

"In the kitchen," Miss Isabel had said. I could only hope Brent hadn't disconnected it.

Back to the kitchen. I felt along the wall in the darkness, pressed a switch, and light flooded the room. There it was on the wall, a black relic of another time with a long dangling cord.

My hand shook as I pressed the numbers.

"I need help at the Spirit Lamp Inn on Deer Leap Road. I was attacked, and there's a woman. In the attic... There's a killer on the loose."

Dear Lord, I sounded like a babbling idiot. I forced myself to repeat the message coherently, to answer the dispatcher's questions, to emphasize the need for haste.

From the front of the Inn, I heard the door slam shut. Heavy footfalls. An object clattered to the floor.

I dropped the receiver and scanned the kitchen desperately, looking for a hiding place.

Where can you hide in a kitchen?

The appliances, sink, and cupboards were flat against the wall. A half-open door revealed a staircase. Leading to the basement? That was no escape route.

The footsteps were closer, louder, a pounding in my head. I imagined a powerful man with heavy strides, coming toward the light that shouldn't be on.

Brent, come to investigate a disturbance on his property? Crane?

If only I dared call out.

I didn't. Somehow I knew the newcomer wasn't either one of my hoped-for saviors.

A weapon?

I'd found a weapon in a kitchen before. Images from the past assailed me. Close calls. Defensive moves. Once I'd foiled a would-be killer by throwing a bowl full of salad in her face. I'd overcome another with a blow from a heavy rolling pin.

I needed a cast iron frying pan. Something lethal. A knife? A cook would have knives.

Hurry!

I threw open two drawers before I found a carving knife, as lethal a weapon as I could hope for. I grabbed it and was suddenly out of time.

The man stood in the doorway. Dressed in black, he wore a ski mask that concealed most of his face. Only his eyes were visible, and I couldn't match them to a face in my memory.

Bruce or Ted?

I couldn't tell. But he knew me.

"Resilient, aren't you?" he said in a tone that was even more chilling for his casual, almost amused tone.

I couldn't recognize the voice.

Useless to create an excuse, even if I could think of one. He knew me, and he held a gun in his black-gloved hand.

I had the knife, clutched in my hand, out of sight; he had the advantage.

Get him to talk.

I moved back a step, felt the counter cut into my waist. Could I plunge a knife into the chest of another human being?

If I had to.

There were only about two yards between us. I'd have to spring at him, be faster than his bullet.

It wouldn't work.

"There's no point in killing me," I said, trying for a conversational tone. "Miss Isabel is too confused to make trouble for you. She thinks she's in her room hosting a tea party."

He gave a short, rude laugh. "It's an act. Isabel was always good at pretending. She remembers all right. And now you know. Sorry, Jennet. I liked you. You shouldn't have got mixed up with us."

"I called the police," I said.

He looked at me, disbelief etched in his sneer. "Sure you did."

"On the phone. Right over there. They'll be here any minute."

"Then I'd better work fast."

In mystery fiction, the villain explains his motivation, lets himself be distracted, gives his victim a chance to turn the tables on him. If this were a novel, I would know how to proceed.

But this was life. All my killer said was, "Goodbye, Jennet. Nice knowing you."

And fired.

And fell in a burst of flying white china. He lay sprawled on his back. The gun, as if it had grown wings, flew across the room and landed in a corner.

What happened? Had the shot hit me? Why was I still standing?

An enormous bowl lay in shards around his head. A stream of fruit spilled out: apples, pears, bananas, and oranges rolled across the floor... The shot had pierced one of the jars on the counter. Honey oozed out. Thick, golden, gooey, a mess pooling on the floor. I could imagine it sliding down my throat, and the sensation made me ill.

I stared, still clutching the knife, still hearing the gunshot. Over and over.

A small woman in a pink blouse tottered in the doorway gloating. She had duplicated my long ago maneuver with the salad.

I found my voice. "Miss Isabel?"

When I'd last seen her, she'd been shivering with my coat for a blanket, drifting in and out of consciousness. She had claimed she couldn't stand. Was that an act, too?

I had a dozen questions. "Where did you find the bowl?" I asked.

"On the table in the hall," she said. "A stupid place for it, really, but handy in this case. It'll be all right now, Cynthia," she added. "He's dead."

~ * ~

But he wasn't dead, and it wasn't all right.

He could come to at any minute. We were still in danger. Miss Isabel had saved the day, but she was still a crazy woman, and she didn't seem too steady on her feet.

I didn't believe for one moment that her calling me Cynthia was an act. I should humor her though.

"Rope," I murmured. "We need rope to tie him up."

Or drag him down the basement stairs and shut the door. Or hit him with something. I still held the knife. With a shudder, I shoved it back in the drawer. Louise must have a rolling pin. All those pies she made...

Relax, I told myself. *Just hide the gun.*

As I picked it up, I heard the siren. Soon now I could turn the whole mad affair over to the authorities, but... I had to suppress the urge to burst into hysterical laughter.

After all this drama, after skating closer to Death than I ever had before, I still didn't know whether the killer was Bruce or Ted.

Fifty-seven

Lieutenant Mac Dalby of the Foxglove Corners Police Department, Crane's friend and my sometime nemesis, looked down at the fallen man.

"Who is he?" he asked.

"Ted," I said. "Or Bruce."

A meager smile crinkled his grim countenance. "Once again, Jennet. What happened here? Women in the attic? Killers on the loose?"

I searched for a chair but didn't see one. All right. I'd have to stand a little longer and hope I wouldn't fall.

"One woman plus me and one killer."

I told him the story, thinking all the while how melodramatic it sounded. How incredible.

A tea party that turned into a death trap, a woman whose grip on reality was tenuous at best, a bowl of fruit. One of the officers who'd accompanied Mac had stepped on a pear, squishing it. The whitish pulp made me queasy. I looked away.

He frowned. "Are you all right, Jennet?"

"My head still hurts," I said. "I don't know what he hit me with. If I had my purse…"

Amazing to be dreaming of two pain pills and a glass of cold water at a time like this.

"You'd better get checked out at Emergency," he said. "Crane would never forgive me if..."

"I'm fine, or I will be. Take care of Miss Isabel first."

"Nothing's wrong with me," she said. "I just want my tea. Where is it, Jennet? You promised."

"Soon," I said. "This goes back a long way, Mac, to the murder of Cynthia Lauren."

"The woman whose bones turned up in the backyard?" he asked.

I nodded. "I'm pretty sure we're looking at her killer."

"We are," Miss Isabel piped up. "I saw him do it. And the ghost. Don't forget the ghost, Jennet."

"A ghost story?" Mac shook his head. "Why am I not surprised? Weren't you facing down a gun a few weeks ago?"

"At my school," I said. "That gun wasn't pointed at me."

But it might have been.

"I expected to see my husband," I added with a glance at the door.

"I had a word with him on the way here. He just got home and found you gone. He left you a message..."

On my cell phone. In my purse. Crane would have thought I was still with Miss Isabel, drinking tea. But, no. He should have known I wouldn't forget about...

The dogs! Who'd been home to feed them and let them out? I glared at the man on the floor who had regained an uneasy consciousness. One of the officers had pulled off his ski mask when I wasn't looking.

"It's Bruce," Miss Isabel murmured. "I remember now. I saw his face, and he saw me."

"I can't drive home, Mac," I said and told him about my missing purse.

"Let's look in my room." Miss Isabel linked her arm in mine. "That's the only place it could be."

At times she sounded lucid. Later, maybe tomorrow over tea and fresh pastries, I wanted to talk to her.

Perhaps I'd finally find the motive for Cynthia's murder. I also wanted to know what had stoked Miss Isabel's memory into life at this particular time. And how had she ended up in the attic? And why she had the heart charm in her possession.

All interesting questions, but they didn't need to be answered right away.

~ * ~

I found my purse on the floor of Room Three just beyond the door. Its contents had spilled out on the floor. My cell phone with the voice mail I'd never heard, a small pill box containing the coveted aspirin, a compact, and the precious keys to the Taurus.

I stuffed my possessions back inside and turned to Miss Isabel. "Is my coat still in the attic?"

"I don't remember. It must be."

"Maybe one of the men will go up for it. I never want to set foot in an attic again."

"Neither do I. Not anymore. Not ever again."

Mac was waiting downstairs to follow me home in his patrol car. In spite of her half-hearted protests, Miss Isabel had agreed to go to the hospital. Bruce had stumbled his way to a patrol car, an officer at each side.

It was over. Well, mostly over.

Miss Isabel's room felt different. Empty? Yes, but it was something else...

Warm! That was it! The room was almost too warm. Not even an elderly lady who complained about cold temperatures could find this suite uncomfortable.

Because Rachel was gone! Of course she had moved on to another plane. Why would she stay? Her friend, Cynthia, was buried in sanctified ground. Cynthia's murderer would pay for his crime, or so I hoped. The Spirit Lamp Inn would lose its otherworldly mystique. Brent could make of his property what he would.

While Miss Isabel gathered a few necessities for a hospital trip, I took one last look at her room: the table, the tea kettle, the silver tea service and trays. The strawberry tarts looked as enticing as ever, but somewhere along the way I'd lost my appetite. All I wanted was to be in my own home surrounded by my loved ones. Now, thanks to Miss Isabel, that was going to happen.

~ * ~

Crane and I stayed up late that night, sitting close to each other while our fire blazed and the collies slept. I didn't have to worry about them. Seeing that neither Crane nor I were home at dinnertime, Camille and Gilbert had taken care of them.

I was blessed with my friends, unlike some people whose relationships were soaked with poison.

"You have to stop risking your life, Jennet," Crane said.

He spoke in his stern deputy sheriff voice. I hadn't heard it in a while, and I didn't want to hear it now. It chipped away at the romantic cloak that enclosed us. After all, it wasn't as if I'd courted danger—this time.

"The school shooting couldn't be helped, and today I went to the Inn for a tea party," I said.

"You've been in danger more than I have," he pointed out. "And I'm the lawman."

I couldn't deny it. My thoughts drifted to the Spirit Lamp Inn.

It was empty tonight. Miss Isabel had been admitted to a room for observation. And Brent? No one knew where Brent was. He hadn't replied to my voice mail.

Until morning when Louise and her crew arrived, the Inn would slumber in darkness and silence. The second story hall would wonder where its haunt had gone.

"Brent is probably out romancing a new lady," I said.

Crane smiled. "Probably."

"I don't want to go back to the Inn ever," I said. "But I have to talk to Miss Isabel. She knows the whole story, if her memory can be trusted."

"Why don't you invite her here? You can have your own tea and bake pastries or buy them at the Hometown Bakery."

"That's an idea," I said. "As soon as she's home."

"I don't think she should be staying at the Inn."

"Maybe she won't want to, after what happened."

"She doesn't have to decide right away."

"Miss Isabel saved my life," I said. "I'll put together the most elegant tea anyone ever gave. It'll be a celebration."

As if she knew the meaning of 'elegant tea,' Candy raised her head and woofed.

It was strange about dogs. They were overjoyed to have Crane and me home after what must have seemed like an eternity. But of the entire brood, Halley alone seemed to know something had almost gone very wrong. She followed me from room to room, lay quietly at my feet, and every now and then nudged my hand.

I leaned down to pat her. My first tri. My oldest collie friend. I didn't doubt that she had known about my close brush with death. Perhaps she had known more than I.

"I dreamed about you, sweetheart," I said.

Crane winked at me. "I hope so."

I didn't tell him I was talking to the dog. But feeling a little bit guilty, I packed an extra measure of passion into my kisses that night.

~ * ~

On Saturday afternoon Miss Isabel came to tea. She was a passenger in Brent's new vintage blue Mustang, a vision in a flowing pink dress and hat. I had beer for Brent. He brought wine.

I'd set the dining room table with my best china and silver and lit the tapers in the heirloom candlesticks. My own delicacies sparkled on crystal plates: banana bread, blueberry muffins, tarts, and, contributed by Camille, cream puffs.

Brent surveyed the table. "What a fancy spread, Jennet. Crane is a lucky man."

"He calls me his multi-talented wife," I said. "But I have to confess. Camille baked the cream puffs."

"Cream puffs!" He eyed them with suspicion. "I'll take some of those tarts."

"They didn't have decent tea in the hospital," Miss Isabel said. "It tasted like medicine. You promised me a cup of tea in the attic, Jennet," she added. "Do you remember?"

I did, only too well. "Better late than never. This will be more comfortable."

Only why was my hand shaking? Bruce was in custody. He had admitted to terrorizing Miss Isabel and me—as a prank—but not to killing Cynthia Lauren.

He couldn't hurt us. Nothing at the Spirit Lamp Inn could hurt us again. Still, I had to set my hands firmly on the table to steady them.

Memories were powerful. This one had even more staying power than the shooting at Marston High School.

"I want to hear the whole story," Brent said, eyeing the beer I'd poured into a crystal goblet. "And I want the truth, Miss Isabel, not one of your fantasies."

"The truth is that I witnessed the murder, but it slipped out of my mind. Don't ask me to explain it. I can't."

"What made you remember?" I asked.

"I saw you wearing Cynthia's charm bracelet. The last time I saw it, it was on Cynthia's wrist. I started having flashbacks, I guess you'd call them. Nothing that held together."

"Start at the beginning," I said.

She took a deep breath. "Bruce and Cynthia had dated for a while, but she broke up with him. He wanted her back. He used to talk about her like she was still his girlfriend. Then out of the blue, he stopped. He never mentioned her again."

"Well after she vanished…"

"That's what I thought," she said. "I was wrong. He wanted to distance himself from her memory."

"I don't understand," I said. "How did you all end up at the Spirit Lamp Inn? From what I read, Cynthia and Rachel stopped there to shelter from the storm on their way home from a trip."

"That's true. Well, it was one of those coincidences. It wasn't unusual for Bruce and Ted to drive out to the Oaken Bucket for dinner. They knew the owner."

"So Bruce would know how to find the attic," I said.

"I assume so. I was there that night with my gentleman friend for dinner. By chance I met Cynthia in the ladies' room. She told me she wasn't feeling well. My guess is that Bruce ran into Cynthia by accident just as I did and tried to bully her into dating him again.

"I stopped by her room to see how she was and heard quarreling. The door was half open, and I saw him strangle her. I must have screamed because he turned around and saw me. That's all I remember.

"Then tonight Bruce came to my room. He said he had a surprise for me. Suddenly I knew. Just like that. And he could tell I remembered."

"What about those invitations you sent me?" I asked.

"The first one was legitimate. The second one he made me write. I should have resisted. I'm sorry, but I was afraid."

"I understand," I said. "I was afraid too."

"I want to know about the silver heart charm." That was Brent.

"Cynthia used to wear it on a chain to go with her bracelet. She had it on that night. When Mister Fowler showed it to me, well, I waited for an opportunity and took it. I planned to look for the chain. It seemed like Cynthia's jewelry was scattered all over the Inn. I thought if I could find it all, I'd know what happened to her. Well, it made sense to me at the time."

"But how did the chain get in the crate?"

"Bruce would know," Miss Isabel said. "Or maybe Rachel."

But Rachel was gone.

~ * ~

The next day fickle Mother Nature gave us soaring temperatures. Well, they soared into the high forties. The sun melted a modicum of snow, and a scent of spring rode the air.

Which was all wrong. It was December. Christmas was coming. I didn't want the snow to melt, but as I took Candy, Halley, and Misty down Jonquil Lane, I exulted in the remembered fragrance of daffodils.

Always quick to take advantage of clement temperatures, I led my trio down the Lane to Sagramore Lake Road. As we neared Deanna Reid's house, I wondered how she and Sparrow were getting along.

Speak of the Devil! But that wasn't fair. I didn't have any proof that Deanna had done anything except give voice to her threats.

She came out of her house with a pretty tricolor collie running in circles on the end of her leash. My dogs set up a clamor. What could we do but stop? I wanted to talk to her anyway.

"Hi, Jennet," she said. "Isn't it a glorious day?"

"It sure is," I said. "So this is Sparrow."

The tri wagged her tail with great collie enthusiasm.

"Are you still planning to buy a tricolor puppy to show?" I asked.

"Maybe, if one becomes available. That way, Sparrow will have a companion. May we walk with you?"

"Of course. I heard about your ex-boyfriend. Did they find out who shot him?"

"It wasn't me," she said quickly," but I'll admit I was happy to hear he was dead. Is that terrible of me?"

"I don't think so," I said. "You feel what you feel. If he had never stolen Sparrow, you might have been able to summon up an ounce of sympathy for him."

"I'm glad you understand," she said.

We walked in silence for a while, the dogs trying to sniff out the wonders that lay beneath the snow and the humans dodging ice patches that were slow to melt.

One of the houses had a forlorn untenanted look. Its snow hadn't been shoveled, and the uncurtained windows gave testimony to emptiness. A slip of paper, possibly a foreclosure notice, was attached to the front door.

The place reminded me of the Spirit Lamp Inn when I'd first seen it. Suddenly I remembered. This was Molly and Jennifer's mystery house whose owner had moved in and promptly vanished.

"The owner never came back?" I said.

"Apparently not. She must have changed her mind."

I wondered. If Molly and Jennifer had been out, I could have asked them. Ah, well.

Some mysteries were never solved. Others remained just out of reach for decades, only to be solved in the end. Still others had simple solutions.

Anyway, this one belonged to Molly and Jennifer. For myself, I would enjoy this brief false spring and walk with my beautiful collies and enjoy the company of a woman I once hadn't even liked.

Life itself was a mystery. Sometimes it was wonderful.

Meet

Dorothy Bodoin

Dorothy Bodoin, a full-time writer of mystery and romantic suspense novels, lives in Royal Oak, Michigan, with her collie, Kinder, who provides plenty of inspiration for the fictitious collies in her books. Prior to attending Oakland University where she earned Bachelor's and Master's degrees in English literature, Dorothy worked for two years as a secretary in southern Italy for Chrysler Missile Corporation.

After graduating from Oakland, she taught high school English for several years and during that time wrote short stories and a Gothic novel, *Treasure at Trail's End,* later published by Wings ePress. Her first published work was *Darkness at Foxglove Corners,* the first in the Foxglove Corners Cozy Mystery Series.

VISIT OUR WEBSITE
FOR THE FULL INVENTORY
OF QUALITY BOOKS:

http://www.wings-press.com

ings
ress, Inc.

Quality trade paperbacks and downloads
in multiple formats,
in genres ranging from light romantic comedy
to general fiction and horror.
Wings has something for every reader's taste.
Visit the website, then bookmark it.
We add new titles each month!

CPSIA information can be obtained
at www.ICGtesting.com
Printed in the USA
FSOW02n0856140517
34257FS